His lips touched hers briefly before she opened her mouth and slid her tongue toward his.

Desire hit her like lightning, shooting through her veins in a hot bolt. His hands held her steady as he explored her mouth. She groaned against his lips. The fingertips of his right hand moved from her shoulder to trail the outside of her breast, down her rib cage, and over her hip bone. He reached into the neckline of her low-cut dress and found her nipple. She gasped into his mouth as he pinched, twisted. The pain shot through her, straight to her sex. She was getting wet.

"Come to the show tonight, Ruby," Mark said.

"Yes."

"I'll leave a pass at the door. I want you to find a spot to the right of the stage and wait for me there."

"Yes," she breathed.

"If any men approach you, I want you to ignore them. If you don't do as I say, I won't be happy."

A shudder ripped through her body. How would he respond if she displeased him? Her pulse jumped with excitement. A part of her wanted to find out what he'd do. Would he punish her? She'd never been punished like that...

Bound to Please

LILLI FEISTY

FOREVER

NEW YORK   BOSTON

Cover design by Giorgetta Bell McRee
Cover design by Claire Brown

Forever
Hachette Book Group
237 Park Avenue
New York, NY 10017
Visit our Web site at www.HachetteBookGroup.com.

Forever is an imprint of Grand Central Publishing. The Forever name and logo is a trademark of Hachette Book Group, Inc.

Printed in the United States of America

First Printing: May 2009

10 9 8 7 6 5 4 3 2 1

For my mother.

Acknowledgments

Kate Pearce and Robin Rotham, thank you for encouraging me when I was just starting out. Crystal Jordan and R.G. Alexander, you keep me going. Nicole, you've been with me since the start and I love you. Red Garnier, you inspire me in so many ways. Dana, thanks for the tough love. Gemma Halliday, you are an amazing CP (yeah, you're one of mine now, sorry). You rock for ignoring your kid to critique my revised manuscript in three days. I also want to thank Gwen Hayes, Karen Erickson, Shelli Stevens and Lacy Dances for being damn good, understanding friends. Jax and every single member of Romance Divas, you all are my lifeline.

Eden Bradley, you're the other half of my brain. I could never survive without you.

Without a doubt, I need to thank my amazing editor, Amy Pierpont, and the most wonderful agent in the world, Roberta Brown.

Bona, thank you for always inspiring the crazy best friend who inevitably starts out as a transvestite at the beginning of my books. Pam, thanks for wearing that vintage seventies dress and sharing lap dances with me.

Robin and all the other folks who frequented the Power Exchange in San Francisco, thank you for being part of some wonderfully naughty memories.

And thanks to the Babettes, the most insane, supportive book club ever. You know what you'll be reading for our May 2009 selection. And Marty, Vanessa, and Robyn, thank you for being my adoptive family for over twenty-five years.

I also appreciate Jason Quever from the Papercuts and Pan American Recording Studio for answering all of my questions. Jason, you are not allowed to read past this page.

And J. You're the best friend a girl could ever have. I love you.

Bound
to Please

Chapter
One

Have you ever been spanked?"

Ruby Scott choked on her chocolate martini. "P-pardon me?"

Meg, her best friend, business partner, and apparent perv, jerked a few nods. "You know. Spanked, flogged, whipped. Whatever."

Ruby blinked. Sure, they'd talked about sex in their ten years of friendship, and it wasn't like Meg didn't know Ruby had a kinky side. But she'd never gone *there*. Until now.

Meg gave her a little push on the shoulder. "Come on! I really want to know about it. About S and M."

Ruby glanced around the room, checking that the night was running smoothly. It was. She was, after all, known for being a highly organized and efficient event planner. Tonight was no different: Waitstaff scurried by, bartenders polished oversized martini glasses. Music blared from invisible speakers at the perfect volume. Guests hadn't started to arrive yet, but Ruby could feel everything falling into place for tonight's party.

Instead of enjoying the buzz around her, Ruby turned back to her friend and took a rather large swallow of her drink. "Um...first of all, don't call it S and M. You can call it SM, BDSM, D/s—"

"Can we discuss the lingo later? I just want to know what it's like. To get spanked." Lowering her voice, Meg leaned in closer. "Or to spank someone else." Meg's cheeks were downright flushed with titillation.

"Why the sudden questions, anyway?"

Leaning back, Meg tucked a lock of ebony hair behind her ear. Looks-wise, they were polar opposites. Ruby's hair was black, but naturally so. Meg had an olive-skinned, curvy shape while Ruby was pale, and her body was, for lack of a better word, skinny. And despite their shared interest in vintage, Ruby was the only one who actually wore retro dresses. Meg still shopped at the junior department; it was really quite handy that punk rock was back in style.

Now Ruby's post-punk-rock friend's brown eyes sparkled behind layers and layers of black makeup. Tonight her outfit consisted of a short black dress, black wrist-length gloves, and shiny patent pumps with buckles on top. Meg was not about to go gently into that goth night.

She crossed her legs, which were enclosed in spider-print tights. "I was just thinking of ways to spice things up a bit between me and Emmett. Do something different. You and Ash used to be,...you know. Into that stuff. Kinky stuff." One of the bartenders had moved a bit closer and Meg whispered the last word, as if *stuff* was more acceptable than S and M. "I just thought you could give me a few pointers."

"Do we have to talk about this now?" Ruby asked. "The band's going to be here any minute. And"—Ruby waved a pointed finger—"I think I need to check on those hors d'oeuvres." She slid off her barstool.

Meg wrapped her hand around Ruby's shoulder in a death grip. "Just one tip?"

"Yeah. Stay away from artists and musicians."

"Are you nervous to see him tonight?"

By "him" Meg meant her ex, Ash, who was supposed to show up to this little shindig, but, knowing him, if he came at all he'd be late. Ruby wanted as many hot names at this party as she could get, and the fact was, Ash Hunter was about the hottest name in the San Francisco art scene right now. Kinky sex was definitely *en vogue*, and the übercool were snapping up Ash's shibari rope-bondage photographs as fast as he could produce them. Thank God Ruby had posed for him before he'd become famous, and he'd promised to keep those images private.

"I'm actually not nervous to see him. I'm glad he's doing so well." Ruby smoothed her pencil skirt, a purchase from Meg's now-defunct vintage clothing shop. "Really."

Meg raised a brow. "C'mon, Ruby...you haven't even dated anyone since Ash. Are you sure you're over him?"

"Absolutely." She nodded vigorously. "I'm sick of these artistic types. I need a man with a real job, a man who wants a wife, not an accessory. I want a man who wants a stable, normal life."

Meg raised her glass and took a sip. "Good luck with that."

"What? You have it with Emmett. I want what you have."

"Anyway." Meg crossed her arms in front of her chest. "You're really not going to tell me anything about the kinky stuff? What it's like?"

Ruby shrugged. "To be honest, I don't know. We didn't...I mean, we never..."

Meg's eyes went wide. "But what about all that bond-age? The photographs? Come on, you can tell me!"

Ruby gave a frustrated sigh. "Ash was only into bond-age. There was never any . . . *spanking*." She felt her neck heat, which was ridiculous considering she and Meg used to share everything, including the details of their sex lives. But that was before Meg married, before Ash. With a start, Ruby realized they hadn't talked like this in months.

She touched Meg's hand. "Hey, honey. Is everything okay?"

"Yeah! Definitely." If Meg's smile was a bit too bright, Ruby ignored it for now. "I was just, you know. Curious." Meg shrugged. "We've been married a while now. It's normal. Right?"

"What's normal?"

"To want to spice things up in the bedroom."

"Sure. Absolutely." Ruby nodded furiously, but what did Ruby know about being married?

Still, the idea that Meg's marriage was less than per-fect made Ruby uneasy. Not quite sure how to reassure her friend, she said, "Ash never spanked me, flogged me, paddled me, or anything like that." The words came out in a rush. She inhaled. "He just tied me up." Secretly, she'd wanted Ash to do those other things to her, but she'd never been able to voice her desires and she couldn't bring her-self to tell Meg now, either.

"So he tied you up and then had sex with you?"

The sound of glass breaking whipped Ruby's atten-tion to a bartender who had just picked up, and obviously dropped, their empty glasses. With a scowl, Ruby grabbed Meg and led her to a small round table in the center of the room. "Listen. To be honest, the sex itself was pretty vanilla."

"Vanilla?"

"Traditional."

Meg's shoulders drooped. "Oh."

Bizarrely feeling as if she'd let her friend down, Ruby wanted to say more. But just then the first of the guests came through the door, and she gave Meg's hand a squeeze. "I promise we'll talk more about it later. But this is a big night for Emmett, and I want everything to be perfect."

For tonight's party, Ruby had booked a monochromatic bar across from the building where Emmett and Meg lived and where Emmett had his recording studio. For the food, she'd selected an array of Mexican-Vietnamese-Italian fusion appetizers, and the bartenders had been instructed to keep everyone happy with the latest rage in cocktails, the chocolate martini. Ruby's connections in L.A. had told her '80s hair bands were back in style in a retro-kitsch way, so she herself had created a play list that lent an absurdity to the whole event.

Or maybe that was just her perspective.

Regardless, it was her job to make it work, and she'd done her job well. She always did.

Ruby followed Meg's gaze to Emmett. He was walking through the door with a small group of people. Two men, one gorgeous redheaded female. The detached air about them shouted "rock band," and Ruby barely refrained from rolling her eyes. Why did all artist types have to be so aloof? Was it in their DNA?

Whatever. Luckily, this was an early event, and she could be home in a few hours with nothing but a nice bottle of wine to keep her company. Heaven. But now she had to work.

And reassure Meg about her sex life.

Her friend was still staring at her husband, the tallest, lankiest one in the room. "Emmett really wants to record the Riders. Says they're amazing, the most talented group he's seen in a long time. He's become good friends with Mark, the head of the band, and says he's not just a good guy, but one of the most talented musicians he's ever met."

Ignoring the amazing band, Ruby focused on her friend. "Emmett's the best at what he does. I can't imagine they'd choose another producer."

"This could take him to the next level, not to mention make him happy. I really hope this happens." Meg did a quick wave around the room. "Anyway, you did a fabulous job with the pre-party. As usual."

Compared to the productions Ruby had been planning lately, this was a small party. But it was for her best friend's husband, so Ruby had put a lot of extra energy into it. After all, they were selling San Francisco itself because if the band did choose to record with Emmett, they'd be living here for as long as it took to make the record. She wanted tonight to be flawless, hip, and cool.

But more than that, she wanted her best friends to be happy. "Listen, sweetie. If you want to know more about kinky stuff, I'll help you. I'll tell you everything I know." *Which isn't much.* "I'll take you to the sex store. We can look at floggers, paddles, whatever your little heart desires!" Ruby beamed and nodded in what she hoped was a reassuring manner, despite the fact that she really had no idea what she was talking about.

Ignoring the way her pulse skipped at the thought of

going back to the fetish shop, she went on. "I can be your tour guide into the wonderful underworld of kink! Where every perversion is at your fingertips!" She punctuated her sentence with a quick *snap!*

That snap seemed really loud because Meg had gone oddly quiet, looking over Ruby's shoulder. Ruby slowly turned to follow Meg's gaze, and for some reason the hairs on the back of her neck stood on end.

Emmett was staring at her as if she'd grown a second head. And beside him was one of the most gorgeous men Ruby had ever seen. Tall, lean, with a bad-boy gleam in his deep brown eyes. He'd obviously heard her, but the only thing that gave him away was the nearly imperceptible tilt at the corner of his luscious mouth.

Tour guide into the wonderful underworld of kink!?
Fuck. A. Duck.

Chapter Two

"Ruby, meet Mark St. Crow. He's the head of the Dark Riders." Emmett gave her a look that she knew meant *Kiss his ass.*

And her first thought was *Okay! If you insist.* Because the man standing before her made her heart race. Made her feel all tingly and they hadn't even spoken yet.

His head was shaved and gleamed in the dim light, clean and shiny. She'd never been with a bald man; she wondered how the skin would feel beneath her fingers, if she'd be able to trace the bones of his skull. Her fingers curled at the thought.

She uncurled them and held out her hand. "Nice to meet you." Their palms met and her pulse jumped.

She took her hand back.

Young. He looked so very young. But, at thirty-seven, it seemed everyone got younger every day.

He gazed at her through black-rimmed glasses. *Damn.* She'd always had a thing for glasses on a man. She'd had a serious crush on an art history professor in college who wore them. At night, she'd study nineteenth-century Italian paintings, then go to bed and think of him as she used her hot-pink bullet vibrator.

For fuck's sake, don't think about that*!*

"Ruby. Do you know there are at least forty songs with your name in the title?" Mark asked.

"Um, actually I didn't. So you get points for an original twist on an old line." She cringed. Why had she said that? She could almost feel Emmett's censure, but when she turned she discovered he, along with Meg, had vanished.

She looked back to see Mark raising a brow over those bloody glasses. "So are you saying I'm not original?"

"I don't know yet. Can you name all the songs?" Was she flirting? That sounded like flirting.

"Probably. But I want to get paid for my talents. Fortunately, I work cheap. A beer ought to cover it. I'll even get it myself."

She raised a hand to protest. "That's really not necces—"

"Be right back."

She watched him walk away. Tall and sinewy, his black T-shirt showed off a solid torso, and the short sleeves gave her a nice view of well-defined, tattoo-covered arms. Faded, low-slung jeans—not too tight—wrapped around long legs that carried his form with a confidence that drew her attention. He looked too young for that kind of confidence. So young he could get away with leather bands circling both his wrists and make it look hot.

In fact, he had a lot of leather on his body. Bracelets, belt, boots. All black, all worn. The sight of all that leather sent a thrill through her, which she quickly stomped down.

Now he was walking back across the room with his gaze fixed on her. Like she was some kind of target, like he was some kind of predator. Hell, he probably was. Young, gorgeous, talented. She'd go down like a gazelle under a lion's attack.

He handed her a chocolate martini, and she could swear she smelled the leather from his bracelets. Which made her remember the wall of leather at the sex shop. There was a specific smell to this type of leather. Woodsy, freshly cut. Sexy.

No, no. Don't think about that…

But of course she did. She thought about the time she'd gone with Ash to the fetish store to purchase suspension equipment. Ruby had been drawn to the wall of floggers and paddles and other mysterious implements; her palms had dampened as she approached all that leather. Nervous and excited just to see the tools, all lined up in neat, erotic rows. She'd wondered how the leather would feel striking her skin. Would it sting a lot? Or a little? Would she like it? Her hand had trembled as she ran her finger over the soft strands of a buckskin flogger.

"You like them?"

"W-what?"

Mark shook his wrist. "These. You were staring at them."

"No. I mean yes. They're lovely." *Lovely?*

That damn brow of his went higher.

She felt hot. All over. Which compelled her to take a calming sip of the drink he'd handed her. As a rule, she didn't drink at her own events, but so far she'd broken her own rule twice in one night. First with Meg, now with Mark. *Mark something St. Crow.*

"Do you have a middle name?" she asked.

He tilted his head. "Why?"

"Um. Just wondering." Seriously, her legs were trembling.

"Let's sit." Was he reading her mind now?

He led her to a table in a corner. And the only reason she took the seat he offered was because of Emmett. Really, it was. Emmett wanted to record this band, and, as his wife's best friend, she felt an obligation to do whatever she could to help out. And if that meant making small talk with a young man who wore black glasses and smelled like leather and looked at her like she was the only woman in the room, so be it.

She stifled a shiver.

"You cold?"

"Nope. Uh-uh. Not at all." In fact, she was burning up. *Conversation. Make conversation.* "So. You're in a band." *Real clever.*

"Yup. Sure am." Why did he always seem to be holding back a smile?

She went on. "What do you play?"

"Everything. Piano, guitar. The Bazantar—"

"You play the Bazantar?" she said, her eyes wide.

"On occasion. You know what it is?"

"It's a five-string double bass, invented by Mark Deutsch."

He stared a second too long. "Wow. I'm impressed."

"So am I. That you play it, I mean." She cleared her throat. "Anyway, what else do you do?"

"I sing. I'm a bit of a control freak about performing, actually."

She couldn't help but find that interesting. Mark St. Crow was a control freak. He seemed the opposite of her, and yet she often referred to herself with that same exact phrase. Well, everyone referred to her that way, didn't they? "What kind of music does your band play?" she asked.

"Rock and roll. Punk. Electronic. Everything." Now he did smile before he tilted his beer bottle to his lips. She surmised that, by now, he must have realized she had no idea who his band was. It didn't seem to bother him.

Which was even more interesting. But she shook the thoughts out of her head. She really should be checking in with the caterer, mingling. So she had no idea why she asked: "Didn't we have a deal? Were you going to name forty songs with the name Ruby in the title?" So now she was asking him to serenade her. *Niiiice.* Not flirting at all.

"This might not be in chronological order; I'm a bit rusty."

"I understand."

He coughed into his hand, cleared his throat. Made a show of it. She bit her lip, trying not to laugh at his silliness. With all this charm, no doubt he had girls falling over him every night. The thought sobered her up, and she straightened in her seat.

Suddenly she had the distinct feeling that she was being watched and she looked up to find the woman Mark had arrived with staring at her. Tall, with a supermodel's figure and sparkling green eyes, the redhead was stunning. And, judging from the intense expression on her face, she disapproved of Mark talking to Ruby.

"What's up?" Mark asked.

Ruby tried to shrug indifferently. "Your girlfriend doesn't look too happy."

"That's Yvette, my singer. She's not my girlfriend."

"Are you sure she knows that?"

"Yeah. I already ventured down that road, and it didn't work out so well. Hit a dead end so, to speak." He chuckled, his laugh was deep and husky and made her soften even more.

So, he'd been with Yvette. Who cared? Ruby had no idea why it mattered that Mark's gorgeous, talented, soon-to-be-famous ex-girlfriend was staring at them like she would be perfectly happy if a hole opened up and swallowed Ruby alive.

"Don't mind Yvette. She's just overprotective. We go way back."

"I don't mind," Ruby said as Yvette turned away. "Not at all. It's great to have good friends. Anyway, I should be going. I have to check on...things." As if she didn't have every detail, down to the exact number of hand towels in the bathroom, under control.

His hand on her knee made her pause. "But I haven't finished my side of the deal yet. So sit back and listen, my darling Ruby."

She flicked his hand away. "I'm not your darling anything."

"I know. It's a song. By Mossa."

"Oh."

"House music."

"I don't listen to house."

"Understood. It's not nearly as good as the hair-band music you have going on here."

She bristled. "Eighties rock is *back*."

"Sadly."

She agreed but didn't say it. And she really wished he would stop smiling like that. It did funny things to her stomach.

He opened his mouth to speak, but she interrupted. "So you're on. List every song with Ruby in the title. And, just for fun, how about you do it by genre?" She smiled innocently.

"A bit of a challenge, but I'll give it a try. What should I start with? Not house. Rock? Alternative? Jazz—"

"Jazz." Ruby loved jazz and was quite sure this young rock star would be stumped. Which, bizarrely, would please her.

"Jazz it is. Okay, then. *A-hem*. Of course we have 'Ruby, My Dear' by Thelonious Monk; 'Ruby, I Need You' by the Steel Brothers; 'Ruby' by Ambrose Akinmusire; 'Ruby' by Art Farmer; 'Ruby' by Jimmy Smith; 'Ruby' by Benny Carter—"

She froze. "You've heard of Benny Carter?"

"You seem surprised."

"I am. Not many people know jazz."

"How do you know so much about jazz, Ruby So Sweet?"

"My dad turned me on to it." She just stopped herself from adding, *before he left*. "When I was a little girl. Not many people have heard of Benny Carter."

"My father was a jazz musician. Upright bass. I'll never forget the first time he caught me listening to the Ramones. I thought he'd have a heart attack right there in my bedroom."

Ah, yes, the Ramones. Their album had come out when Mark was what? Ten?

She asked, "Was he a successful musician? Your father, I mean."

"In his time. Played with some of the greats. Monk, Brubeck, Hancock."

She leaned back, studying the way he coolly listed some of the greatest names in jazz. "Impressive."

He shrugged, and for just a second his eyes flashed with an emotion she couldn't place. "At the time. He gave it up when I came along."

"Really? Why?"

His laugh was wry. "The usual. Mom didn't like the late nights, the travel. The unpredictable income."

"That's understandable."

He eyed her over his beer. "Maybe. Anyway, he taught me everything I know about music. So, Ruby baby. Shall I continue?"

Nodding, she settled into her chair and listened. And listened. And listened. Finally, she waved him to stop. "Fine! I get it. There are a lot of songs with the name Ruby in the title!"

"As there should be."

She rolled her eyes and bit back a grin. Yeah, he was a charmer, all right. And she'd fallen right into his trap. But why her? Why had he picked her to flirt with? Glancing around the room, she saw half a dozen gorgeous young things, some of whom she'd hired herself as eye candy. And that they were. In her vintage suit and high-buttoned shirt, Ruby felt downright dowdy in comparison. At least her red peep-toe pumps were sexy.

Straightening her blazer, Ruby took a deep, calming breath. But then she looked up and her heart stopped. Because Mark wasn't just looking at her, he was scrutinizing her. She found herself pinned under his gaze as if he'd tied her to the chair.

He took a slow swig from his beer. "I noticed the tattoo on the back of your neck. It's nice work."

She wore her hair in a high ponytail, and her hand

went to the cherry blossom tattoo at the top of her spine. "Thank you."

If possible, his gaze became even more intense. "It looks familiar. In fact, it looks exactly like something on a piece of art I bought recently. Here, in San Francisco."

She felt the blood drain from her face. No. It couldn't be. Ash had promised to never sell any of the photographs he'd taken of her. He was a narcissistic, chronically late, tortured artist who, on occasion, cheated on his girlfriend. But he wasn't evil.

Was he?

Mark went on. "The thing is, this piece I bought? It's of a woman, bound in rope. It was one of the sexiest things I'd ever seen." Still watching her, he took another casual swig from his beer. "Until now."

She met his gaze, silent for a minute. Then she started laughing. High-pitched hysterical giggles that had him looking at her with an expression of confusion.

Finally, her laugh died out. "So that's what this is about."

"What 'what' is about?"

She flapped her hand between them. "*This*. You talking to me. You think I'm easy because I posed—*past tense*—naked in erotic photographs. You think I'll tie you up, let you worship my shoes or something." She pushed herself to her feet. "And this is exactly why I didn't want anyone to know it was me in those pictures. You let someone take a few nude photographs, and the next thing you know, guys are begging you to spank them—"

A firm grip on her wrist stopped her midturn, midsentence. He was standing now and she jerked her chin up, confronting his stare.

"Ruby, I'm never the one begging to be spanked. Trust me on that."

He used two fingers to tilt her chin up just a fraction, and the scent of his leather bracelets assaulted her. His brown eyes told her everything: There was nothing submissive about Mark St. Crow.

He said, "You're vibrating."

She shook her head. "I'm not."

That smile again. "You are." He slid his free hand into her blazer pocket like he had every right to do so, and the heat from his arm made her shiver more than she already was. Releasing her wrist, he placed her phone in her palm. The phone that was, in fact, vibrating.

"You might want to get that. Could be important."

"Right. Thanks." Without looking at the caller ID, she turned away and flipped the cell open. "This is Ruby."

"Are you okay?"

Glancing over her shoulder at a grinning Mark, Ruby took a few more steps away from him and scanned the room. "Meg? Where are you?"

"Hiding behind a palm tree. Did you know these things are fakes? Anyway, I saw the way Mark was holding your arm. Is everything all right?"

She looked behind her to find Mark still watching her. She turned away. "Yes. Fine. Turns out Ash sold one of those photographs, and guess who happened to buy one?"

"No way!"

"Way."

"So why was he holding on to your wrist? Does he

think you're easy or something 'cause of those pictures? Fuck the recording contract. I'm gonna kick his ass."

"No! No. It's fine, really." Ruby didn't know how she knew this, she just did. And she couldn't help the fact that a part of her was enjoying their banter. Enjoying him. Yeah, as a musician he was a sworn-off species, but that didn't mean she couldn't enjoy a little flirting, did it? She was thirty-seven. Even if the lighting was soft, it felt good to have a hot young guy hitting on her. Not to mention her wrist still burned from where he'd held her. And that excited her even as it freaked her out.

"Really, Meg. It's fine. Thanks for checking, though." She flipped her phone shut and faced Mark. He was, of course, still staring at her. But now he was sitting again, sipping his beer. Looking innocent. But there was nothing innocent about him. And there was something in his eyes that made her go liquid inside. Made her heart flutter. *Flutter*.

Shit.

Stiffly, she sat back down, picked up her drink and took a sip. She wasn't stupid. She knew what was being offered. A one-off with a gorgeous young man who made her pulse race. A fast fuck with a man who purchased erotic art and probably thought she had more experience than she had with BDSM. A man who'd said he was never the one begging to be spanked, worded in such a way to imply there was, in fact, someone who had begged for such a thing.

She couldn't get that smell of leather out of her nose.

His gaze darted to the patio door and back to her. "Have a cigarette with me," he said, and she looked up to find those intense brown eyes of his boring into hers.

"I don't smoke."

"Neither do I."

A heartbeat later, she nodded.

Mark placed his beer bottle on the table, and then he took her hand. She loved the feel of his dry, strong fingers laced with hers. Loved the way he confidently led her through the crowd. Even as she broke rule number two—never leave your own event—she loved the way her heart hammered as she followed him onto the terrace. Besides, if anyone needed anything, she was just outside the door.

On this empty patio. All alone. With Mark St. Crow. Her heart started to race in a way it hadn't in a long time, in an anxious pace that made her palms moist.

But then his hand was on her arm, stroking softly. The feeling passed.

She met his gaze and her heart quickened, but in a much more pleasant manner than it had just a moment ago. Were they going to do it now? Have sex? Here?

It suddenly dawned on her that she was about to have a quickie on the patio with a man she'd just met. Why else would he have led her out here?

Why else would she have let him?

Just do it and get it out of your system!

Hell, they were halfway there anyway, right? He'd already seen her at her most vulnerable. The man possessed pictures of her, not just nude, but in bondage. Rope wrapped around her breasts, her arms, between her legs. Totally bound. God, he'd seen more of her than any man had in over a year.

Turning, she smiled shyly at Mark. "You've seen me naked."

"Don't think I'm not thinking about that." The corners

of his mouth lifted in a mischievous smile as he took a step closer to her.

She lifted her chin a fraction, then jumped into the unknown. "Do you just admire the art you buy, or do you play?" Her entire body seemed to shake as she waited for him to answer.

His hand went to his belt buckle, where he lightly stroked the brass. "I'm interested in all aspects of power exchange."

And she wanted to give him that power over her.

How had he brought out this side of her so fast? Because she wanted to sink to her knees before him, give herself to him right then. She'd forgotten what that craving was like, how encompassing it could be.

She shook her head. All this talk about leather and bondage and spanking had her head spinning, had her acting crazy.

Instinct told her to run, but then he pulled her to him and cupped her face between his hands. "I'm going to kiss you, but only if you promise to come to my show and then wait for me afterward."

"What if I hate the way you kiss?"

"You won't."

"You're so sure of yourself?"

He lightly stroked the top of her ear. "Yes."

She had no intention of going to his show, but he didn't need to know that. She pulled him down toward her. She loved the way a man's neck felt in her palm, and she closed her eyes and savored the seconds before their first kiss. Then his lips touched hers briefly and she opened her mouth, slid her tongue gently toward his. She tasted him. Took pleasure in the easy way they connected.

She'd forgotten what a kiss could be like. How it could make her legs tingle. How it set loose butterflies in her belly. How it melted her.

His hands were roaming her back, pressing her body against his. Desire hit her like lightning, shooting through her veins in a hot bolt. Their kiss became harder, more intense. His hands held her steady as he explored her mouth, and she groaned against his lips.

Slowly, he moved his fingertips from her shoulder to graze the outside of her breast, down her rib cage and over her hip bone until his hand clenched around her upper thigh. With two steps he had her backed up against the wall. She went limp as he covered her, until she was sandwiched between his hot body and the hard concrete, still warm from the day's muted sun.

His hands were in her hair, loosening the strands. Stroking and pulling, pulling until she gasped from the sharp sting. Her legs quivered and he brought her closer, tilting her head so he could run his tongue across her teeth in just such a way it sent little quivers shooting through her. When he brought her hands together and stretched her arms to hold them high above her head, she allowed it.

How easily she followed his lead. How easy it was to let him direct her. *How could this be happening so fast?* The feeling was too intense, and it was exactly what she was afraid of. Letting go, craving something she couldn't control. Craving the *need* to let go.

So why did it feel so good?

He released her arms, but she kept them over her head

and she felt his hands at her chest, steady as he undid the first few buttons of her blouse. Still he kissed her. His knuckles were warm on her skin as he spread the fabric and then his fingertips found her nipple. She gasped into his mouth as he pinched, twisted. The pain shot through her, straight to her sex.

Ash, the others, had always been gentle.

She realized she did not want Mark to be gentle.

She was getting wet. Wet between her legs, but she didn't want him to touch her there, not yet. She wanted to feel the void, feel the want. The journey was as good as the destination, and she wanted to enjoy every moment of the ride, make it last.

Which was bad. Very bad. This was supposed to be a quickie, nothing more. She pulled back. "Do you have a condom?" .

He stepped between her legs and yanked up her skirt, lifted her up and she wrapped her legs around his hips. She held him between her thighs as he pushed his denim-clad erection against her panties, which were now moist and damp. "Mark. Please tell me you have a condom."

"Yeah, I have one in my pocket." He sounded so calm. How could he be so calm when she was so quickly becoming undone?

"Thank God." She rubbed her pulsing sex against him, sliding against the buttons of his jeans, letting them grate at her swollen flesh through her underwear. The muscles in his shoulders bunched beneath her hands, thrilling her. She could come, just like this, with a stranger.

He continued to kiss her, stroke her, wrap her hair in

his fist. Grind his cock between her legs until she was begging him. "Please, Mark. Condom."

"Come, Ruby."

"I will, I promise. As soon as you put on the condom and we...you know. *Do it*." She whispered the last two words.

He shook his head, and—*damn him*—he seemed to be biting back a smile. Again. "No, I mean come to the show. You obviously like the way I kiss."

She was panting as if she'd been running, and she had to fight to catch her breath. "Why do you care if I go later?"

By now her neat ponytail was practically nonexistent, and he wrapped a lock of hair around his finger. "Because then I can see you afterward."

"But—"

He gave her hair a gentle tug, and fuck it, her sex clenched from the sharp pain. Like a puppet, she responded to his every touch.

"Listen, Ruby. I want you."

"Here I am. Take me!" She wiggled a bit against his body as a prompt.

His eyes searched hers, darting back and forth. "I want more than a quickie against a wall. I want the night with you. And I have a feeling you want more, too."

Everything in her froze. "Like what? What do you think I could possibly want?"

Leaning in, he kissed her earlobe. "I think you want to give yourself over to me. I think you want to feel my hand on your ass. I think you want to know what it would be like to be owned by me. Just for one night."

Speechless, she stared over his shoulder at the

jasmine growing in a pot in the corner. She bit the inside of her cheek. He was wrong, so wrong. She *so* did not want those things.

So why was she trembling? Why was her pussy throbbing just from those simple words? Why were her nipples tingling beneath her satin bra?

And, most important, why were her insides melting into a puddle of lust with each passing second he breathed against her ear?

This was such a bad idea.

But the alternative was going home to her vibrator, which sounded much less appealing.

"Fine. I'll go," she said.

Her reward was another kiss that blew away any reasonable thoughts left in her head.

He slid her down his body and put her on her feet. Then he straightened her skirt and fastened one button between her breasts. How could he look so controlled when she felt anything but?

And then, with his hand, he encircled her throat, his palm pressing against her clavicle, and something calmed inside her. His eyes were dark as they drilled into hers. "I'll leave a pass at the door. There will be a spot reserved for you near the stage. Where I can see you."

"Yes," she breathed, loving the way his hand enclosed her neck. Loving *everything*.

"I'll tell the bartender to have a drink waiting for you. If any men approach you tonight, I want you to ignore them. Do you understand?"

She nodded. She couldn't help herself. She liked the feelings Mark had set off inside her too much to say anything at all, especially the word *no*.

Pinned to the wall, his large hand on her throat, she sank into him as he kissed her again. His mouth gently belied the rough grip he had on her body, and the juxtaposition of sensation nearly killed her.

How could she deny herself this? After all, it was just one night.

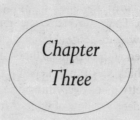

Chapter Three

"You scared her," Mark said.

From across the limo, Yvette grinned. "Did not."

"You did. I'm a big boy, you know. I can take care of myself."

She shrugged and shook back her hair. "I just don't trust all these girls coming out of the woodwork. It gets worse every day."

Mark ignored the bite of irritation he felt at Yvette's words. "Ruby isn't like that. She's an event planner. She was just doing her job."

Yvette barked a laugh. "Fucking you is part of her job description? Nice work if you can get it."

"You always get testy before a big show. Don't take it out on me."

Pulling a bottle of wine out of a built-in chiller, she poured herself a glass. "Isn't she a bit old for you?"

"I didn't notice."

"At least she seems to be aging well."

"Fuck off."

If Ruby was older, it didn't bother him at all. In fact, as he approached thirty, he was starting to look for more mature women, women who knew what they wanted and didn't play games.

"I would if I could," Yvette said. It was just the two of them in the limo. Their third band member, Jake, had to get to every show early to double-check that his drums hadn't been fucked with. Jake got a bit OCD when it came to his drums, which was funny because the guy was so relaxed about pretty much everything else.

Yvette took a deep swallow of wine. After a minute she said in a softer tone, "You're right. I'm sorry. This effing stage fright is killing me."

"You know the more freaked out you are, the better you perform."

She grunted and drained the rest of her wine.

Mark was the opposite. He got off on the crowd, and the bigger the better. The only other time he felt such a rush was when he was giving a woman pleasure through domination. Which was what he wanted to do to Ruby. Later. If she'd let him.

She would.

Adrenaline raced through his veins, releasing a rush that hit him like a drug. She'd done this to him, riled him up. He tapped his booted foot on the floor of the limo, unable to keep still. Between Ruby's response to him and the upcoming gig, he was pumped. Ready.

Ruby. Her sweet body had felt so good under his hands, and the way she melted against him when he kissed her, the way she gave herself over to his control—it got him hot as hell. She was so beautiful in her delicate submission.

"When was the last time you got laid, anyway?" Yvette asked with a smile.

He had to think. "Um, Seattle? Maybe it was Vancouver. It was a blonde, that much I remember." The Riders had just finished their first big tour, and everything was blending together: the gigs, the towns, the women. Just one giant blur of time, with nothing standing out except the exhilaration of performing in venues that seemed to get bigger in each city they played.

Mark had a hard time picturing Ruby becoming part of that blur. With her huge blue eyes, gorgeous black hair, and delicate frame, she had immediately caught his eye when he'd walked into the trendy bar. But it was so much more than her looks that had his cock as hard as granite. He smiled. Hell, she knew what a Bazantar was and probably knew more about jazz than he did. And it intrigued him that she seemed to have no idea who he, or his band, was. She seemed perfect.

An insane desire to discover her flaws overcame him. Maybe she snored or didn't recycle. Maybe she was a horrible driver. Maybe she wore flannel pajamas instead of the silk lingerie he could so easily picture her in.

"So, you ready?"

He glanced back to Yvette. She was on her second glass, but the wine seemed to have calmed her a bit; her fingers weren't their usual preshow fidgety selves, and she didn't look quite as ready to crawl out of her skin.

"Yeah. Should be a good crowd." Ruby had promised to come. He couldn't wait to play for her, couldn't wait to see her again.

Yvette grinned at him. "So. This Ruby is *different*."

Sometimes it seemed Yvette could read his mind, and it could be downright annoying. He decided to change the subject. "You're just jealous because I get more girls than you do."

She leaned back into the limo seat and gave him her

sassiest smile. "You're just looking for the perfect girl to replace me."

"Maybe I was. Ten years ago, when I met you and I thought a pair of perky tits and angel's voice equaled perfection."

One of Yvette's signature husky laughs burst from deep inside her throat. "And when I heard you play the first time in that dive bar? I did consider switching teams."

He took off his glasses and polished them with the edge of his T-shirt. "Well, I think the fact that I don't possess a vagina would have been a pretty large deterrent for you."

She nodded sagely. "Indeed."

"Anyway, I finally accepted the fact that I'd never get in your pants. I'm cool with it now. And you can have my leftovers."

"Mark, even I don't have the stamina to take up your leftovers."

"Not many do."

"So." Yvette gave him a playful nudge. "You gonna get some later?"

Yvette loved to hear the details of Mark's encounters. "I don't know. She said she'd come to the show."

Yvette raised a brow. "Huh."

"What, *huh*?"

"I saw you come back from the patio with her. You definitely had her all a-twitter."

Mark grunted.

"You keeping this one on the downlow or what?"

"No." He slid his glasses back on. "Maybe. I don't know." Normally he shared everything with Yvette. But for some reason he wanted to keep this thing with Ruby between the two of them. He didn't want to share her. In any way.

She grinned. "Interesting."

"What?"

"*Mark has a girlfriend,*" she began chanting in a sing-song voice. "*Mark has a girlfriend.*"

He couldn't help but laugh. "Fuck off! I just met her, and we leave town in twelve hours. Not to mention the small fact that we live on opposite sides of the country. I'll never see her again after tonight." Oddly, that last sentence was hard to say, or think.

"Unless we decide to record here. Then we'd be here a couple of weeks. And I gotta say, I like Emmett's setup. Very old-school. Hardly any digital."

Mark had already been leaning toward recording here, but he had to admit the thought of seeing Ruby while he did so was helping cement the deal. "He said he could fit us in as soon as we want."

"I'm game, and Jake's down with whatever."

"Yup."

So that was it, then. They'd be here for a couple of weeks, and he could see Ruby again. Reaching for the stereo controls, he turned up the volume until a loud, steady thump from a White Stripes tune blasted through the speakers and filled the limo.

Had he only just met Ruby a few hours ago? Already, he felt like he *knew* her. He knew she loved his hand around her neck, and a bit of pain with her pleasure. But she fought it; he could feel her struggling with her desire to submit to him.

She also loved chocolate. When she swallowed a bit of chocolate from her cocktail she'd closed her eyes, savored it in her mouth. He'd had a sudden desire to feel her tongue on his cock, licking the tip just as she'd done that glass.

He could have. On the patio, she'd wanted him. *Begged* him to fuck her. It had taken every ounce of willpower to say no. But, from the moment he'd seen her, he'd wanted more. He'd wanted to see her bound, in real life. Not just in a photograph.

Subspace. When a person gave over so completely, it produced a trancelike state for the submissive, and Mark couldn't stop thinking about taking Ruby there. Seeing her on her knees, ready for him. Building her up until she was begging him to spank her harder and harder and harder.

His balls went tight, his cock stirred. Anticipation coursed through him, and he couldn't keep still.

Tapping his fingers on the edge of the window, he tried to turn his thoughts to the upcoming show. The idea of getting on stage further energized him. Yeah, he was a thrill junkie. Always had been. And meeting Ruby was the biggest thrill he'd had in ages.

Ruby had just said good-bye to the last guest when Meg yanked her by the arm and pushed her into the women's restroom. Releasing her, Meg nailed her with a wide-eyed gaze. "Did you make out with Mark St. Crow on the patio?"

Clutching the countertop, Ruby dropped her head and breathed deeply. *In and out, in and out.* Finally she managed, "Oh my God. I think I did."

Arms akimbo, Meg gasped. "You naughty little minx!" She stepped closer and lowered her voice. "How was it?"

Ruby glanced up and realized she couldn't see anything

because her hair was a mess. Straightening, she gathered her hair and started redoing her ponytail. "It was..." She felt her cheeks heat. "Holy cow. I don't even know how to explain it."

"Come on, honey. You just made out with a gorgeous young musician. I want all the details, and the more sordid the better."

Turning, Ruby rested her backside against the counter. Although she'd been trying to keep her feelings under control, now her entire chest felt like it was about to explode from excitement.

After breaking up with Ash, she'd immersed herself into her work, and despite the fact that she threw parties for a living, she rarely had any time for fun herself. She couldn't remember the last time she'd felt this young, this energized.

She gripped the counter beside her hips. "Oh my God, Meg. Have you ever been kissed like...like you thought your legs would buckle? When he kissed me my knees actually felt weak."

"Oh, I remember that feeling," Meg said to the mirror, smoothing down her cropped bangs. "It happened the first time Emmett kissed me. Still does, sometimes."

"This isn't like what you and Emmett have. This is just tonight."

Meg tossed her bag onto the counter. Digging through the contents, she pulled out a shiny black tube of lipstick. "So, the night's not over for you two lovebirds, then?"

"He wants me to go to his show."

"You gonna go?"

Gazing in the mirror, Ruby lifted her chin, half expecting to see proof of where Mark had wrapped his hand around her neck. But her skin was pale and unmarked. Oddly, she was disappointed.

"*If* I went, I'd need to go home and change first. This suit doesn't exactly scream sex or rock and roll or...sex." She stole the lipstick from Meg's fingers, twisting the tube until the shiny red cylinder pushed up. "Have you ever noticed lipstick is really phallic?" She applied the crimson makeup to her lips.

Meg ignored her question. "You're not going home to change. I know you; if you go home you'll stay there."

"But I can't go like this." Through the mirror, Ruby scanned her ensemble: pencil skirt, blazer, and a blouse that still had the top three buttons undone. Boring. If she was going to do this, she wanted to feel sexy. Ergo, she needed a sexy dress. And shoes. Definitely shoes.

Meg took back her lipstick and leaned in close to the mirror. For some reason the woman refused to admit she needed glasses. "I have an entire collection of gorgeous dresses right next door. I can have you dressed and ready to go in ten minutes. Tops."

It was true. In fact, it was their shared love of vintage clothing and costumes that had brought the two women together. Meg had owned one of the best vintage-costume shops on Haight Street, and Ruby had become addicted to shopping there. When Meg closed the shop, the women had gone into business together using Meg's extensive collection of props and Ruby's extensive experience in planning events. They currently housed all their supplies in a spare room next to Emmett's recording studio.

Smiling slyly, Meg dropped the lipstick back into her purse. "You know. If the band does decide to record here, Mark will be in San Francisco for a few weeks. At least."

Ruby stared at Meg. "I hadn't exactly thought that far ahead. But it doesn't matter. I'm going to the show, and possibly seeing him afterward. *If* anything happens—"

"Which it will."

"I'll have had a one-night stand with a rock star."

"You lucky bitch." But Meg was smiling, and her eyes sparkled. "Just promise me one thing."

"The last time I promised you something I ended up with food poisoning."

"I really thought that taco stand was cleaner than it looked. Anyway, promise me you'll tell me all the details tomorrow? Even if he, you know...spanks you. Or something."

"Meg! Why would you think that?" And why did the thought of Mark spanking her make her insides go all quivery?

Meg shrugged. "I've just heard rumors he's into that kind of stuff."

Obviously, he was. But it was good to know Mark didn't keep it a secret; it made him more trustworthy somehow.

Meg clasped her bag shut and strode to the door. "Now come on, I have the perfect dress in mind. Let's go get you sexified." She grabbed Ruby's hand and tugged her out the door.

*Chapter
Four*

Emmett was busy talking to Mark's "people," so Ruby and Meg went to the show by themselves. True to his word, Mark had left passes at the door, so when the girls arrived at the venue they were able to bypass the long line snaking around the block.

"Oh my God!" Ruby said, eyeing the procession. "These kids all look like they're in high school!" Ruby's doubts about the night had been escalating, and feeling like she was old enough to be most of these kids' mother wasn't helping.

But Meg grabbed her arm and yanked her inside. "You're the one Mark St. Crow wants. Plus, you look fucking hot." Meg looked over Ruby's figure with the appreciative eye of a clothing connoisseur.

Ruby ran a damp palm over the silky fabric. "Are you sure? This is so different from my normal style." Meg had talked her into a red seventies-era disco dress. It was low cut and very, very clingy. "Are you sure I don't look too slutty?"

"Slutty can be highly underrated." Meg gave her a Cheshire cat grin. "And those shoes? They have CFM all over them."

Ruby glanced at the strappy gold sandals on her feet. She

wasn't used to heels quite this high, but she had to admit they were making her feel sexy. Not to mention, they also gave her five-foot-two frame some much-needed height.

Ruby grimaced. "They hurt like hell."

"It's a bitch being beautiful." Giggling, Meg took her arm and muscled her way up to the crowded bar.

A tall bartender with multiple eyebrow piercings caught her eye. "You Ruby?"

She blinked. "Yeah. How'd you know?"

"Mark said you'd be with a goth girl wearing spider-webs on her legs."

Meg raised her hand. "That would be me. I'll have a Lemon Drop, please. And my friend will have—"

"A chocolate martini," he finished, turning to pull two bottles from the shelf behind him.

Ruby felt Meg's gaze burning a hole into her face. "What?"

"Um, Mark St. Crow has your drink waiting for you at a show. That's what."

"Is that bad? Does that mean I'm a groupie?"

"It means he really wants you to have a chocolate martini. And that he's into you."

Ruby beamed. "Do you think so?"

"I do. Come on." They took their drinks from the bartender and started toward the stage.

Ruby reached out and touched Meg's shoulder. "Wait." For some reason she felt her face go hot. "Mark kinda asked me to go over there. He was very specific about it." She jerked her head toward the right of the stage.

"But I see some people we know on the other side."

Ruby's face was burning. But she didn't want to disobey Mark's instructions. "Please?"

Meg looked at her funny but then shrugged and followed her to a reserved table in the far right corner, separated from the crowd by a wooden rail. A little white card with the words *Ruby Darling* sat on the table, which somehow made her stomach do that fluttery thing again. They took their seats.

The venue wasn't big, but it was packed, and the energy vibrating inside the building was nearly palpable. Canned between-set music played, further adding to the sense of anticipation buzzing within the crowd. Ruby picked up on the power of it all, and her excitement level kicked up a notch. She realized she wasn't just excited to be with Mark after the show; she was eager to hear him play.

"When was the last time you were at a live show?" Ruby asked.

Meg looked thoughtful. "God, I don't know. Emmett goes all the time, but I never seem to have the energy."

"And the last thing I want to do in my spare time is go to another event."

They looked at each other for a second before bursting into laughter. "We are so old," Ruby said.

Meg held up her glass. "Cheers to that." Laughing, they sipped their drinks.

Finally Mark's band came onstage. The audience swarmed to the front as Mark took his place behind some kind of mixing machine. The third member, a guy with a bleach-blond Mohawk Ruby recognized from earlier, sat behind a drum set. Yvette slung a guitar over her shoulder, low on her hips, exposing the taut skin of her midriff.

Meg watched Yvette with a contemplative gaze. "I think that's one of the hottest women I've ever seen. If I swung that way, I'd be all over her."

"Gee, thanks."

"What?"

"Well, she's his ex, and I get the distinct impression that woman does not want Mark to be with me." Frowning, Ruby watched as the redhead went to Mark and leaned over his shoulder. She spoke close to his ear and laid her hand on his back, intimately casual.

Meg nodded. "Oh yeah. She's into him."

"Not. Helping." Ruby gave her friend her meanest glare, the one she used for caterers who showed up late.

Meg just laughed and ignored her, watching as Yvette took center stage. When the roar of the crowd died down, Mark dropped a needle onto a record and then the scratchy notes of an old jazz tune drifted through the speakers. It was a soft song, one Ruby recognized, and she couldn't help but sway a little to the tune. Soon the drummer began a steady beat, and a few minutes later Yvette struck a chord, adding a rhythmic harmony that had the crowd moving to the beat. The song built, layer after layer of sounds, driving faster and faster until the entire audience was like one giant beast, captive to the masterful music.

As Ruby was. But not just captive to the music. It was Mark, too, that had her riveted. He had presence, a commanding way about him, and he was very confident in what he was doing, and comfortable being onstage. He seemed to go into a trance, his competent fingers composing right before her eyes, using his mixer and the keyboards to create a sound so unique, it truly sounded like art. The beat pulsed right through her and she felt it everywhere. Her chest, her stomach. Between her thighs. She was so enthralled with his performance, she barely noticed when a young man she recognized as one of Mark's crew dropped a folded piece of paper in her lap.

He then disappeared, lost in the crowd before she could catch him. Puzzled, she unfolded the note and read.

Take off your panties and put them in your purse.
                                                    M.

For a second she just stared at the note. Did Mark really want her to do this? Here? Now?

She kinda wanted to.

Meg tapped Ruby's arm and pointed at the paper in her hand, her brow raised in question. But Ruby wasn't quite ready to share this particular note with her friend, so she just shrugged and tucked it away in her purse.

On edge, already about to explode in anticipation of what was to come—whatever that was—and excited from the music, the crowd, she could barely keep herself in check. Now he wanted her to take off her panties?

He was so bad. She loved it.

But could she do it? What if someone saw? She was just starting to create a name for herself as an event planner. When in public, she needed to behave professionally at all times. No, it was too risky.

But he was watching her.

She picked up her cocktail and realized her hand was shaking. When she brought the martini glass to her mouth a drop of the cocktail spilled over the rim and onto her hand. As she licked the sweet liquid off her fingertip, she glanced up to see Mark's gaze was locked on her mouth as she slowly licked the last drop from her skin.

She wasn't far away, and she could see his expression

tighten. Ha! So he wasn't entirely Mr. Cool, Calm, and Collected. She brought her drink to her lips again, this time using her tongue to lick the rim, slowly. Seductively.

He missed a beat.

She smiled. And savored the anticipation of waiting for his show to end. She was going to leave her panties on. And find out for herself what happened when she disobeyed an order from Mark St. Crow.

Chapter Five

"You didn't take off your panties," he whispered against Ruby's ear as she passed through the door. The chilly air hit her. She couldn't tell if it was from his warm breath in her ear or the slap of cold air, but a shiver raced up her spine.

"I couldn't exactly just whip them off in front of Meg." Not that her friend would have cared. Meg had practically shoved her out the door with Mark, saying she'd catch a ride home with a friend.

He followed Ruby into the alley and a limo pulled up. Soon they were zipping over the hilly streets toward her house in the Richmond District. They bumped along in silence until she glanced his way. Her breath caught. Those eyes of his: Dangerous. Exciting. Tempting. They made her want to unlock all her secrets and lay them at his feet.

And then he pulled her to him, kissing her softly. As he pressed his lips against hers, her head fell back against the worn leather of the limo seat. Her body went limp; he knew exactly how to make her melt, and there was a beauty in letting him.

There was something about opening up with a stranger. No rules, no limitations. Nothing to lose. Now, she sighed as his hand caressed her knee, moved over her thigh and slid under her dress.

"Open for me."

Her dress stretched against her thighs as she let her legs fall open.

Pulling her panties aside, he gently nuzzled his mouth against the side of her neck. "You make me so fucking hot, Ruby. Something about you..."

The limo crested a hill, then dipped over the other side. Her stomach dropped from the quick fall while at that very moment he slid a finger into her moist sex. She gasped.

He pulled out and pushed again, this time punctuating his movement with a sharp nip to her ear. Pure lust surged through her, had her nerves tingling, electrified.

"I want you bound for me. I want to see you so turned on you scream my name. I want you in so many ways, Ruby."

Even now, some part of her brain reminded her that she'd only just met him. Yet she felt safe, safer than she had in so long. With her body melting around his hand, she had no doubt he could give her what she so deeply craved.

She could barely admit it even to herself. But she wanted to be possessed, ruled. To experience the secret desires she'd admitted to no one, not even to Ash. Not even to herself. And this was perfect; a perfect stranger to take her there.

One night. Get it out of your system. Move on.

His chest pressed against her arm, and when he spoke she could feel his voice on her skin. "If we're going to do this, we're doing it right. The way you want it. The way I know you want it."

His hand still cupped her between her legs, warm and firm.

"Yes," she said.

He spoke softly, his hot breath sending thrilling pinpricks over her shoulders, down her arm. "Tell me your limits, Ruby. Tell me how far I can push you."

"I–I don't know." Apprehension and anticipation mingled inside her. She had no idea what to say. And she didn't want to have any limits, not tonight.

"I noticed you looking at my cuffs earlier. Tell me, Ruby. Do you like leather? Do you like being restrained?"

Even now she could smell it on him, and the scent was nearly as erotic as his touch, his voice. She nodded.

"Would you like to feel it on your skin? Striking you?"

When she was silent, he said, "Well, Ruby? Would you like that? Would you give me that privilege?"

She could barely breathe, let alone talk.

"You need to say yes if you want this, baby."

She tried to swallow, but her mouth was dry. "Yes," she managed, and her voice sounded scratchy.

He kissed her then, and she felt the pad of his thumb lightly on her clit.

"Oh," she said. "Yes, Mark."

"But you're a little naughty, aren't you? A little feisty." He pushed deeper into her pussy, until his finger was buried in her wetness. "That's okay. I like that in a girl. It's more fun, don't you think?"

His finger worked her, and she bit her lip, trying not to groan. "I'm not all that submissive," she gasped.

"I know. Earlier, at the show, why didn't you take off your panties?"

She sank even farther into the leather seat. "I don't know."

"Don't you?" He cupped her sex, his palm pressing perfectly on her clit.

She bit back a moan. "I couldn't...it was too public..."

He made a tsking noise. "You're a bad girl, Ruby." He slid another finger inside her. "Now I'm afraid I have to punish you."

"Yes. Please," she said, her body clenching around his fingers. It was starting. The thoughts in her head were evaporating like drops of water under the desert sun. Soon there would be nothing. Just him.

Giving herself over completely—it had been so long, and she was beginning to wonder if she'd ever let herself go one hundred percent. Because this was so different from anything else and it hit her like a shot of tequila, with a prickly heat that coursed through her veins, warmed her blood.

"Tell me you're mine tonight."

"You had me at hello."

"My naughty little Ruby." His low, hot voice breathed into her ear, making her shiver. "But it's an act. You've wanted to give yourself to me from the second we met."

She stilled. "For some reason, around you..."

"What? Tell me what I do to you, Ruby."

"You don't understand; I'm normally not like this. I'm normally very responsible."

"You think we're being irresponsible?"

"Yes."

She inhaled sharply when he slid his hand out of her pussy. He replaced her panties over her damp sex and then, arranging her dress over her thighs, he gently straightened the silky fabric. Then he grinned. "You're so sexy when you fight your desire for me. It'll be that much more fun when you're screaming for me to spank you harder."

She was about to argue, but he touched her lips gently, silencing her. With the hand that had been inside her he traced her lips with his fingertips. The scent of herself on his skin made her squeeze her thighs together, hoping the pressure would help ease the throbbing ache between her legs.

It didn't.

She closed her eyes as he pushed one finger into her mouth. Then two fingers. She tasted her own, acidic essence on his skin. She sucked him deeper, tasting and licking, hoping to tease him a little as he'd done to her. But it wasn't working; she was only getting hotter, wetter. Weighed down with wanting him.

He withdrew his hand, leaving her empty and filled with need. It took her a minute to focus after she opened her eyes. She could smell him, their scents mingled. She inhaled deeply, wanting to cement his unique, spicy scent into her nostrils. Knowing these memories would make her recollection of this night all the more real after he left.

He took her hand, lifted it to his lips, and kissed the back of her wrist. She wanted more, wanted him to take her finger into his mouth and lick her, suck her like she'd done to him. But instead he dropped their hands onto his lap and held them there for the rest of the ride home.

Her heart hammered the entire time. The tension in the limo was heavy, and the scent of sex and leather was making her breathless.

Finally they came to a stop. They got out of the limo, and she led the way to her Victorian apartment building. Her hand trembled as she unlocked the front door, and her legs trembled as they made their way up the marble steps to her apartment. Once inside, she placed her purse on the hall table and walked to the living room, her heels clicking on the hardwood floor as she crossed the room, the sound echoing in her ears.

She turned to face him. "Can I get you something? A drink? Coffee?"

"I'm good." He took in her place, inspecting her one-bedroom, second-floor flat. She followed his gaze to the huge bay window, beyond which the lights of the city sparkled. Even though tonight the fog muffled the view, San Francisco twinkled in colorful, blurry lights. It was this scene that had sold her on the tiny place nearly five years ago.

But the outlook didn't interest him as much as her music collection. Soon he was flipping through a crate of records she kept next to her ancient record player. "You really do like jazz."

She tucked a loose strand of hair behind her ear. "They were my dad's."

He looked up. "You close with your folks?"

"Not really. My dad left when I was sixteen. When Mom tracked him down, she left to be with him. Now, I get the occasional e-mail or postcard. I think they're in Thailand at the moment."

He blinked at her but didn't press her for information, which she appreciated. Instead he slipped a record out of a sleeve and gently placed it on the turntable.

Ruby loved the first few scratchy seconds right after

the needle dropped onto vinyl. Silently they listened to the static, and then the soft piano of a Thelonious Monk tune drifted through the speakers.

Mark stood, and she followed his gaze to the black-and-white picture hanging over the fireplace. It was a photograph of a woman's back. Rope came down from her neck, winding around her shoulders and across her arms, multiple times, ending with one knot that held her wrists tightly at the base of her spine.

Mark glanced at her. "You?"

She nodded. Her walls were filled with the black-and-white photographs she'd taken during her college years at RIT. But there was one that wasn't hers, the only photograph she'd kept from her time with Ash. Of course, Mark had honed right in on it.

It didn't show her face or even her tattoo. But he knew it was her. He already knew her that well. Even her own sister had never made the connection, which was why she'd kept the photograph on her wall.

"Gorgeous," he said.

She laughed nervously. "That's because you can't see my face."

He turned to her then, his gaze sharp. "I never want to hear you talk about yourself that way, Ruby. Understand?"

All she could do was nod.

Rooted to the floor, she stood stock-still as he approached her. Then he was kissing her again, with that gentle yet commanding way that turned her insides to mush. She barely noticed the firm hand on her shoulder, pushing her to her knees.

She closed her eyes, felt the wool of the Persian rug scratch the skin of her knees. The floor grounded her as she turned inward, mentally preparing herself for whatever he wanted to do to her.

For the millionth time she wondered how this was happening—how she'd let it happen. And yet, it felt powerful somehow. Mark said he would push her, but, more important, she was pushing herself to explore these fantasies she'd been hiding for so long.

"Are you ready?"

Her belly quivered with nerves and anticipation. "Yes." She braced herself on the floor.

She heard his boots thudding as he circled her. "Can you follow instructions?"

"Yes."

"Then why are you still wearing your panties?"

She speared him with a look.

Legs planted in a wide stance before her, he held his hands clasped before him. Despite his commanding posture, he smiled at her. "There will be rules. Such as, no dirty looks."

She tried not to roll her eyes.

"Also. Don't move unless I tell you to. Don't speak unless spoken to. Unless of course, you want me to stop. If you want me to stop, you can say . . . Chihuahua."

"Chihuahua?"

"You want me to stop already?"

"No . . . but Chihuahua?" She tried not to laugh.

He also seemed to be holding back his humor. "You just broke a rule. Such a bad girl, but I'll enjoy punishing you for it."

She bit her lip to keep from telling him to go fly a kite.

His smile faded, became more serious. "Now, are you ready, Ruby darling?"

Every muscle in her body seemed to tremble as she took a deep breath and met his stare. Last chance. She could still run away. Scream Chihuahua.

And always wonder what it would have been like.

She took a deep breath and straightened. "I'm ready."

"Take off your dress."

Her arms trembled as she lifted the hem of her skirt up over her thighs, her black panties, her back. He finished the job by raising the dress over her head, and then she was exposed except for her black lace panties and gold stilettos. She felt goose bumps trickle up her arms.

He took her hair in his hands and moved it aside, draping the heavy length over her shoulder. She felt a hot kiss at the back of her neck, right over the cherry blossoms tattooed at the nape.

His soft lips and warm breath calmed her shaky body. She closed her eyes, listening as he moved. She heard the clinking of brass as he unbuckled his belt. Then the sound of leather sliding across cloth reached her ears. Her breath caught in her throat.

Softly, so softly it was like a whisper, he took the strap of black leather and drew it over her skin. Around her neck, over her collarbone, across the back of her shoulders.

Ash had used only soft hemp rope. So much heavier, this leather. It scratched her skin like the music coming from the old vinyl scratched her ears, and there was something distantly comforting in the sensation.

As he caressed her skin with his belt, she absorbed its commanding weight, knew Mark held that exquisite power in his hands. The scent of buckskin would never seem innocent again, would always remind her of Mark.

He took both her arms until they were straight behind

her back, rigid. She wore no bra, and her nipples tingled as she arched forward.

Binding her with his belt, he wrapped the leather around her arms from elbow to wrist, until she heard the final clink of him fastening the buckle. Then, she was as he'd wanted her. Bound. His.

Shaking, she waited to see what he'd do next. She heard his footsteps on the hardwood floor, but she dared not turn around to see what he was up to.

Then he was back, his hand resting gently on her head, caressing her. Calming her.

"The first thing I noticed about you was your hair. I had to keep my hands behind my back to keep myself from burying my fingers in it."

She felt a brush oh-so-gently moving through the strands of her hair. It tingled her scalp and seemed intimate somehow. As he continued to brush her hair she felt her nerves calm down, just a little.

He continued for a moment before taking the boar bristles and lightly skimmed her ribs, down her spine and then her buttocks. The sensation was prickly and should have been unpleasant, but it wasn't. In fact, the feeling became more lovely by the second as he scraped her ass, one side and then the other, running the brush over the edge of her panties. He increased pressure until the bristles scraped her skin, causing her to inhale sharply. It hurt, and yet the pain only made her more aware of how turned on she was. Her eyes closed, she felt his breath at her ear.

"You're the one bound, Ruby. But you have all the power here. Don't forget that."

She nodded, unable to speak.

He scraped her ass again with the brush. "Such beautiful skin, so pale. It's going to look even more beautiful after I'm done with you, and you're going to love it. You're going to love looking at your skin and knowing I put those marks on your body. Aren't you, baby?"

She squirmed and he chuckled.

"I was very disappointed earlier when you went against my order for you to take off your panties."

"I know," she breathed.

Lean over the chair. Rest your body on the cushion."

Kneeling, she leaned facedown across the cushion of the overstuffed chair. Her nipples tingled against the fabric. Her arms, bound by Mark's belt, were stiff behind her.

Now she was utterly exposed, vulnerable. She'd given herself over to him, given him that authority. Why was it so freeing to be so helpless? What was it about Mark that made her want to give him this? Give him everything?

He'll be gone in the morning.

She pushed the thought away. The fact that he would be leaving just made her more determined to take advantage of every second, to experience this night with him as intensely as possible.

Something dark fell over her eyes, blinding her. She inhaled the now-familiar scent that made her knees weak. Mark's shirt. He was using his shirt to blindfold her.

"Oh, God." The sensation was killing her. She couldn't see; she couldn't move. She could just smell him, hear him...

"How are you doing, darling Ruby?" he asked.

"Never better." She tried to sound droll, but her voice

trembled, giving her away. "Fuck it. Please, Mark. I need..." She had to feel him. She couldn't *feel* enough.

"What do you need, Ruby? Tell me."

"You. I need to feel you. On me, inside me."

"Oh, but I think you need something else. I think you need a little more sensation than a cock filling you up."

His graphic language set her sex on fire. He seemed to layer her pleasure, much as he'd layered his music during the show.

He took the bristles again, ran them over her ass and upper back, across the backs of her thighs, until she was trembling again. Until she was raw.

It was never like this before. Being bound by Ash seemed so incomplete in comparison; this was what she'd been craving. Mark had every nerve in her body alive, made every sensation amplified.

Now he used the brush with a heavier touch. She squeezed her eyes shut as he scoured her skin. Her body shook from needing him, needing him to strike her. She could feel her own endorphins kicking in, turning the pain to pleasure, but she wanted more. Wanted something harder.

"You like that, Ruby, don't you? I can feel you trembling. But you know I'm just preparing you because you know the first slap won't be gentle."

Good. She didn't want it to be. She had no idea how she knew that, but she was very certain that she did not want a gentle hand. She wanted to feel. She wanted to feel *everything*.

With the back of the brush, he struck her with a stunning precision that thrilled her very core. Sharp pain singed the entire right side of her ass. Still, she did not cry out. Instead she begged. "Please—"

"Sshh."

She bit her lip.

The next slap was harder and hurt. Hurt so much she couldn't keep her voice inside.

He slapped her again, with more force.

"Fuck!" Her entire body responded in a rush of bitter-sweet pleasure.

"Do you want more?"

"Oh, God—"

The back of the brush stung her again; the slapping sound resonated in her small apartment, drowning out the soft jazz.

"Ask for more."

"Please, more—" She screamed, her body twisting, writhing.

He obliged. Beautiful pain ripped through her; her pussy throbbed from it, her mind reeled from it. And each time he struck her ass she inhaled him again, thankful for the shirt he'd used as a blindfold. Her senses were limited to scent and pain and sound, and just when she was going to come from it all, he stopped.

"Please, more . . ." She was begging. Begging him.

"I think you've learned your lesson." His voice sounded dark and gravelly, hoarse. She rubbed her crotch against the edge of the chair, hoping for even the tiniest bit of friction of release.

"Oh, no, you don't." He yanked her hips back and tugged down her panties until the elastic stretched just above her knees. The air chilled her wet pussy but then he was there, his warm tongue licking her, exploring every moist inch. She backed into his mouth, pressed against his face. He licked her from clit to anus, again and again, until she was screaming nonsense, screaming his name. And when he shoved his fingers deep inside her she came in a hard rush that left her shattered.

She didn't remember him unbinding her or lifting her, but then she was in his arms, cradled against his chest as he dropped into the chair. He gently untied the blindfold and her gaze fell on his exposed skin.

It seemed strange that this was the first time she'd seen him undressed, and she drank him in. He had little body hair to detract from his lithe frame. When her eyes fell on his nipple rings her sex gave a little throb. She wanted to lean down and take one into her mouth. How hard would he like her to tug? He knew so much about her, yet he still remained a mystery to her.

And it was already early morning. So little time remained to explore this man, Mark St. Crow.

Sitting in the chair, he held her in his lap, nuzzling her hair, her ear, her neck. Held her with such tenderness it melted her insides. She loved the way he could dominate her and nurture her in the same moment. He kissed her eyes, licked away the tears her release had brought forth.

Taking her arms in his hands, he massaged her wrists. "Been a while, baby?"

She nodded. "Yes. Since..." She glanced at the portrait on the wall.

"He broke your heart, then?"

"No. He just couldn't give me what I needed."

"And I can." It wasn't a question; the fact that she was still quivering inside from her orgasm was all the answer she needed.

Mark reached down to pull her panties over her knees and her heels. He threw them next to her dress. "Why me?" His brown eyes searched hers.

"I liked you. I trusted you." She smiled. "And I'm insane, obviously."

"I'm glad I met you tonight, Ruby." His fingers skimmed a lazy circle around her nipple until she felt the tip harden under his touch. And then, a stirring between her legs.

Her ass still stung from earlier, and she couldn't wait to see the marks on her skin. What was that about, anyway? It seemed so wrong, and yet there it was.

She began to suspect this was a huge mistake, this little tryst with Mark. This feeling, this afterglow, could be addicting.

"Do you ever stop thinking?"

She met his gaze. "What do you mean?"

"I can see it in your eyes, the little gears churning."

"It's just that I never—"

"Do things like this. I know." He kissed her softly on the lips. "But I'm so glad you did."

Through his jeans she could feel his erection pressing against the side of her hip. He'd taken off his glasses and now he slid them back on. She reached up and gently traced the frame. "Can you see without them?"

"Barely."

"I think they're sexy."

"Yeah?"

She nodded.

With great care he took her head between his hands and lowered his mouth to hers. "I want to fuck you now, Ruby."

"Yes. Fuck me." She'd never spoken this way before, but with him she couldn't hold anything back. Like somehow it was easier to be herself with this stranger than with her family and friends.

Lifting his hips, he tugged off his jeans and boxers and kicked them aside.

"Put your hands on my shoulders."

She did.

He took his cock in his hand and stroked down and up, slowly. Her pussy responded immediately with a steady, pulsing throb. She watched as he tore open a silver packet with his teeth, removed the condom and slid it over his erection. His hip bones were sharp and angular, his stomach flat. She loved watching the muscles of his body as he moved.

"Slide onto me, Ruby."

She closed her eyes as he guided her. This was it, what she'd been waiting for. She slowly sank onto his body, and when he was inside her, she cried out from the satisfaction of it.

He filled her completely, physically and emotionally. She was dying to give herself over to him. Using her pelvis, she rocked against him back and forth, until she saw a little drop of sweat on his brow. Lust pooled inside her, between her legs.

"Don't come," he said.

Her hands clenched his strong, smooth shoulders as he lifted her up, then down, directed her. Every nerve in her body screamed, wanting release. Her own cries of ecstasy, animalistic and unlike anything she'd ever heard herself utter, contrasted with the soft jazz music, elevating the erotic energy already coursing though her body. Her orgasm, just out of reach, throbbed from her clit to the depths of her sex and deeper still.

She watched his eyes darken, his lids lower, and she fought the urge to lick the drop of sweat off his brow. She couldn't take that initiative. Even now, with her riding him, he controlled her. His need to control and her need to submit seemed to pulse between them, like a living thing.

He leaned forward and took her nipple into his mouth. She arched against him, and when he bit her flesh she nearly died.

"Mark, please." She loved to hear herself beg.

He looked up and his gaze was hard on hers. "Do you want to come?"

"Yes, please…*please.* I want to come."

He removed her right arm from his shoulder and kissed the tip of her index finger. "Then fuck me."

He sucked her finger into his mouth and she ground against him, moving until her clit rubbed his pelvic bone. *Yes, right there…*

"Mark!" She threw her head back as the climax ripped through her, tore her apart. And only then, with her finger on his tongue and her gaze locked on his, did he allow his own release.

She didn't know how long she lay on top of him, a panting heap. He traced his fingers over her back, stroked her hair.

After a while she glanced over her shoulder at the photograph Ash had taken of her. Yes, it was beautiful. But it was like looking at an image of someone else. It was the image of someone trusting and foolish. It didn't feel like her at all.

Now, suddenly, she was sick of the picture, sick of it in

her home, sick of it on her wall. She suppressed the urge to stomp across the room, rip the thing down, and throw it out the window.

But then she remembered the photographs Mark had purchased. She thought of him looking at those images, and it softened her. Just thinking that he might look at them, that he would remember her a little, made her heart melt.

She kissed Mark's cheek and closed her eyes. She wouldn't think about that. Not now, not while she still lay slick and warm in his arms. There would be time for that tomorrow. After he'd gone.

Emmett finally walked in the door at two in the morning. Meg sat at their concrete counter, sipping decaf. Waiting.

He closed the door silently, tiptoed through the entry, and stepped into the open living area before he saw her. "Meg? What are you doing up?"

She smiled. "Waiting. For you."

"Oh." He looked past her shoulder. "Great."

Sliding off the barstool, she let her robe drop to the floor, leaving herself dressed in nothing but a sheer black negligee. "I was hoping we might...you know...do it."

He ran a hand through his hair. "God, Meg. I'm exhausted."

She clenched her fists. "You never used to be too exhausted for sex."

"That was before we bought this place, before the new studio, before..."

"Before what?" She swallowed down the ball of panic in her throat.

He shrugged, his shoulders bunching underneath his

sweater. One of the things she'd loved about Emmett was his body, how he looked in clothes. He was tall and skinny and still wore Converse high-tops. He had spiky black hair and reminded her of Sid Vicious. All those things, combined with his sweet personality, had made her fall for him at first sight.

He came to her and placed a quick kiss on her forehead. "I'm sorry, babe. I promise, tomorrow I'll have more energy." He turned and walked away to their bedroom.

Tomorrow. How many times had she heard that? Swallowing back tears, Meg picked up her robe and followed him to bed.

Chapter Six

Ruby was trembling in Mark's arms.

He held her tightly, stroking her back as he kissed her nipples. He could feel the muscles of her arms spasm beneath his hands as she recovered from what they'd done.

What they'd done. He was flying high still but beginning to crash. Didn't matter. What mattered was Ruby in his arms, open and vulnerable and needing him to care for her.

He knew he'd taken her further than she'd ever allowed herself before, and now, with this petite beauty in his arms, he felt so much more than an obligation to be a responsible dom. The desire to protect her came from somewhere deep inside, and it was unfamiliar and primal.

He stroked her silky hair, and she smiled up at him, still dreamy. He wanted to see that look again, wanted to look in her eyes and see everything right there. It seemed that if he just searched her eyes long enough, he'd know all her secrets, her deepest fantasies. And fuck if he didn't want to be part of those desires.

Wrapping her in a soft blanket he'd found draped over the couch, he laid her on the oversized chair.

As she rested her head against the back cushion she

looked at him, her eyes wide and dark and so open; for a second he had to look away.

Then he leaned down and kissed her forehead. "Be right back."

She nodded and closed her eyes.

Grabbing his jeans and T-shirt, he found his way to her bathroom, went inside and closed the door. He ran a hand over his head.

His hand was shaking.

Fuck.

Thinking about the fact that he had to leave in just a few hours made something go crazy inside him. He didn't want to go. He wanted to be with her the whole damn day. Make her breakfast, learn how she took her coffee. Make love to her again. Make love to her slowly and sweetly. Watch her come again and again.

He tossed the condom into the garbage and went to the sink. In Ruby's bathroom, there wasn't a stray hair to be found, and soap, toothbrush, and tissue box were arranged symmetrically. Even her makeup brushes seemed to be arranged in order; they stuck out of a glass vase like a bouquet. Her bathroom represented her perfectly: feminine and controlled. Each little glimpse into her life— from her orderly bathroom to her alphabetized record collection—came at him like tiny revelations. He didn't want to be this fascinated by these little things, but he was.

He picked up a bar of soap and brought it to his nose. Jasmine. *Ruby.* He turned on the faucet and lathered the soap between his hands, rubbing until a rich foam coated his palms. He washed his hands, his face, took his time. He massaged the silky soap into his skin, scrubbing up like a surgeon.

Why was it so hard to think of leaving?

Here he was, in the bathroom of a girl he'd met less than twelve hours ago, sniffing her soap and trying to memorize the scent.

This was a fucking first.

He rinsed the last of the soap off his hands and face and dried himself with a soft towel. Then he pulled on his jeans and yanked his T-shirt over his head.

Taking a deep breath, he opened the door and stepped back into the hallway. And when he rounded the corner to her living room her eyes fell directly on his, as if she'd been watching for him, waiting for him.

Two steps and he was there. "Baby, you okay?"

She nodded and gave him a little smile. "I think I'm still trying to process what just happened."

He got on his haunches, brushed her hair off her forehead and kissed her nose. "I'm going to put you to bed." Sliding his arms under her, he lifted her body to his chest, and as he did so she held his gaze, her dark eyes wide. Fuck, she was beautiful.

He held her tighter to his chest and ignored the strange feelings boiling inside him. It was natural for a top to feel protective. He kept telling himself that as he walked to her room, kissed her temple. He inhaled the jasmine scent of her hair, tried to fill his lungs and his head so he wouldn't forget her scent.

Her room was easy to find—it was past her bathroom and down a hallway peppered with photography. As curious as he was about her, he couldn't look at them. He didn't want to know if there were any other images of her that her ex had taken. He didn't want to think about it. Couldn't think about it.

Still wrapped in the blanket, he placed her on the bed. His gaze fell on her bedside clock and he looked away. It was morning. Time was passing fast, too fast.

She was trembling, her legs and arms shaking. He tucked the blanket tighter around her body.

Sitting on the bed next to her, he brushed a lock of hair off her face. "That was pretty fucking intense, yeah?" God, she was stunning even with her eye makeup smeared, her eyes bloodshot, and her hair messy. It was too much, too good. His throat closed up.

She blinked a few times. "I don't even know what to say. With Ash it was so different. Not like this at all."

At the mention of her ex's name he frowned. The thought of her with another man made his stomach tighten.

"I'll call you tomorrow night, I mean tonight. We have to meet with some suits in L.A., but I can call you as soon as we check into our hotel."

She shook her head. "No, you don't need to do that."

"I *want* to do that."

Closing her eyes, she pulled her hand out of his. "Really. It's fine. This was really ... great."

"Great?"

"Yes."

"That's it?"

She narrowed her gaze, her eyes becoming more focused. "Yes. What else do you want it to be?"

"Ruby. I want to see you again."

"You mean next time you pass through San Francisco? When will that be?"

He searched her eyes, not sure what he was looking for there. "We've decided to record here. Starting right away, so I'll be here a few weeks."

She pulled the blanket to her chin. "That's great." But she sounded less than happy, and Mark waited for her to go on.

"This was supposed to be a one-night thing. Nothing more," she said.

"I'm not saying it will be."

She sat up. "Exactly!"

He stood and pulled a worn quilt off a side chair, came back to her and tucked the second layer around her body. "Baby, you are making my head spin." He couldn't help but think that if this were any other girl, he'd have been out of there already. And yet here he was, practically begging to see her again.

"Listen," she said, placing a hand on his. And when she looked at him her expression was downright placating. "This was, um, very pleasant, and you're a really nice guy."

Now *she* was giving *him* the nice-guy speech? When had he totally lost control of this night?

She smiled at him. "Tonight was new and intense, and I could just fall—" She bit her lip and looked away.

His heart missed a beat. "Fall for what, Ruby?"

After a deep breath she straightened and met his stare. "For a guy who'll be gone by the end of the month. By the morning."

It was like a punch to the gut. But what could he say? It was true.

Still, he wasn't ready to leave her yet. "Listen, let's talk about all that later. You've had an emotional night, and I just want to make sure you're okay."

"I *am* okay." She lifted her chin, a gesture he was coming to love and hate all at once. "Seriously. I'd rather you go."

"Why are you fighting this so hard?"

Wide-eyed, she looked incredulous. "Fighting what, exactly?"

"This." He waved his hand around the room, as if that frustrated gesture would explain everything.

"Don't you see? I'm not fighting anything. I'm old enough to know how this works. Tonight, it's me. Tomorrow night, it'll be another girl."

Her words made his blood run cold. "Is that how you see me?"

Nibbling her bottom lip, she just looked at him, her silence all the answer he needed.

Running a hand over his scalp, he took a calming breath. And truthfully, he couldn't even deny her words. He had too many notches on his belt to refute what she'd said. But this was different; so different, he had no idea what to say.

She spoke to him as if he were a stubborn child. "Listen. I feel something right now, right here." She pointed to her chest. "I don't know if it's because of what you did to me or something more. But I do know that I hate saying good-bye. More than anything. And the longer you stay, the harder it's gonna be. So please. Just go."

He shook his head. "It would be totally irresponsible for me to leave you now. It's a dominant's responsibility to care for his submissive." The words sounded rote, mechanical. And desperate.

"I'm fine. Please, Mark. Go back to your hotel. Get some sleep. *Please. Just go.*"

"It doesn't feel right." And it didn't. The total wrongness of the situation hit him like a punch in the gut. Just a short time ago he'd been flying after what had been a nearly perfect night with a nearly perfect woman. And now that perfect woman was kicking him out of her apartment.

When had he lost control?

The feeling was unfamiliar and unwelcome. His heart beat a disturbing rhythm in his chest, and he wanted to run. Run away from this feeling.

Run away from her.

"Fine, baby. Whatever you want." He spun on his heel and stalked toward her living room where his boots and jacket lay next to the chair. He tried not to think about Ruby's naked ass as she'd bent over that chair. Tried not to picture the marks he'd left with his belt.

His marks. He laughed wryly as he yanked on one black boot. She was right. He'd never see her again. They'd already fucked; what did he care if she wanted him gone? Usually he was dying to sleep in his own bed. This wasn't any different.

He stood and slid the belt back through the loops of his jeans.

Then, shaking his head in the silence, he left.

Chapter Seven

Ruby heard her front door shut. Not a slam, but not soft, either. It was the sound of a person sure of where he was going. It was the sound of Mark leaving.

Just as you asked him to.

She took a deep breath and looked at her open bedroom door. She heard a car go by, heard a siren in the distance. The city was alive, breathing, but inside her flat everything was quiet and still. Dead air.

Fuck, fuck, fuck.

Had she made a mistake sending him away? But she'd meant what she'd said. She hated saying good-bye. It sounded so lame, so neurotic. But hey, she'd never claimed to be normal.

Even now, as sensation returned to her overstimulated body, she realized she enjoyed the way her ass throbbed from Mark's impromptu paddling. And it turned her on all over again.

What was wrong with her?

Have you ever been spanked? Meg's question bounced around in her head.

Twelve hours ago, that answer had been no; nothing but a secret fantasy, and now ... it was very real.

Flopping back onto the mattress, she smiled a secret

smile. She'd just had her first spanking. From Mark St. Crow, up-and-coming rock god.

Maybe she could have handled things differently, been more diplomatic instead of freaking out and kicking him out. But it was for the best, it really was. If she'd let him stay, she wouldn't have known if he truly wanted to be there, or if he was simply being a gentleman by staying the night.

He'd been irritated that she'd made him go, but hey, that was probably because it had never happened before.

He'd get over it. Just as she would get over him.

She stepped over the edge of the mountain hot spring. Steam rose in billowing, hot clouds around her. With such pristine water it was hard to tell where the bottom was, but the water was too tempting. She jumped in.

The spring was hot, but it didn't burn her. Instead it seeped into her bones as she floated on her back. She tried not to think about how deep the water was because when she did fear pierced her. Deep waters terrified her, always had.

Her eyes popped open. She heard her sister's cry, but she couldn't see her. She began to swim, following her sister's voice. But then the water started to surge in a whirlpool, and Ruby was spinning, spinning, being sucked down, her sister's name a silent scream in her mouth...

The phone pulled her slowly out of the dream. Her heart still pounded as she reached across the bed to pull her cell off the nightstand and she flipped open the phone without even looking at the caller ID. "Hello?" Her voice sounded scratchy, sleepy.

She glanced at the clock. 10:30? She never slept this late, even on a Saturday.

"Hey, gorgeous."

She bolted upright and cleared her throat. There was only one man who called her that. "James. It's so nice to hear from you." There, that sounded normal. And awake. "How are you?"

"Good. Listen, I was wondering if you had time to get together. With me."

Her pulse fluttered. Was he asking her on a date? After months of flirting and not-so-subtle innuendo, was he finally doing it?

James Cleaver was CEO for a very successful Palo Alto software company. She'd planned their Christmas party last December, and it had been amazing, a winter wonderland like something out of a fairy tale. With an endless budget and free rein, Ruby thought it was her best event ever. She was dying to get more jobs like that—high-end, high-class, and high-budget. It was exactly the kind of event she wanted her company to be known for.

Not to mention, high-end parties brought high-end guests. At thirty-seven, Ruby was feeling her clock ticking, and she wanted to meet a good, responsible, successful man. James Cleaver was all those things. He even had the perfect last name. At the Christmas party, he'd asked her to dance three times, and she was sure he'd call her afterward for a date. Now, four months later, he was.

And of course it was at that exact moment she remembered all the things she'd done last night. With a man who was the polar opposite of James Cleaver. As if to taunt her, her ass suddenly began to sting, and she saw herself bent over a chair, her ass in the air as Mark spanked her. Her body immediately responded in a hot flush, and she squeezed her thighs together in an attempt to hammer down the sensations coursing through her.

"...spring fling. You know, as kind of a company morale thing. I have some ideas for the theme, but I know you'll make it amazing."

James continued, but now Ruby couldn't concentrate. Last night, she'd had Mark St. Crow between her legs. She'd obeyed his commands, let him paddle her ass.

"Ruby?"

Harder! She squeezed her eyes shut, trying to get Mark out of her head. "Very nice ideas. Indeed." But all she could think about was melting under Mark's hot kisses, his warm hands.

"Great. I'm happy you like it so much," he said with a laugh. Not for the first time, Ruby noticed James had a very nice laugh.

She tried to picture James, in his khaki pants and starched shirt, wielding a whip at her. She giggled.

"Are you laughing?"

"No." She put her fingers to her lips, took a deep breath, trying to get the image of a BDSM James out of her head. "Um. It's just that I think everyone will whip."

"Pardon?"

"Flip. Definitely." She nodded as if he could see her. "Everyone will flip over this idea."

"I'm glad you think so."

Awkward silence. She couldn't think! Finally she said, "Can I call you on Monday and we'll set up a time to get together?"

"Yes, I'm sorry. It's Saturday. Sometimes I forget people actually have lives. I'm at the office. Of course," he said with a chuckle.

The guy seemed to always be at the office, which was strange because he was charming, attractive, and wealthy. He was one of the most desirable bachelors she knew.

"I'll talk with Meg, and we'll put together some ideas," she said, pulling a pad of paper and pencil off her nightstand.

"I'm so glad you like the rock-and-roll theme."

Fuck. A. Duck. Is that what she'd just agreed to? After last night, she'd had enough rock and roll to last the rest of her life! She began doodling skulls on her pad of paper. "It's very fresh, very, um...hot."

"And so when I saw the paper this morning, I knew you were just the person to call."

She paused her doodling midcrossbone. "I'm sorry, what paper?"

"Oh, I guess you haven't seen it. The *SF Review*. There's a picture of you and Mark St. Crow at a bar. I didn't know you two were such good friends."

"Oh, shit."

"Is something wrong?"

"Oh, it, it's just that Mark really isn't a friend of mine." *Just my one-night dom.* "He's really just an acquaintance; we're not involved in any way." *Other than when I had him between my legs last night.* "I mean, I'm not sure what the paper said, but I only met Mr. St. Crow last night." *And five minutes later I was begging him to fuck me.*

She began scribbling large X's across the skull.

"Don't worry, gorgeous. I'm sure you're just friends

with the band." But his tone had *wink wink* all over it. "But maybe you could ask him if they'd be interested in playing this private party?"

She wanted to say no. So badly. But the more high-end events she planned, the more successful her company would become. "Sure, James. I'll see what I can do."

Frowning, she flipped her phone closed. The last thing she wanted was a reason to call Mark. She wanted last night to remain a nice, naughty memory.

One night of craziness.

One night of bliss.

One night that would never, ever be repeated.

What she needed to do was focus on the fact that James Cleaver wanted another party. A spring fling. What she really wanted was to persuade him to have a spring fling with *her*. Maybe he was just too shy to ask her out on a real date.

Placing her phone back on the nightstand, she wondered what a sweet, vanilla guy like that would think of her posing for an erotic photographer.

Well, there wasn't any reason he needed to know about it.

Which reminded her, she needed to make damn sure there weren't any more pictures of her out there. Since he'd never shown up last night, she hadn't been able to tell Ash off. She made a mental note to do so ASAP. Meanwhile, she needed to talk to Meg. They had an event to plan.

Ruby exited the taxi on Union Street, in front of a colorful and fragrant flower stand that had set up shop on a corner. Tilting her chin, she let the sun warm her skin.

She didn't mind the San Francisco fog; it made clear days like this sparkle in comparison. Everything and everyone seemed so much more alive and vibrant, which was exactly how Ruby felt as she wound through the crowded sidewalk. Today Pacific Heights was busy with families pushing shiny ergonomic strollers and twenty-something women carrying shopping bags that looked as expensive as whatever contents lay inside.

Many of the cafés had placed tables outside on the sidewalks, and as Ruby walked toward Savor, she glanced at the patrons enjoying a meal in the sun. She smiled at a toddler attempting to scoop scrambled eggs into her mouth and nodded at two elderly, dapper men sipping from foamy white cups as they watched people walk by.

Just another normal day in San Francisco. But she felt anything but normal.

All morning she'd been wondering about Mark, wondering where he was. It was damn annoying, really, and, for the millionth time, she shook thoughts of him out of her head.

Instead she focused on the people around her. A couple sipping mimosas caught her eye. They had scooted their chairs very close together, so close they were touching shoulders. Their voices were low and their faces close together. Intimate. She'd never experienced that kind of obvious love, with Ash or any of the boyfriends she'd had before him. She was beginning to wonder if she was even capable of it.

Looking away, she picked up her pace. Two cafés later she found Meg sitting at a small metal table outside Savor.

"Hey, Megs."

Meg stood and gave her a hug. "Hey, sweetie. I ordered your usual."

Ruby hung her purse on the back of a wooden folding chair and sat down, trying not to wince. Her skin still showed crimson scratches from the hairbrush bristles, and her bottom was sore from the spanking Mark had so deftly given her. He hadn't bruised her, but she was still red. Some part of her wanted to stay that way. Marked. It was the only connection she had with him, and she didn't want it to fade. Each time she felt the pain she remembered exactly how those marks had gotten there, and each time she recalled the scene her heart skipped and her sex began to throb.

Note to self: Spanky-spanky with Mark St. Crow? Not as easy to get over as one might think.

"So why this emergency brunch meeting, anyway? I hope it's because you're going to fill me in on all the naughty details of your night with Mark St. Crow." Meg took a big sip of her foamy latte.

Ruby reached for her own latte and shook her head. "I got a call from James Cleaver today. He wants us to plan a spring-fling theme party for his company!"

Meg's eyes went wide. "Oh my God! That's awesome!"

"Well, there's a catch. He wants the Riders to perform."

"You're kidding."

"No. He wants it to be a rock-and-roll party. Big venue, big budget. Very high-end. Spring-fling rock theme."

Meg leaned back, and Ruby could see her eyes sparkling with excitement. "I have *so* many props for a party like this. We can go over the top. Very glam, very glittery."

"I know!" Ruby said excitedly. When it came to parties, the two friends shared the same brain, which was why they'd been able to work together so long without killing each other.

Ruby picked up a menu and pretended to read it. Even though they had an office at Emmett and Meg's place, they often met at Savor for "official" meetings. They found it was easier to be creative with the help of Savor's excellent lattes.

"Any word from the SF Opera?" Ruby asked.

Meg shook her head. "Not yet."

"Damn. That could have really blown us into the stratosphere of event planning."

"Well, James Cleaver isn't exactly small potatoes."

"True. Speaking of which." Ruby peeked over the top of her menu. "Maybe you can call the band's manager and see if they'll perform?"

"Um, no?" Meg said.

"Why not? You're the one with the in."

"You know why. We're a lot more likely to get a band like the Riders to play a private event if it's arranged outside the booking agent. And as it happens, you just spent the night with the leader of this particular band. Ergo, you need to call and ask him."

"Um. Well—" Ruby laughed nervously. "I may not be the best person to ask Mark for any favors at the moment."

Meg narrowed her gaze. "Why? What did you do?"

Holding the menu like a shield, Ruby slumped down into her chair. "Nothing?"

"I repeat. What. Did. You. *Do*."

"Fine. I kinda kicked him out."

"Kinda?" Meg crossed her arms over her chest.

"No." She nodded. "I pretty much kicked him out. Totally."

Meg was scarily still. "Please tell me you fucked him first."

"Meg!"

"Well, did you?"

"Of course. I'm not a total idiot."

Meg leaned over and rested her elbows on the table. "How was it?" she asked in a low, dead-serious voice.

Just thinking about Mark between her thighs excited her. She grinned. "It was amazing."

"So. Let me get this straight. You fucked him—amazingly, I might add—then kicked him out of your bed?"

"It sounds much worse when you say it like that," Ruby mumbled.

Leaning back in her chair, Meg started laughing. And laughing. When her guffaws finally died down, she said, "This is great. Perfect."

"What are you talking about?"

Meg pulled her oversized black sunglasses down her nose so she could give Ruby her Scary Stare over them. "How many times do you think Mark St. Crow gets booted after a quick fuck?"

"It wasn't that quick." Ruby shifted in her seat. "And, not many, I'd suspect."

"So you've just turned the tables on him. It's probably killing him. A guy like that, not being the one on top?"

Ruby refrained from pointing out that last night, she had, in fact, been the one on top. On the chair, anyway.

Meg gestured toward Ruby's purse. "I bet he calls you today."

"No way. That is *so* not going to happen. I didn't even give him my number."

"I'm sure that won't stop him from getting it. And when he does call, you ask him to play this event."

Ruby just rolled her eyes. "Meg, you're crazy."

Meg tapped her temple with a fingertip. "Crazy like a fox."

Swatting her friend with the menu, Ruby had to laugh. "Seriously, I really didn't plan on seeing him again."

"And would it be such a bad thing to see him again?" Meg asked.

"Actually, yes." Ruby went back to hiding behind her menu.

"Why?" Meg was nothing if not persistent.

"Because. He's just…"

"What?" Meg asked.

"Too much. It's too intense." *He* was too intense. The way he looked at her as if he knew her, the way he *did* know exactly what she wanted him to do to her. It was too much.

"So?"

"So? Meg, you don't understand."

"Understand what?"

"This is not a normal relationship. He's not vanilla. And BDSM is more extreme; it makes you vulnerable. It makes *me* more vulnerable, anyway. And I just can't go there with a twenty-nine-year-old musician who lives three thousand miles away, and that's when he's not on tour." Ruby sipped her latte, hoping Meg would be satisfied with her explanation.

She wasn't. "So you really never want to see him again?"

Ruby was *dying* to see him again. "Nope. Never." She said, shaking her head vigorously.

"Then I suppose this would be the wrong time to tell you the band is going to be recording at Emmett's studio starting, like, now." She put a hand to her mouth. "Oops! Looks like I just did."

So what Mark had said last night was true. Ruby's heart skipped with a combination of fear and excitement. She was getting really sick of this particular feeling.

This was so not good. She was at Meg's all the time, and now Mark was going to be there, too? She felt sweat break out under her breasts. She knew that she'd never be able to look at Mark without remembering exactly how she'd let him dominate her.

It would be torture.

"So, aren't you a little excited to see him again?" Meg asked.

"Yes. No. I don't know."

"What's there to know? He's hot, he's into you—"

"But—"

"The sex was good." Meg shrugged. "I don't see any problem. None whatsoever."

"Meg. I barely know him, and I'm already in a gossip column. I don't like that. I don't even like him."

"Come on, Ruby. I saw the article. It wasn't bad. In fact, it was awesome publicity for us. Next time do something scandalous so we make a national paper!" After a second Meg smiled gently. "You wanna know what I think?"

"Not especially."

"I think Mark could really shake up your neat, orderly existence, and that freaks the shit out of you. I think you freak out whenever you get vulnerable, and something about Mark got you real vulnerable real fast."

"Give me a break. You make me sound like a control freak!" Just then their server, Bree, arrived with two plates of food.

"Here ya go, girls," she said, placing their plates on the table.

Meg smiled warmly. "Got a minute to chat with us, Bree?"

Ruby and Meg spent so much time at Savor, they'd gotten to know Bree pretty well. Still, Ruby recognized a diversion tactic when she saw one. Didn't matter. Meg was wrong, and Ruby didn't have the energy to argue with her about it.

"Yeah, I have a few minutes." Bree pulled a chair over to their table and straddled it. With her short, spiky hair, androgynous body, and gorgeous face, Bree was simply striking. She wore a tight T-shirt and black skinny jeans, and both her wrists were weighed down with dozens of silver and black bracelets that jangled as she crossed her arms over the back of the chair.

"So what's going on, ladies?" Bree asked. "You two have been in heavy conversation since you got here. Work stuff?"

Meg grinned mischievously. "Ruby spent the night with Mark St. Crow."

Ruby kicked her best friend under the table, and Meg yelled, "Ouch! What? It's not like it's a secret; your picture's in the paper!"

Bree simply raised one eyebrow at Ruby. "No shit?" Ruby wondered if anything ever fazed the cool server. "His band has a wicked-hot singer."

"You know the Riders?" Ruby asked. Was she the only one in the world who hadn't heard of the band?

Bree nodded. "Yeah. I read an interview in *Gaydar* last year. Yvette sounded interesting, so I've been following her career."

Ruby paused with a bite of omelet halfway to her mouth. "Wait a minute. Did you say *Gaydar*?"

"Yeah. Why?"

"Is Yvette *gay*?"

Bree nodded. "As a blade. You look shocked."

"I am. It's just that Mark implied she was his ex-girlfriend."

"Well, from all I've read, that woman hasn't slept with a man since she turned sixteen. She's very open about her sexuality, which is pretty hot."

Ruby chewed her eggs thoughtfully. "So, if she's not his ex, why does she hate me?" For some reason it was better if Yvette was a jealous ex-girlfriend. If Yvette wasn't in love with Mark, why had she given her the evil eye all night?

"No idea," Bree said. "So. Mark St. Crow. I can see why you think he's cute. In a breeder kind of way."

Ruby tried to look indifferent. "It was a one-night stand. Fun was had by all. Now it's back to normal life." Ruby shoved a bite of toast into her mouth.

Bree and Meg just stared at her.

"Seriously, it's true—oh, look. My cell's ringing, be right back." Seeing an unfamiliar number, Ruby jumped up and stepped into a jasmine-covered alcove. "This is Ruby."

"Hey, baby."

Her heart stopped. "Mark?"

"You sound surprised."

"Well, after what happened last night, when I, you know..."

"Kicked me out?" he said, and she could practically see him grinning that wicked smile of his.

"Yeah," she said. And part of her felt guilty for asking him to leave, even if she knew it was for the best.

"Emmett gave me your number."

"Right." Of course he did.

"I just wanted to say thanks for last night."

She smiled. "You forgot to leave a tip."

"Well, lucky for you I'm going to be back in San Francisco sooner than I thought. I can give you lots more tips. In fact, I can't wait to tip you again. Tip you over my knee, over the side of a bed, the kitchen table—"

"*Mark!* What's gotten into you?"

"As I recall, last night I was into you."

"Oh my God. You're awful." So why was she trying so hard not to laugh?

"I want to see you again. I'm recording with Emmett, so plan on it."

Staring at the jasmine, she fought for patience. "Mark. Listen. What happened last night...it can't happen again."

"Why not?"

The simple question hung between them as she considered her words. "Because, I have other priorities right now." *Which do not include falling for a bad-boy rock star.* "I don't have time for this."

"Make time."

"I can't."

"Why not?"

"Because I just *can't*." A couple passing by looked startled as she shouted the last word. Turning, she lowered her voice. "Listen, I admit I was curious to know what it would be like to . . . you know, be spanked. So thank you for that."

"Um, you're welcome?"

"But I don't want to do it again." *Not with you, anyway.*

"Why?"

"Because." Her voice sounded weak even to her own ears. *Shit.*

"Because why?" He asked again in a serious tone she responded to.

"If you must know it's because I liked you too much. I mean, I liked *it* too much."

"In my world, you can never have too much of a good thing."

"See?" she said. "That's exactly what I'm talking about. In my world, you can."

She heard him take a deep breath and then, "Do you ever let go? Oh, wait. It's all coming together now. The only time you do let go is when you're bound. And I bet you never let go like you did with me. You were mine within minutes. No wonder you're so freaked out."

"That isn't true!" Why did everyone keep saying that she was freaking out? "I don't freak out."

"Tell me something."

"No."

"Are you sore this morning? On your ass? Can you see where I left you marked?"

"No, and no." But just his words made her body burn with lust, and she knew he'd see right through her lie.

"I don't believe you. I think you love it. I think just the thought of submitting to me makes your toes curl."

Her mouth was so dry she couldn't answer. Arrogant bastard. Why did he have to be so fucking right?

"You're so *freaked out* because that dickhead bondage guy never gave you what you really desired. But I did, didn't I, Ruby?"

"You got lucky."

"I agree. I got fucking lucky the second I saw you last night. And I'm going to get lucky again."

"You really are one of the most egotistical men I've ever met."

"No doubt. And yet you trusted me on the most intimate level, didn't you?"

She nodded absently. And then, "Why me? You can have any girl you want. Why are you working this hard for *me*?"

"Because just like I gave you something you wanted, you did the same for me. I'm not asking you to marry me here. I'm just saying I want to see you again."

Every fiber of her being was yelling no, telling her to run away as fast as she could and never look back. And yet, there was a part of her that so badly wanted to see him again. To submit to him again. Just the thought made her insides quiver.

"Fine. But I'm only agreeing because I know you're too stubborn to give up, and I suspect that once the chase is over, you'll move on."

A long pause, and she wondered if she'd gone too far. But then he said, "Oh, Ruby." His voice was deep, husky. "Baby, I can't wait to prove you wrong."

Her body should *not* be trembling from those words.

Her pussy should *not* be moist. And her toes should *definitely not* be curling.

But even if she did have the self-discipline to say no to Mark, there was the little matter of getting the Riders to play at James Cleaver's party.

"Fine." Straightening, she cleared her throat. "Meanwhile, I have a favor to ask."

Chapter
Eight

Don't make me regret this."

Mark looked up from the notebook in which he'd been jotting down the lyrics for a new song. Because apparently the world needed one more song with the word Ruby in the title. "What?" he said, eyeing Yvette.

She sat on the edge of the hotel bed, her guitar resting on her lap. "Recording this album in San Francisco."

They'd left San Francisco a week ago, and last night had been their final tour date. Now they were returning to San Francisco later that day to start recording with Emmett.

"What are you talking about?" He tried to hide his irritability at being interrupted midthought. He'd had this melody in his head, and some lyrics, and he needed to work it out.

"Oh, come now. I'm not above eavesdropping. I know you've called her or sent a text message to her every day this week."

It was true. He'd wanted to hear Ruby's voice, to know she was thinking about him. She always kept it short, but at least she answered, even if he had a feeling she did so just because he hadn't yet given her the okay on her party. Yeah, he was milking that one for all he could.

And, he was dying to get back to Ruby. The thought made him shift, his balls suddenly tight.

"You know how intense recording can be; we need all your focus on this album. Don't let her get in the way."

He gripped his pencil. The problem with having such a close relationship with Yvette was that she knew exactly how to piss him off. But all he said was, "This is a girl I've met once."

She strummed a chord. "I would like to declare an official position on your interest in a certain dark-haired girl to whom you seem to have become attached."

"Is that so?"

"Don't do it."

Using the tip of his pencil, he stabbed a hard beat on the notebook.

"Thanks for the advice, but I think I can handle it."

"Aha! So you admit there is something to handle?"

"Yvette. Watch it."

"I did. Last weekend. I watched you miss a beat because you were smitten with a girl in the audience." ·

He slammed his notebook shut, annoyed that he hadn't gotten his thoughts on paper. "Are you saying you've never had an off night? Because that's not true. In fact, I've noticed the bottle of wine you drink before each show isn't exactly helping your performance."

Green eyes blazing, she stood. "What are you saying?"

"Maybe you should lay off the booze for a bit. You're getting sloppy."

"At least I didn't speak for the band and agree to play some stupid yuppie party, all to get in some chick's pants. It's not cool."

The tension in the room grew as they stared at each other. But Mark wasn't about to back down, even if it struck him as strange that he was fighting with Yvette about a girl. In all their years together, this was a first.

He had no idea why he was so attached to Ruby after such a short time, but he wasn't fighting it. In fact, his feelings had been inspiring him to create new material, which was what he'd been trying to do when Yvette had interrupted him.

Finally she gave him a grin. "God, that was so cliché. I can't believe we're arguing about girls and alcohol."

Mark decided to let it go. "Yeah." He ran a hand over his scalp. "Listen. I know you want this record to be perfect, and trust me, so do I. But stop stressing. We have thirteen new songs, and Emmett really seems to get us, our style. I don't know about you, but I'm excited to get started."

"So am I. But let's just remember the real reason we're going to San Francisco and not be distracted by sweet pussy."

She must have seen the murder in his face because she backed down. "Hey. I've said my piece."

"Yeah. You have. Now drop it."

She did, taking her seat on the bed. Soon the tinny melody of her unplugged electric guitar filled the room. Mark returned to his notebook, letting her rhythmic tune lull him back into creative mode. He wanted to finish this song and hopefully get it on the record. But he wondered how Yvette would react when she heard the title. He traced the words over and over until they formed thick block letters.

RUBY MINE.

*   *   *

"So...are you looking for anything in particular at the sex store?"

It was Saturday and, at Meg's request, they were in a taxi headed toward Bindings, San Francisco's biggest sex shop. Meg shrugged. "Not sure. I just know I need something."

Ruby caught her friend's wistful look. "Hey, is everything okay?"

Meg seemed to be considering the question. She finally said, "I know you think Emmett and I have the perfect relationship. And in some ways that's true. But..."

"Meg. What's going on?"

"I think he's having an affair," she said in a blank voice.

Ruby's heart stopped. "No! He would never do that to you."

"Really?" She just raised a brow. "Because he doesn't seem to want to have sex with *me*...and I've discovered things on his computer. Not just porn, but strange porn."

"That doesn't mean he's cheating, Meg."

"We used to have sex all the time." The taxi driver coughed and Meg lowered her voice. "I mean *all the time*. We were freakin' bunnies. But these past six months it's dwindled to nothing. And he comes home late, and he seems so distant. And he's mingling with a new crowd. People who are used to a different, faster lifestyle. And they're all so *young*." Meg's eyes looked watery. "The whole thing scares me."

Ruby could barely process that her friend's marriage was in trouble. In fact, for the past year she'd been waiting for Meg's announcement that she was pregnant, but it never came.

"Have you tried talking to him?" Ruby asked.

"Sure, but he just clams up."

"So you think going to the sex shop is gonna help?"

She shook her head. "I have no idea. But maybe he needs something I haven't been giving him. Maybe I can get some ideas. I don't know. It was either this or Botox. And you know how much I hate needles."

"Oh, honey." Ruby gave her friend a hug. "I'm sure it's nothing. But if you want to do this, I'll do what I can to help."

Meg returned the hug and chuckled. "Well, at the very least I can have fun trying to save my marriage."

"Is this it?" Meg sounded apprehensive.

Ruby eyed their reflection in the one-way mirrored door. "Yup." The word *Bindings* was painted directly on the building, but otherwise there was no indication that there was actually a sex shop inside.

"Hey," Ruby said, opening the door. "You're the one who wanted to go sex-toy shopping."

Meg followed her inside. "And you're the one who knew exactly where to take me."

"That's because I came here with Ash to buy props for his photo shoots. I wasn't here for anything fun." Like . . . leather paddles, for example.

Meg just shook her head and gazed around the store. The front area was dedicated to kinky apparel: leather pants, silk corsets, and an entire row of cruel-looking shoes that were clearly meant for entertainment purposes only.

Meg walked toward a black latex dress and fingered the fabric. "So," she said. "Here we are."

"Uh-huh." Ruby paused a minute, breathing. The scent of leather assaulted her, reminding her of belts and boots and cuffs. Of Mark. She took a deep breath. "Here we are."

"Can I help you, ladies?" They turned to find a tall, burly man approaching. He wore a leather cap, heavy-looking leather chaps over jeans, a white T-shirt, and a black leather vest. He sported a graying handlebar mustache over a friendly smile.

Meg stepped forward. "Hi. I'm new to all this kinky stuff. Can you tell me where I would find some tools for spanking and the like?"

Totally unfazed with her candidness, he motioned for them to follow him into the back room. It was about three times as large as the front space and was filled with instruments and garb, all meant for exquisite torture of a willing sub. And helpful tools for a firm dom. Ruby's entire body seemed to become erotically charged just from being there.

And there was that back wall. The one she'd seen when she'd been here with Ash. The wall with the rows and rows of leather tools. Just looking at the display made her heart race, and she approached the collection like a moth drawn to a flame.

The man in chaps stopped in front of the display. "So. Are you two ladies looking for floggers? Canes? Paddles?"

Eyes wide, Meg pulled down a ten-inch leather paddle. Made of black leather, the handle was round and had eight holes dotting the wide end.

"Oh, that's a nice one," said the salesman. "Black latigo

leather. Firm but flexible. Speaking from personal experience, I can tell you it delivers quite a nice whap, thanks to the holes."

Meg's eyes glittered. "Really?"

"Yup. Here, see for yourself." He turned and stuck his bum out a bit. Pointing at the fleshiest part of his ass, just inside the edge of the chaps, he said, "Go on. Give it a tap."

"Are you sure?" Meg's voice was high-pitched and excited.

"Just remember to keep away from the tailbone."

"Okay." She brought her hand back and gave the man a light pat on his rear.

"Good job. Now do it harder."

Meg studied her target as an archer would a bull's-eye. Then she pulled her hand back and efficiently brought the paddle down on the man's ass. The leather hit his jeans with a loud *whapping* sound, as promised.

"Good job," the man said. "Now really put some *oomph* into it."

She did, swinging her arm in a precise arc that ended with a very loud thud.

Smiling, the man straightened. "You're a natural."

Meg beamed. "Really?"

"Definitely."

"I'll take it."

The man turned to Ruby. "And you, sweetheart? What can I help you find this fine afternoon?"

"Oh. Um. I'm j-just looking." But her heart was racing and her skin was on fire. Just being surrounded by all this leather put her on edge, had her libido all fired up.

"Let me show you something." Why don't you just

see how this feels." Reaching up, he plucked a small black flogger off the wall. "Yeah, this one is real nice." He winked. "Also, you can put it in your purse. It's quite portable."

About eight inches long in total, the handle was wrapped with a leather ribbon, and the flogger had six raw-leather strands and six feather-covered ones.

He took her hand and held it palm up. She watched as he drew the straps slowly, lightly, across her open hand. It felt even more sensual than she had imagined, and as the man continued to wisp the tails across her skin, shivers raced up and down her spine.

"You like this one."

She nodded; her mouth was too dry to speak.

He released her and held out his arm, forearm up. "But it has a nice little sting, too." *Slap.* With an expert flick of his wrist he snapped the flogger against his own skin. He did this three more times in quick succession and then stopped. They all watched as a pink welt appeared on his arm.

Ruby smiled. "Wrap it up. I'll take it."

Chapter Nine

Mark had been calling and texting her every day, and then on Saturday, nothing. Now it was Sunday, and Ruby went about her morning as she always did. Woke up early. Took a long jog through Golden Gate Park. Stopped at the grocery store for her weekly provisions.

Her sudden craving for Ben & Jerry's had absolutely nothing to do with Mark. Definitely not. She had no idea why she'd thrown the carton into her basket as she'd zipped down the frozen-foods aisle. At least she'd been able to resist the chocolate ice cream and had gone straight for the vanilla. If she bought the chocolate, she'd eate the entire pint. Best to stay away all together.

She wasn't disappointed he hadn't called her. The marks on her ass had faded now, and she was thinking it would be best to avoid any more of the BDSM stuff. It was like chocolate: She needed of all it or nothing. And yeah, so far, the all thing hadn't worked out so well. There was just something too intense, too vulnerable about it. Falling for a guy like Mark would be so much more powerful than falling for a vanilla guy. Therefore, when Mark left—and his type always did—it would be extra painful.

She was home now, staring out the bay window. But she suddenly needed something, and the ice cream was calling her name. In the kitchen, she yanked the freezer door open and pulled out the carton. Leaning back against her kitchen counter, she spooned in a heaping mouthful.

With a start, she looked at the spoon. She never ate ice cream out of the carton. What had gotten into her?

Her kitchen phone rang, making her jump. Along with the cherry-print wallpaper and green Formica countertops, the phone was vintage, and when it rang it was louder than a fire truck's siren.

"Hello?" she said, for some reason uneasy.

"Ruby, it's Mark."

The spoon clattered to the floor. "Mark?"

"Yeah. Remember me?"

"Barely," she said, trying to sound nonchalant. "How did you get my home number?"

"I have my ways."

"Hmm."

"Right. So, listen. I was thinking we could take a drive this afternoon."

"When did you get back to San Francisco?"

"Today."

"I see." He hadn't mentioned exactly when he was returning in any of their conversations.

"Are you busy?"

"Yes." She nodded. "Very busy." *Eating ice cream out of a carton.*

"I heard there's a great spot just north of here, right on the water. Let me take you to dinner."

"I don't know…"

"Come on, it'll be fun."

She really shouldn't, but he hadn't agreed to the Spring

Fling yet, and this might be the perfect opportunity to nail him down.

And if her heart was racing just at the thought of seeing him again, that was her heart's problem. "Fine," she said. "Okay."

"Great. Pick you up in thirty minutes?"

"Sure."

"Oh, Ruby?"

"What?" she asked, his tone making her more alert.

"Wear a dress and don't wear any underwear."

"Mark!"

But he'd *already* hung up.

Ruby was waiting on the curb when the red Ferrari turned the corner and purred up her street. When it stopped in front of her, she had to pick her jaw up off the ground. Leaning down to look through the passenger-side window, she found Mark grinning at her.

"I see you're not going crazy with your newfound wealth."

He shrugged. "Company loaner. I guess they were out of Pintos. Hop in."

She opened the door and slid into the luxurious leather seat. She took in the chrome dials, sleek design, total opulence. The engine hummed quietly beneath her, a mix of restrained power, youthfulness, and extreme indulgence. Kind of like the man driving it.

"I take it you've never been in one of these before?"

She clutched her bag tightly on her lap. "In fact, I have."

Putting the car in gear, he smoothly accelerated. "Yeah?"

"My father was a mechanic. For a while he worked for

a very wealthy man, maintaining his fleet of luxury vehicles and boats."

They pulled onto Nineteenth Street and continued south. She hated talking about her parents, so she changed the subject before that particular conversation continued.

"Tell me about the record you're about to make." She truly was curious. She'd downloaded the band's previous two albums from iTunes and had been impressed by their modern, cross-genre sound. She could see why they were so popular; they could potentially be played on nearly any major radio station.

"What can I say? It's gonna be a kick-ass record. Like bluesy, and scratchy with a bit of hip-hop and Tom Waits thrown in."

"I love Tom Waits."

He glanced at her, an eyebrow cocked. "Really?"

"Why are you so surprised?"

He shrugged. "Because his music is so chaotic, so uncontrolled." He gave her a quick glance. "So unlike you. But then you like jazz, too. And that's a very spontaneous type of music." He eyed her vintage fifties yellow dress with a raised brow, and she wished she'd left the top button undone. As if her primly buttoned dress proved his point, he grinned and faced forward.

She bristled. "I'm not the controlled priss you seem to think I am."

He gave her a bone-melting grin. "Oh, baby. I know you're not. I knew that last weekend when you had me between your legs. I still have scratches on my shoulders from your nails."

Her cheeks burned as she reached over to turn up the air-conditioning.

"You hot, baby?"

"I'm not your baby. Or anything else."

"But you did wear a dress for me."

"It wasn't for you. I always wear dresses." She left out the fact that she never wore dresses on Sundays.

"And what about the panties? I hope you followed that direction as well."

God, for such an expensive car, the air-conditioning really needed some help.

"Ruby?"

"Of course I'm wearing my underwear!" She didn't mention that she'd been tempted to follow his orders, but she just couldn't bring herself to do it. She tugged the hem of her dress lower.

He shook his head in that way of his—the way that let her know she was in trouble.

She needed to change the subject again, and now that she finally had him cornered, she wanted a definite answer about James Cleaver's event. "So, Mark, I was wondering if we could discuss the Spring Fling—that's what we're calling it, by the way."

"Shoot."

She turned to face him, watched his long legs as he shifted into a higher gear, pulling them onto Highway 1. She swallowed; why did just watching the way he controlled the car heighten her awareness like this?

She said, "Can I get a confirmation from you?" She really needed him to say yes. James had sent her the guest list, and it included some very impressive potential clients. She needed to wow them.

"What's the company again?" Mark asked.

"Boxware. Maybe you've heard of them?"

"Um, yeah. I'm young and a musician, but I'm not stupid."

She felt her face flush, but this time from embarrassment. "Sorry. Anyway, the founder is a guy named James Cleaver. He's young, hip, and very into keeping his employees happy. He's a wonderful man."

"Is that so."

She nodded. "So are you interested?"

"Possibly."

"Great. Right. Talk to the band. Get back to me." She tried not to sound overly eager.

"Actually, I think I can speak for the band and agree—"

"Wonderful!"

"Under one condition."

"What?" she asked skeptically.

"You take off your panties."

She gasped. "I'm not going to take off my underwear for a job!" She knew she should be outraged. He was, after all, using sex to get his way. But instead she felt a buzz of excitement shoot through her.

"Oh no?"

"No." She hoped she sounded convincing.

He shrugged. "Up to you."

Crossing her arms over her chest, she stared straight ahead. She needed to convince Mark to play at the Spring Fling, but was he really going to agree only if she obeyed him? And if she did obey him, what did that make her?

Instead, she focused on the coastline whizzing past the window. The two-lane road hugged a cliff, at the bottom of which the Pacific Ocean crashed against rocks and sandy beaches. The sun was just starting to set, lighting up the ocean in an orange-and-yellow blaze.

They passed a marina, and she couldn't help it—her gaze darted among the sailboats, searching for forty-foot craft with the word *Ruby* painted on the bow with big, scrolling letters. But of course, there was no boat. Twenty years had passed since she'd waved good-bye to her father as he'd sailed for the South Pacific. Problem was, Hawaii hadn't been enough. He'd kept going. And Ruby had kept waiting.

"You're a jerk."

Mark slanted a glance her way. "Pardon me?"

"Using sex as an advantage over me. It's disrespectful and unfair."

He slanted a grin at her that made her stomach do a flip. "You seem to have a strange attachment to your underwear."

"I do not!"

"First during the show, now tonight. What do you think will happen if you go without underwear for a few hours, anyway?"

"That's not the point!"

"Just seems like a funny thing to get all uppity over. You know damn well your panties are coming off at some point tonight. Why not now? Then we both get what we want."

"Just because I let you *you know what* me one time does not make you my boss. Or my dom."

"You weren't complaining last weekend."

"I thought I'd never see you again. I told you, that was—"

"An aberration. I know."

"You are a very frustrating man."

Reaching over, he lightly touched her thigh. She jumped at the warm contact, hating the way it sent tingles down her leg. "Come on, baby. I'll play this show, all you have to do is take off your underwear."

"You want me without my underwear? Fine." She pulled the lace down her legs, over her sandals, shoved them into the glove box, and slammed the thing shut.

Glaring at him, she settled back into her seat. "There. Happy now? See you at the Spring Fling."

"That's a good girl. Funny thing, though."

"What's that?"

"Looks like you locked the glove box. And I don't have the key."

Mark handed the Ferrari keys to the valet at the Ritz. The luxury resort was located on a dramatic piece of coastline in Half Moon Bay. Reluctantly, Ruby took his hand as he led her to the front steps.

The girl was on edge. With her neat hairdo, prim dress, and shiny clutch, she was sensibility personified. The only thing that gave away her sexy side was the strappy heels on her dainty feet.

He wondered what happened to that girl he'd met nine days ago. Now she had a wall around her ten feet thick. So much different from that woman who'd melted in his arms on the patio.

But it was all a facade. There was a connection between them, nearly tangible, and he knew it wouldn't take much to have her belonging to him once again.

He was known for his patience, but he'd been waiting for this all week, and their time apart felt like the longest foreplay ever. He was ready to explode.

They entered the grand lobby of the Ritz, but instead of heading for the restaurant, Mark pulled her into a side hallway.

"Mark, what are you doing?"

"This." He pressed her back against a wall and kissed her. It took all of two seconds before she started kissing him back, wrapping his neck in her cool hand and holding him steady. Her little tongue tasted him, gently at first and then more eagerly. Yes...here she was, here was that girl who'd given herself to him last week.

He pressed his hips against her, showing her exactly how much she turned him on. His cock was hard and heavy, and for a moment he considered just booking a room, ordering room service, and spending the night fucking her senseless.

Instead he continued to kiss her, running his hands through her hair, trickily loosening the strands of her ponytail so he could bury his fists in the silky black waves.

When he pulled away he was happy to see a small smile on her face. It was her first one of the night; score one for team St. Crow.

She put a hand to her head. "What did you do to my hair?"

"I like it down."

"It's a mess."

"It's perfect." He heard the sounds of footsteps so he stepped back. Blushing, Ruby looked to the side, her silhouette casual, as the strangers passed them.

When the intruders had gone, he brought the back of her wrist to his lips and kissed it. Her skin tasted sweet and decadent, like chocolate. "You know you can trust me to never push you too far in public. I need you to trust me, Ruby."

She looked at him for what seemed like forever before she shook her head in apparent wonderment. "Yes. Somehow I do know that I can trust you. I must be crazy."

"No. You just like what I do to you, don't you?"

"You mean make me question my sanity? Actually, no. Not so much," she said, and then she laughed, a nervous little chuckle that made his cock twitch.

"You're not questioning your sanity. You're questioning your intense need to give yourself over to me."

"You forget that I was with a bondage expert for nearly a year. I'm not some novice groupie."

He leaned closer. "Tell me. How do we compare? Me and *him*? Now that you've had a glimpse of true surrender, what do you think?"

He saw the struggle in her eyes and wondered if she would answer him. But then she shrugged. "I like it. With you, you cocky bastard. It scares me how much I like it."

"Aw, sweetheart." He brought her into his arms. "No need to be scared. You trust me, remember?"

She laughed against his chest. "I barely know you."

But when she said the words, he realized he wanted that all to change; he wanted to get to know her. But fuck. He didn't want to hurt her, not Ruby. The very nature of his life meant he'd spent a total of twenty nights at home in the past two years, which was, frankly, just fine with him. It was a very handy excuse when it came to relationships. *Sorry, babe. See you next time around.* But now he had a hard time picturing himself saying those words to Ruby.

And these feelings? Lust could run deep, but he knew

it didn't last. What lasted was the music, and when you sacrificed one for the other, it never turned out well. That was a lesson he'd learned early on. His dad only needed a few beers to start reminiscing about the "good old days" before he'd settled down. Or rather, been forced to settle down. A wife, a kid. A "real" job.

"Come on," he said, taking Ruby's hand. "I'm starving. Let's eat."

"What's this?" Inside the dining room of the Ritz, they'd been led to a table with the best view of the Pacific Ocean, and after Mark had pulled out her chair, she'd sat down to discover a small box at her place setting.

A small box that happened to be a very unique shade of robin's-egg blue. Her pulse jumped with a feminine excitement she couldn't tamp down. "Is this for me?"

He looked almost sheepish as he dropped his napkin onto his lap. "I don't see any other girls around."

She was quite sure her smile must have been downright goofy, but she couldn't hide it. "This is a Tiffany's box," she said, stating the obvious but unable to say anything else.

"Yeah, I hear girls like this kinda thing."

"Yeah. They do," she said, her smile stretching even wider.

"Go on, open it," he said, as if he'd given her something as trivial as a newspaper.

Her fingers hovered over the shiny ribbon as she glanced up. "Are you sure?"

"Just open it."

Slowly, drawing out the moment, she undid the little bow and pulled the ribbon aside. Then she delicately separated the lid from the box and pulled out yet another velvet case. Her heart beating wildly in her chest, she opened the small box.

With a gasp, she glanced up. "What's this?"

A dainty silver chain sparkled against the blue velvet lining, coming to a V in the center, where a small pendant dangled. "It's a lock," she said as nerves took flight in her belly.

"A *diamond-covered* lock. 'Cause I'm classy that way," he said with a wink.

"W-what does it mean?"

He took the box from her hands, got to his feet, and came around to stand behind her. "It means that, whenever you wear it, you're mine."

Her heart thudded in her chest. She wanted to wear it, and not just because it was a gorgeous piece of jewelry from Tiffany's. No, there was more. She wanted to be owned, by Mark. Sure, it was just a fantasy, and a fantasy that seemed so very wrong, but she couldn't help it, and knowing it was temporary somehow made it okay.

Behind her, his hands were warm on her skin as he pulled her hair aside and fastened the necklace. "It's not a real lock, you know. There's not a key. You can take it off any time."

"Well, I guess I can wear it," she said, lightly stroking the pendant now hanging between her collarbones. "Tonight."

He pressed his lips to the nape of her neck, and then his teeth nipped gently at her cherry blossom tattoo. "Good girl."

Trying to calm her racing heart, she looked for a menu. "I don't have a menu. Or any silverware. You'd think in a

place like this, they could give a girl a knife and a fork."
God, she sounded like such a dork, but she couldn't seem
to stop babbling.

"You don't need a knife or a fork, not tonight."

She looked up to find Mark giving her one of those
heart-stopping grins of his. The one that usually meant he
was up to something.

"Actually, I do. To, you know. Eat?"

"Trust me."

She rolled her eyes, wondering what the man had up his
sleeve. He seemed to have ordered ahead of time, because
a bottle of champagne had been chilled and poured, and
then a waiter approached, holding a tray.

"Shrimp cocktail." The server placed a large glass in
front of her. The inside of the glass was filled with red
sauce, and five large prawns hugged the rim.

"This looks divine." She looked up. "Aren't you going
to eat?"

His eyes were dark, unreadable. "I think I'll just watch
you for now."

Shrugging, she picked up a prawn and dipped it into
the cocktail sauce. Then she brought it to her lips and
took a large bite. The shrimp flesh was salty, like the sea.
The red sauce was perfectly spicy and set off the subtle
flavor of the seafood. Blissful. She looked up again and
saw that Mark was watching her eat, studying her. She
licked a drop of sauce off her lips.

"You missed a spot," he said, reaching across the table.
He dabbed the corner of her mouth with his fingertip, then
slowly, gently, ran the pad of his fingertip over her lips.

The entire time he held eye contact with her and didn't
look away. And she didn't want him to. She wanted to look

him in the eye as she sucked his finger, as she'd done the other night. It was insane, how easily he excited her.

"Under My Thumb." Her mother had always hated that song, said it was degrading to women. And yet she'd been totally infatuated with Ruby's father, so much so that she would literally follow him to the ends of the earth. Ruby would never be so emotionally dependent on a man. Ever.

"Ruby," he said, and she snapped out of it.

"What?"

His expression was more serious than she'd ever seen it. "I was kidding earlier, in the car. I'd never ask you to trade sex to get some business deal."

Something inside her softened as she searched his eyes for pretense. She saw none. "Thank you, Mark. I needed to hear that."

They fell silent and Mark picked up another shrimp, dipped it into the sauce, and brought it to her lips. She opened her mouth, let him feed her. Let him go as slow as he wanted to. She licked her lips, held his gaze. Soon her nipples were hardening under her bra, and her skin felt hot. Suddenly she wanted to feel his fingers on other parts of her body. Her neck. Her breasts. Between her legs.

He picked up her champagne glass and tilted it to her lips. She tasted the bubbly liquid, rolled it around on her tongue. It tickled her nose and she smiled.

"You are so fucking sexy, Ruby."

Uncomfortable, she waved his words away. "No, I'm not."

"I told you not to put yourself down."

"I'm a lot of things, but sexy, or pretty, isn't any of them."

"If you think that, why did you pose nude?"

She straightened. "For one thing, I never thought those photographs would be sold. And..."

"And what?"

All these sensations—the food, the view, the scent of the sea—seemed to open her up, and she found herself admitting things she hadn't ever before, even to Meg. For some reason, maybe because of what they'd done that first night, she felt like she could tell him anything about this part of herself.

She shifted in her seat. "I felt sexy posing that way. Like I was being decorated, celebrated."

"You should be celebrated, Ruby."

"No—"

"Don't argue with me." His tone was firm, but he was smiling and waved a shrimp in her direction as he spoke.

He glanced out the window to the endless ocean and then at her. "You grow up around here?"

She nodded. "Actually, about one mile from this very spot. Of course, there wasn't a Ritz-Carlton here then. In fact, I spent many hours on this beach that's been so neatly tamed. When I was a girl, you took your life in your hands just to get to the water."

"So, you were a risk-taker, then?"

"No, not really. But my parents loved the ocean, and we spent a lot of time here and at the marina. We were always in the water, always sandy and salty. My mom always said my sister and I were part mermaid." But Mom had been the one to disappear into that liquid sunset, not Ruby or Claire. While their folks had been off sailing the world, the girls had been landlocked.

"Where are your parents now?"

She sipped another few drops of champagne. "Being a

mechanic was just something Dad did to pay the bills. He was really an artist himself, a free spirit; he painted, played music, wrote. Our house was always full of artists. But Dad could never stay in one place very long. He was always going on sailing trips." She shrugged. "One day he never came back. Mom waited an entire year before going after him."

"Did she find him?"

"Yeah. But Dad was never happy in one place. The sea was in his blood. So even if they came back, they never stayed long. I think they felt more at home on their boat than anywhere."

"How old were you when your dad left?"

"Sixteen. Claire was thirteen."

"Your parents left you to fend for yourselves when you and your sister were teenagers." He said it as a statement, not a question, and his tone was rough.

"It wasn't that bad. We were mature for our ages, and we knew how to take care of ourselves."

"How did you afford to live?"

"Luckily the house was paid off. And they sent checks sporadically. I also had a grandmother in Florida who did what she could."

"Did you work?"

She nodded. "I got a job assisting an event planner after school." She tried to smile casually. "And the rest, as they say, is history."

"You never thought about doing anything else? For a living?"

"Yes, I went to college and studied photography. But even at school I found I was always planning parties, mainly keggers," she said with a laugh. "I guess it's in my blood. I came back to this because I love organizing things, watching a series of plans come together. And it's always a party; who doesn't love a party?" She looked away, thinking she'd revealed way too much about herself. "Anyway, enough of that. So, you'll really do the show for Boxware?"

He paused, and she wondered if he'd ask more personal questions, or say no. But then he smiled. "You took off your panties, even if you did lock them in a loaner car. But a deal's a deal. We'll do it."

"That's wonderful. Thank you, Mark, really." She gave him her very best flirty look. "So, what would I have to do to get you to agree to a little preparty with James and some other high rollers?"

"I'm sure I'll think of something, baby." He took her hand and softly rubbed the pad of his thumbs over her knuckles. A lovely quiver of anticipation rushed through her. "After all," he said, "we have all night."

Ruby licked the last bit of butter off her fingertips. Mark had broken open a stack of crab legs and lobster tails and fed them to her in small, butter-dipped bites; she hadn't been allowed any silverware during the entire meal. Now she was partway through a delicious plate of strawberries and melted chocolate. Thank God it was Sunday, the only day she cheated on her diet.

Mark watched her eat. "You enjoying yourself tonight, Ruby?"

"It's been tolerable," she joked, licking a drop of chocolate off her finger.

His eyes were dark, dilated behind his glasses. He liked it, liked watching her eat like this.

Leaning over the table, he handed her a strawberry.

The look in his eyes caused an aching throb between her thighs. He said in a low voice, "I want you to dip this in the chocolate sauce and then pretend it's my cock, Ruby. Lick it like you mean it. Show me what you'd do if it were my own flesh in your mouth."

Her body temperature spiked up a notch, and her eyes darted around the room. "Mark, no. I can't." But the sound of her voice was breathy, high, and revealing.

He grinned in that wicked way of his. "Can't you? You sure about that?"

Oh, he was so sure of himself. Knew exactly how far to push her. But the gleam in his eyes nailed her right in her core, promising sinful pleasure whether she obeyed or disobeyed.

Fuck it.

She dipped the strawberry in the chocolate. His eyes on her mouth, she brought the fruit to her lips, let her tongue dart out and lick the top. A bit of chocolate dripped and she caught it with her tongue, imagining how his cock would drip when he was excited. The image made her sex pulse and she squeezed her thighs together, painfully aware of her nakedness beneath her dress.

She let her eyelids lower as she tasted the chocolate, leisurely licking around and around the pointed tip until the chocolate had dissolved in her mouth.

"Fuck, Ruby."

She loved his eyes on her; the only other time she'd felt comfortable under such scrutiny was when Ash had looked at her through the lens of his camera. But this was so different. With Mark, there seemed to be an energy between them that pulsed like electricity.

She took a bite of the strawberry. The sugary fruit burst

into her mouth, and she felt a corresponding tug between her legs. Tart, juicy, sweet.

She met his gaze and paused at the look in his eyes. Gone was the playful twenty-nine-year-old musician. Before her was a man, a gorgeous man who radiated confidence. And lust. Lust for her.

Fuck me.

She wanted him. Now. She took another unhurried bite of the strawberry and didn't care if her eyes were begging for it, for him.

But his hands were steady when he picked up another piece of fruit and dipped it into his glass of champagne. "Spread your legs a little for me, Ruby."

"W-what?"

He handed her the strawberry. "Do it."

She was too turned on and too lost in this entire crazy night to deny him. So, pulse hammering, she inched her knees apart.

"Good girl. Now take the strawberry and touch yourself with it. Touch that gorgeous pussy of yours."

Her fingers trembled as she took the piece of fruit.

"No one is watching, Ruby."

How had he known she'd been wondering that? He always seemed to know what was on her mind, and she didn't even look around to see if he spoke the truth. She didn't need to. Instead she reached between her thighs and gently touched the strawberry to her damp flesh. She nearly moaned.

From a fucking strawberry. But the cold bite of the champagne was a shock against her hot skin and she felt her body react, felt herself melting into the upholstered Ritz-Carlton dining chair.

"Now tell me, baby. Aren't you glad you took off your panties?"

"Don't," she managed, but she loved it and she spread her legs a tiny bit more.

"Then tell me. Tell me I was right."

She slid the strawberry a bit higher, her legs going slack. "You were right. You were *so* right."

"Are you wet, then, baby?"

"Yes." And it was true. She was slippery. *Slippery when wet.* The thought made her giggle, and she touched her clit with the tickly tip of the berry.

"God, Ruby. You go so easily."

"Go?"

"Yeah. You fight so hard, but then, fuck. You belong to me in an instant."

"No...I don't belong to anyone." But here she was, wearing no panties, masturbating under the table with a strawberry at one of the most formal restaurants in northern California. "You fucking bastard." She twirled the strawberry in her wetness, coating it, loving the way the tiny bumps caressed her swollen clit, even loving the fact that someone might wonder what she was doing with her hand beneath the table. She could climax from just that, from him getting her to this point.

"Give it to me."

Her eyes fluttered open. "What?"

"The strawberry. Feed it to me."

"No," she said with a smile. "This feels too good to stop."

"You disobedient girl."

"Sometimes," she agreed. Then she waved the fruit under his nose. His shoulders looked tight, his biceps flexed as he watched her. The veins in his neck visibly pulsed. She paused with the strawberry just beyond his lips, and when she finally saw him breathe, she moved as if to feed him. His mouth opened, eager as a baby bird. But then she pulled back. Bringing the strawberry to her own lips, she opened her mouth and bit through the tart flesh of the fruit, tasted her own juices mixed with the sweet berry.

She ate the whole thing, tasting, chewing, swallowing. Smiling. Her lips burned from his gaze. Yeah, she would pay for this later.

And she couldn't wait.

*Chapter
Ten*

You know, I played guitar once."

After she'd finished the last of the strawberries, she expected him to whisk her into a broom closet or some other nook and ease this need between her thighs. But instead he'd led her outside, past the valet, and away from the hotel. Now they were strolling along a narrow, man-made path.

He liked to torture her, that much was obvious.

Still, part of her was enjoying the easy way they talked as they walked along the smooth cement trail that ran beside the wild coastline. But even the Ritz gardeners hadn't been able to tame the wild vines of jasmine that still grew along the perfectly rounded edge of the concrete, the flowering vine's perfume mixing with the sea-salt air. This scent made her nostalgic, made her think of home.

"So you're a musician, then?" he asked.

She shrugged. "I was never very good, but I got blisters trying. My dad loved music. He taught me how to play." Growing up, it was one of the few things they did together, one of the limited activities they shared an interest in, so she'd taken advantage and spent as much time as possible learning about music. "I think that was why I always found myself going out with boys who were in bands."

"You're a groupie?" he said teasingly.

"No. I swore off musicians when I turned thirty. Along with sculptors, potters, and painters. And writers. They're the worst."

"You really have dated quite a few creative types."

"It's a disease." She thought of James Cleaver and wondered if she'd finally found a man who met her requirements. He'd become even more flirtatious on the phone over the past week, yet she'd been unable to get as excited about this turn of events as she thought she should be.

Mark squeezed her hand. "Oh? So you only date photographers now."

"Nope. I eliminated them, too."

He chuckled and they kept walking.

"Anyway, my parents were total hippies. Always had people around, playing music. During the summer of '75 Jerry Garcia would come and jam with my dad. I was only five, but I knew even then that I was witnessing something special."

"Wow, 1975. I wasn't even born yet."

She gave him a playful punch. "Brat."

"So I've been told. The ladies don't seem to mind my rakish disposition, though." He tilted his mouth in one of those killer grins of his.

She said, "Speaking of the ladies, I have a question for you."

"Shoot."

"When did you know you were . . . you know? That you liked to be dominant."

Out of the corner of her eye, she saw him give a start. "Wow. That was a strange conversation segue."

"I'm known for them. Sorry."

Slowing his pace, he regarded her dubiously. "Seriously? You want to go there?"

She tucked a stray strand of hair behind her ear. "Seriously."

"Fuck, I don't even know. I did tie my girlfriend to my bed when I was sixteen."

"Why am I not surprised? And you just...kept exploring?"

"Kinda. I really got involved about five years ago."

"Why then?" she asked.

"I just needed something...more."

"Like?"

"Christ, Ruby," he said, running his hand over his scalp.

"Tell me," she said.

He blew out a gust of air. "Because sex had become routine, easy."

"Oh."

"See? You don't want to know."

She tugged his hand, urging him to keep walking, talking. She did want to know this part of him.

"Tell me," she said.

"Shit. Okay. Well, I just always liked being in charge, having control over someone, over their pleasure. At first I couldn't believe I actually enjoyed inflicting pain on another person. But then I accepted how much they liked it and it fed me. I get off on making people get off, I guess. In music, in sex."

She smiled. "So, big, bad rock star Mark St. Crow is really just a people pleaser at heart."

"I can't help it if it pleases some people to be spanked with a hairbrush, doll. I just do what I can."

She was glad the dark night hid her blush. She coughed. "I bet. So five years ago you started getting into, uh, spanking people."

"Yeah. We put out our first record, and our venues got bigger and bigger. Our band became more well known. Soon I had girls...er...well..."

"Go on." She could take it. She *could*. This thing between them was temporary, and she was curious—and curiously turned on—to learn about his voyage into BDSM.

"Girls were everywhere. I could have sex ten times a day if I wanted to."

"Hmm."

"Do whatever I wanted to them."

"Right."

"They wouldn't say no to *anything*."

"I *get* it." She pulled her wrap tighter around her shoulders.

"But straight sex wasn't doing it for me, and more and more I realized it was the power exchange I craved." His strong shoulders jerked a shrug. "I get off on it, of knowing I can bring someone total pleasure."

"You really are confident in your abilities."

"Haven't had any complaints yet." And he gave her that crooked, cocky smile.

They'd come to the end of the man-made path and now stood facing the ocean. In the distance, moonlight reflected an infinite pattern on the water and the waves roared against the cliffs, sounding as if the sea could rear up and suck them away.

After a moment, she said, "I love it when I plan a huge event and everything comes together. I look out in a crowd and see things running smoothly, and I know it's because I left no detail ignored. It's a rush. And when I…submit…I feel a similar kind of power, which is so strange to me. I don't understand it, any of it."

She saw him pull something shiny and metallic from his jeans pocket. It was a knife, and she watched as he quickly sliced through several vines of jasmine. He stood, holding the long strands in his hands.

"Why do you have to?"

"Understand my feelings? Because I want to know! I want to know what's wrong with me that I like pain, that I like to be controlled." She clutched her wrap in her fists. "It goes against everything I believe about myself."

"Like?"

"Like, I don't like to give up control, for one thing."

"I know."

"See? It's so confusing."

"Were you this confused with your ex? The bondage expert?"

Was it her imagination, or did he say those last two words with a slightly bitter edge?

"Not at the beginning," she said. "But then yes. As things progressed, as I found myself more and more willing to do whatever he wanted. Then I started wanting him to do even more. And then…"

"What happened?"

"One day I found some other girl's bra in the laundry."

"What a dickhead."

"Doesn't matter. His first love will always be his art. Just like yours will always be your music. Women will always be secondary to guys like you, and, frankly, I look at the whole thing with Ash as one big close call."

"Guys like me, huh?" He faced her. "So, you think there's not room for both? Women and music?"

"Do you?"

"No." He stepped closer. "But this is about you. I see your problem now."

"What?"

He took her chin in his fingers. They smelled like jasmine and melted butter.

"You're scared of letting go, afraid of getting your heart broken." He leaned closer, his lips a breath away from hers. "That's why you resist your deepest desires. It's the ultimate vulnerability, right?" His gaze dropped to the pendant at her throat. "But you love to be ruled, don't you? You'd get on your knees for me right now if I wanted you to."

"Probably," she said against his lips. "Even though I know I shouldn't."

He licked her bottom lip, his tongue sweeping slowly, lovingly, over her skin. Now she smelled the jasmine and tasted the butter on Mark's lips. A shudder went through her.

"And yet here you are," he said finally, his breath warm against her mouth, still damp from his kiss. "Trembling for me."

"I'm obviously out of my head."

"Not yet. But give me a few minutes."

"You are such a cocky bastard." But she was smiling, and then she was kissing him, holding him to her. All this talk should have calmed her down, but admitting her most intimate thoughts to him only made her feelings for him stronger, made her body's response to him more erotic.

She was so, so fucked.

But she'd already gone this far, and she knew there was no turning back, at least not tonight. Tomorrow. Tomorrow she'd try to get back to normal. Now, she just wanted to feel his solid flesh against hers, wanted to taste his skin. Everywhere.

Smiling, she pulled away. Then she dropped to her bottom and flung her legs over the side of the cliff. He looked startled, as if he thought she was about to jump over the edge.

She looked up at him. "Don't worry, you haven't made me suicidal quite yet. This may look like a dangerous ravine, but it is, in fact, a way down to the beach."

He eyed the overlook with a doubtful expression.

Sliding her sandals off her feet, she hooked the ankle straps with her index finger. "You're not scared, are you, Mark?"

He peered into the narrow valley. "Should I be?"

"Come on, Mark," she said as her bare feet hit the dirt. "Just trust me."

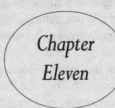

Chapter Eleven

See? You're fine," Ruby said. But it was a ridiculous statement because halfway down he'd picked her up and carried her the rest of the way. Now he placed her on her feet in the sand.

"You would have broken your neck." He bent down to unlace his boots then tugged them, along with his socks, off his feet.

"No way." She threw her sandals next to his discarded boots. "I know that path like the back of my hand."

"That was not a path. That was a cliff," he said, straightening. In the dark he looked stronger somehow, the moonlight emphasizing his sharp jaw and long, lean limbs.

When he'd picked her up to carry her he'd draped the jasmine vines around her neck and now he pulled them, tugging her toward him so he could lower his mouth to hers.

She could kiss him all night, but she pulled away, running ahead along a small creek, the vines falling away behind her. She had a destination in mind, and she knew Mark would follow her lead.

Tucked away, the little cove was dominated by a huge cypress tree, its limbs grandly sweeping the area like protective arms. And it was fitting because she'd always felt safe here; when she was growing up, it had been her little private spot. And now she was here for the first time in years, with Mark.

The soft breeze of the ocean washed over her in a salty caress that made her skin tingle, and the sound of the sea pounding the shore roared in her ears. The sand felt like a thousand little massages on the soles of her feet.

When she reached the dark shadows of the cove, she turned.

He approached slowly, picking up the vines she'd discarded and tying them together as he walked. His feet were pale in the moonlight.

He closed the distance between them, leaned down and kissed her. Slowly, he leisurely ran his tongue inside her bottom lip, then pushed deeper. Everything faded as she fell into him, into this kiss. Desire crashed into her as the waves crashed against the shore. Her pussy went moist, her breasts felt heavy.

When he pulled back she was panting. "Don't stop . . ."

"Take off your dress for me, baby."

She didn't even hesitate. They were in public; anyone out for a stroll could see them in this little cove if they really looked. But Ruby didn't care. She'd used dessert to pleasure herself in the dining room of the Ritz. What was a little public nudity after that?

And she trusted Mark to take care of her. The realization hit her that she was willing to put her own safety in his hands; had she ever trusted anyone so much before? The answer frightened her.

She began unbuttoning her dress. Her fingers shook slightly but she made quick work of it. Soon she had the top half open, and she pulled the dress over her head, tossed it into the sand.

The chilly air hit her skin, bare except for her lacy bra. She shivered.

"Take off your bra, Ruby girl."

Reaching behind her, she unhooked the clasp. Soon her bra was tossed on top of her dress and she stood there before him, naked. He hadn't even removed his leather jacket.

"You make me so fucking hot, Ruby."

She felt her nipples harden into tight little beads as a gentle breeze drifted over her skin. Or was it his words that had her body responding so intimately?

He raked his gaze over her. "Sometimes it's hard for me to keep control around you."

"Then don't," she said.

As he took a step toward her, she thought she saw a rueful smile on his face. "Not an option."

"You're always in control." It wasn't a question.

"Yes." He took both her hands in his, pressed the insides of her wrists together. He still held the jasmine vines, and as he wrapped one of them around her wrists the tiny white flowers released their pungent scent. The fragrance was exhilarating, and she inhaled deeply.

The vine he used was about five feet long, and she watched, fascinated, as he tied a knot around her wrists. The jasmine reflected the moonlight in an ethereal glow, the leaves soft and dark against her pale skin. Being bound in something so beautiful took her breath away.

He finished his knot, leaving himself about two feet of vine, which he used to lead her toward the tree. Like a prisoner, she followed a step behind him, surprised she could walk at all, her limbs were so shaky. Now that he had her under his control, what would he do?

When they reached the tree, he tied the end of the vine over a low branch and tugged until her hands were stretched above her head. Until she had to use the balls of her feet to keep her balance.

After testing the slackness of his "rope" he tied it off, securing her to the tree. Then he stepped back. His eyes were dark, intense, as he scanned her stretched, naked form.

Goose bumps erupted all over her skin. Tied, helpless, bound. For him. For his pleasure; he could use her as he wished. And she wanted him to.

He circled her, and she jumped when she felt his hands on her shoulder blades. "Ssssh," he whispered against her ear. His breath was hot, damp. Her sex started to throb, and each caress of wind chilled the moisture between her legs.

She'd never felt so aware. The ocean roared louder, the air was crisper, the moon shone brighter. And Mark. Mark was...

Pressing his solid body against hers. His erection was rock-hard under his jeans, pushing at the small of her back. "Tell me something, Ruby."

"Anything."

"Do you like it when I touch your breasts?" His hands came around to cup her breasts, and he gently massaged the sensitive flesh.

She moaned. "Yes."

"Tell me what else you like."

"I love it when you pinch my nipples." She'd never said anything like it before, and the words seemed to echo in the darkness.

He took a hard tip between two fingers and pinched her softly. "Pinch you like this?"

"Harder."

She felt his smile against her throat. The bastard already knew she didn't like it gentle; he was torturing her once more. But then he pinched again, harder, this time sending a sharp pain through her body that shot to her pussy. She writhed against the open air, straining against the vines that held her bound.

Then she felt another jasmine vine on her skin, a fragrant whisper across her rib cage, between her breasts, around her neck and back again.

Silent, she waited as he manipulated the vine around her breasts, her sides, her neck. The feel of his fingers brushing her skin, the silky flowers caressing her sensitive flesh, were like erotic pinpricks covering her wherever they touched.

Jasmine enveloped her upper body. It came together in the center of her breasts to spread out again, wrapping around her ribs toward the back. She felt him tie off the vines in the middle of her spine, leaving her in a cupless bra of leaves and flowers.

His hands were on her breasts again, pinching, kneading, pulling. The leaves and stems were slightly scratchy on her skin and somehow heightened the tingling at her nipples.

"Please," she gasped, throwing her head back against his neck. "Touch me . . . I'm so wet."

"If only you weren't so disobedient."

"I'm not . . ."

"You are. I recall asking you to feed me a certain strawberry earlier at dinner. Do you remember that?"

She whimpered. Her pussy was dripping, the juice sticky on her inner thigh.

His hot breath on her ear sent shivers over her skin. "You were a greedy thing, weren't you? You couldn't share that berry with me. And I wanted to taste you so badly, Ruby."

"I'm sorry, Mark; just touch me, please."

He teased her nipple, tweaked until she cried out, the sound drowning in the roar of ocean waves.

"My mouth was watering for it. You had your pussy juice right in front of my mouth. I could smell it." He skated his hand across her rib cage and she felt him span her abdomen, hip bone to hip bone.

"Lower," she begged, squirming.

"Tell me something first." He still held her left breast in his palm, and he squeezed her.

"Anything." *Just touch me.*

"Tell me what you tasted like," he said.

"See for yourself."

"So naughty. So defiant." His fingers inched lower, and she bucked forward. But the evil man did not go low enough. "Ruby darling, maybe you're not as submissive as I originally thought."

"You'll never find out," she said, twisting against him, teasing him.

"We'll see." His voice was even, but his cock jerked against her ass. Oh, how she wanted to feel him inside her. Filling her. Fucking her.

Again he took her nipple in his fingers and twisted until she writhed in ecstasy. "Yes, Ruby. Get even wetter for me."

"Fuck me, Mark. *Now.*"

"I will, but not until you tell me what that strawberry tasted like."

Her face burned, but she ground out the words. "Acidic, sweet. Juicy. It tasted like your fingers that night in the limo."

"Did you like it? Did you like the taste of yourself?"

She bit her lip.

He twisted her nipple.

"Yes! I liked it. And I liked knowing you wanted it and denying you."

"Is that a fact?"

"Yes."

"Why?"

"I love to see you turned on, to know I'm turning you on and torturing you at the same time," she said, not quite believing she'd said it.

So close, his finger was so close to her clit she could feel the heat of his skin.

"Mark, just touch me."

"Where?"

"My pussy. My clit."

"Good girl." His head slanted next to hers, and he released her breast to guide her mouth to his. She sucked his tongue into her mouth as his fingers—finally!—found her pussy, opening her wide.

One finger, then two slid into her. In and out. She fucked him back, barely aware of the unfamiliar sounds coming from her throat; her body had taken over her mind and now she let him take her to the edge and beyond, until she knew her own body couldn't be trusted to hold her upright.

And when she climaxed he was there to catch her.

*   *   *

Mark thought he'd never seen anything so beautiful as Ruby, bound in jasmine and glowing in the moonlight.

She was so small, so delicate. Yet her breasts were lush, filled his palms perfectly. Her hips flared out in gentle curves from a tiny waist. Her hair was wild and long and darker than night, emphasizing her fair skin. Here, on the beach with the ocean crashing in the background, she looked otherworldly, like a nymph from the sea.

Her body still shivered, her vaginal walls clenching around his fingers. He should let her wait, recover. But he'd been waiting so long already, since the second she'd stepped off the curb and peered at him through the Ferrari window. His cock had gone hard at the sight of her in her prim getup; he couldn't wait to see her undone.

And now she was.

"Oh, fuck, baby. I'm so goddamn hard for you."

"I know." She wiggled her backside against his straining cock and he nearly exploded.

"Hang on." With a flick of his knife he released her wrists from the jasmine vines. Then she turned to face him. Her eyes were wide, glossy, and dark.

He took off his jacket and draped it over her shoulders. She slid her arms into the sleeves, but her hands didn't even reach the hems.

"Do you have a condom?" she asked.

Nodding, he pulled a silver packet from his jeans pocket.

"Allow me," she said, grinning impishly. Then she dropped to her knees before him.

That sight alone was enough to make him lose control, and he bit back a groan.

She pushed the sleeves of his coat up to reveal her hands, and he handed her the condom. His balls were so goddamn tight, sweat beaded at his brow. He clenched his hands at his sides, fighting to stay in control. Because it was so hard not to throw her on the sand and fuck her. So hard when her delicate fingers were unbuttoning his jeans, pulling them down his legs, along with his boxers, until his cock was free. Her eyes widened and she licked her lips. "I barely got to see you the other night. You're quite impressive," she said with a naughty grin.

"You can look all you like. Later."

But she took his shaft in her hand, circled him in her warm grasp. He felt himself pulsing against her palm, throbbing for her. When she leaned down and licked a drop of cum from the swollen head of his cock his entire body jerked.

"Is this what you wanted earlier? When I had that strawberry in my mouth? You wanted me to lick it like this?" She licked him some more, slid her teeth across that sensitive part of him, nibbled the swollen head of his cock.

"Mmm. Much tastier than even a chocolate-dipped strawberry. I could do this all night."

"Put the condom on, Ruby."

"Fine," she said in a pouty voice. "But why do you get to have all the fun?"

"Because I'm the top and you're the bottom," he ground out.

"Maybe. I'm still thinking about what you said, that maybe I'm not as submissive as you thought I was. Or *I* think I am."

"Ruby..."

She tore open the condom wrapper and unrolled it over his shaft. When she reached the base he lifted her up and she instinctively straddled him. She was so light he could hold her body and place her exactly where he wanted her, which was with her pussy nestled right against his erection.

With a groan, he slid into her. "Fuck, Ruby. You're so tight... you feel so goddamn good."

She rocked her hips, taking him deeper, as deep as she could.

He backed her against the trunk of the cypress, going into her deeply, then pulling out and entering her again. She smiled. His jacket protected her skin from the bark of the tree as he plunged into her again, harder and faster. Found a rhythm. She reached between their bodies and took both her breasts in her hands, toyed with her nipples until they were hard again. Her arms rubbed against the jasmine vine he'd bound her breasts with, the perfume wafting between them in a rich scent.

"Yes, Mark... don't stop. Don't let go."

"Never, baby. I've got you."

She closed her eyes, arched against him. "Yes, like that."

He grasped her thighs, hard, knowing his hands would leave prints on her skin. But he couldn't let go. He needed this, needed to have her exactly right so he could feel her fully. So he could go as deep as she'd let him. So he could make her his.

She gasped, stilled. Then cried out, cried his name, and he felt her body spasm around his cock, coaxing him over the edge. Making him slam one last time into her before he exploded.

And he heard himself whispering into her ear, nonsensical, unfamiliar words. "Never, baby. Never so good. Ruby, my sweet, Ruby. Mine. Never this fucking good."

After his shudders had stopped, she took his face between her hands and placed a sweet, delicate kiss on his lips. "Promise me something, will you, Mark?"

"Anything." And, to his surprise, he realized he meant it. "Anything," he repeated.

She met his gaze. "When you leave, don't say good-bye. Just go."

Something in him went cold. "Who said anything about good-bye?"

She shrugged, trying to appear indifferent but failing. "Everyone has to leave sometime, right?"

"Good-bye's not forever."

"I mean what I said. I really, really hate saying good-bye. I turn into a blubbering idiot, and I'm wrecked for days. Happens every time. And, despite my best efforts, I think it would be really hard to say good-bye to you."

He just stared at her, took in this beautiful, disheveled, sex-flushed woman named Ruby whose body was still clenching around his cock. She was offering him perfection. Phenomenal sex with a gorgeous girl. The temporariness he always craved, but without the guilt that went with it. She'd give him what he wanted, and when it was time to go, he could just walk away. Without even the bother of saying good-bye.

Yeah, perfection.

So why did it feel like he'd just been kicked in the teeth?

He pulled out of her and set her on her feet. Managed a

smile. "Yeah, baby. Sure." He pulled off the condom and tossed it into a rusty old garbage can.

She snuggled deeper into his jacket. "Great. Thank you."

"No problem." He yanked up his jeans. "Whatever you want, baby. Whatever you want."

Chapter
Twelve

What's that?" The minute Ruby walked into the office Monday morning, Meg's gaze shot to her throat.

Ruby dropped her messenger bag on her desk. "What? Oh, this? Mark gave it to me."

"Well, well, well. That's quite a present."

Ruby shrugged off her coat. "Hey, I've never turned down diamonds," Ruby said with a smile. "It's not like I have a humongous rock on my hand to flash around." Ruby nodded at the three-carat diamond ring on Meg's left hand. "How are things with Emmett, anyway?"

From behind a stack of silk flowers, Meg said, "The same."

"Have you used the you-know-what yet?" Ruby asked, referring to their jaunt to the sex store.

"No, I haven't." Meg shrugged. "Emmett's barely been home, and I just haven't had the opportunity to say, 'Hey, hubs. How's about you bend over for me and let me try out my new paddle?'" She tried to sound flippant, but Ruby heard the sadness in her friend's voice.

"You just need to make time to talk with him."

"I know," she said and changed the subject. "I'm going to call the Riders' manager and hammer out a final date for the Fling." She picked up her phone and dialed.

Ruby let it drop. She wanted to help Meg, but she wasn't sure how. She wasn't even sure if she was handling her own love life with the caution she should be. No matter how hard she tried to tell herself this thing with Mark was casual sex, after last night she knew it was so much more than that. She'd opened herself up to him, physically and emotionally, and he'd gotten into her head.

And she couldn't get that damn smell of jasmine out of her nose!

She went to the bathroom to wash her hands one more time, trying to get rid of the scent, and she returned to their office just in time to see Meg flipping her phone shut. "You're not going to believe this, but the Riders can only perform on the twenty-eighth."

"What?"

"Yup." Meg nodded. "Their manager said they're booked solid after that."

Ruby did a quick calculation. "That's three weeks away."

"Yup."

"Three weeks?" Ruby dropped into the chair behind her desk. "Three measly weeks?"

Meg crossed the office to the bookshelf. "You know, no matter how many times you say it, you're still only going to have three weeks to plan this Spring Fling."

Under the table, Ruby kicked off her pumps. "Hopefully that date works for James Cleaver."

"Speaking of whom, did he ever ask you out?"

"No, but he's becoming more and more flirtatious. I don't know what to think."

"He certainly takes his sweet-assed time. I mean, it was obvious to everyone that he was into you at the Christmas party," Meg said, dropping into a chair opposite Ruby.

Ruby shrugged. "Who knows?"

"Wait a minute. You used to be dying for Mr. Perfect to ask you out. Now you act like you couldn't care less." Meg leaned across the desk. "What's going on?"

"Nothing! I mean, I just don't want to get my hopes up." But the words sounded false and dry. Because it seemed any man paled in comparison to Mark, even Mr. Cleaver.

"Anyway," Ruby said. "Let's just hope James can make the twenty-eighth work."

"You just got the hottest band around to play at a private company event. He's gonna make it work." She went to the door and put her hand on the knob. "So call him. I'll be in the prop room, digging for inspiration."

After Meg left, Ruby picked up the phone and dialed James Cleaver's number. Of course, just when he answered, the steady thud of Mark's music in the next room hit her, reminding her that Mark was just down the hall, recording with Emmett. So close.

"Ruby?"

She snapped her attention back to the phone. "Yes! I'm sorry, James. Emmett's recording today, so things are a bit noisier than usual."

"I completely understand. So, gorgeous. How's my favorite event planner doing today?"

"Great! I'm doing just great." He was flirting, definitely. James Cleaver, who was so nice and normal and perfect. He was reliable, everything she wanted, and he was finally showing an interest in her. So, she should be doing her best to get him to ask her out, not squeezing her legs together, trying to lower her response to being in the same building as a certain musician she wished she could say no to.

She shook her head. "Good news. Great news, in fact. The Dark Riders have agreed to play your show."

Thump thump thump. The music was getting louder, making it difficult to concentrate. Making her hot. She loosened the pink scarf tied neatly around her neck. "The possible problem is that they can only play on the twenty-eighth, just three weeks away."

"Can you put the event together in such a short time frame?"

Can you spend three weeks around Mark St. Crow without falling for him?

"Definitely," she said, nodding to herself. "I certainly can." No more spankings, no more dinners. No more jasmine. She brought her wrist to her nose and sniffed. It smelled like skin, not jasmine.

"Then we're on," James said. "I knew you could do it, Ruby. You're the best, you really are."

"Thank you, James."

There was a long pause, and then she heard him take in a breath. "Ruby, I was wondering if you would go out with me sometime. Maybe dinner?"

"Oh, sure, James. That would be nice." She realized she should be much, much happier with his invitation than she was.

"Great! I mean, how about this weekend?"

Tap tap clink, tap tap clink; the beat had shifted, becoming slower, more dynamic.

"Ruby?"

"Um...," she found herself hesitating. "Let's do it after the Spring Fling. I'm just...slammed between now and then."

"Sure, sure. That sounds great."

She opened her top desk drawer, looking for that smell. "Aha!" On top of a neat row of pencils was a jasmine vine, the end tucked into a small vial of water.

"Pardon?"

"Nothing. So, thanks for the dinner invitation. I'll e-mail you the contract and we'll get started."

"Sounds good. I'll talk to you soon, gorgeous."

She hung up and slumped onto her desk, resting her forehead on a pile of papers. The music was louder now, and it seemed to be vibrating through the entire building, thumping into her forehead like some kind of medieval torture. Each note seemed to carry his presence, made her want to go to him.

Made her want to be tied up again.

Made her want to be spanked again.

Made her want to submit again. To him.

Yeah, she wanted those things, but each time she let it happen, she unlocked her heart a little more. Got a bit more vulnerable. Got a bit more scared.

She yanked open the drawer, removed the jasmine vine, and ran upstairs to Meg's kitchen, where she threw the flowers into the trash can.

Her doorbell rang at seven-thirty that night, and when she answered it she heard Mark's voice through the staticky call box.

"Let me up, Ruby," he said. "You managed to avoid me all day, but you can't run away now."

"I wasn't avoiding you." But she had been. She'd snuck away from the office, waiting until she was sure he was busy playing music before she rushed past the studio and ran down the steps.

Now, she looked down at her sweatpants, old Ramones T-shirt, and bare feet. She'd just settled onto the sofa with some popcorn and chardonnay, convinced that those things, along with an old James Bond flick, would help her forget about Mark. But now he was here, at her apartment building. And she, of course, looked like shit.

"I don't care what you look like."

"How did you know what I was thinking?" she asked the box.

"Because you're a girl. But come on, I've seen you naked; I really don't care if you're not wearing lipstick."

She rolled her eyes. "I'm busy."

"Ruby." His voice held a warning. "Open up."

Open up. How many times had he asked her to open up: her lips, her legs. Her door.

What would be next?

She had yet to deny him. "Fine. But only for a second. I have to get up early in the morning." She pushed the button to let him in.

Turning to the mirror above the table by the front door, she quickly pulled her hair out of its messy pony-tail and was still smoothing it with her hands when he knocked.

"That was quick," she said as she opened the door. "You must have sprinted up the two flights of steps."

But he wasn't the slightest bit winded. Instead he looked as relaxed as ever in his jeans, T-shirt, and black boots. She smelled the leather of his jacket and suppressed a shudder.

He stepped inside, looked her over. His eyes paused at her throat, on the necklace he'd given her, but he didn't mention it. She'd taken it off when she'd changed after work, but she'd felt as if something was missing, and she'd put it right back on.

"You're cute like this," he said.

She shifted awkwardly. At her age, she was beginning to feel uncomfortable being seen without makeup, and she wondered if she looked old to him.

He touched her cheek. "I mean it. You're really adorable when you're all unkempt."

"You're just saying that because you think I'll let you stay here tonight." But she immediately realized what a ridiculous statement that was. Mark St. Crow didn't need to lower himself to flattery to sleep with women. Mark St. Crow just needed to *be*, and women dropped like flies around him.

"Don't worry," he said, stepping closer. "I won't stay long."

"Oh. I mean, good. Because I have an early morning."

His brown eyes sparkled behind the glasses. His irises were black, reflecting the soft light of her apartment. "So you said," he replied. "I just wanted to give you something."

It was then she noticed he was holding a small white box with a red ribbon around it. He handed it to her.

"Another present?"

"Open it."

She pulled on the ribbon and set it on the table. The lid was next, and inside was white tissue paper. She separated the delicate folds until red lace and satin were revealed. "Underwear?" she said, purposefully using a casual word for what had obviously been a very expensive set of lingerie. She wondered if he gave all his lovers such gifts.

"I want you to wear these tomorrow."

She took the panties in two fingers and held them up. "I don't wear G-strings." Not because she was a prude, but because she hated the way they made her feel, like she was walking around with a wedgie.

"You do now."

"Mark, come on." She dropped the red silk back into the box and set it on the table. "I had a great time with you, *both* times, but I don't think we should see each other anymore."

She saw the muscles in his neck tense. "Why?" he asked.

"Because." She blew out a breath. "Because I have to concentrate on work, and you're too distracting." *Because I want to fall to my knees right here in the hallway, and that can't be good.*

He leaned down until his lips were a breath from hers. "How ironic."

"What?" she whispered.

"You inspire my work, and I distract you from yours."

Her palms were damp as she clutched the table for support. "I inspire you?"

He leaned down to kiss her neck, just under her ear, and her eyes fluttered shut. "Yeah, baby. You inspire me, you turn me on. I don't know what it is about you..." His words trailed off as he continued to place hot kisses on her skin.

He took one of her hands and pressed something into her palm. The panties. He closed her fist around the luxurious silk. "Tomorrow. Wear them." And then he kissed her one last time on the lips, pulled away, and walked out the door.

*   *   *

"I need Savor," Meg announced. She'd been gluing little flowers onto translucent wire all morning in preparation for the Spring Fling. "If I glue one more flower I think I'm gonna hurl."

"I'm sure the fact that you can barely see isn't helping. When are you going to get glasses, anyway?"

"Never."

"Fine. I gotta pee and then we can go." Ruby was walking down the hall when suddenly she was yanked into the storage closet.

Mark sat them both on an old bench, and she barely caught a glimpse of him before he grabbed her and bent her over his lap. She squirmed, trying to free herself, but he was stronger and held her down.

"Mark," she said, looking over her shoulder, "what the fuck do you think you're doing?"

"Checking to see if you obeyed." He lifted the hem of her dress, exposing her ass. Then, pulling her boyshorts down, exposing her naked flesh, he shook his head. "You naughty girl." He raised his hand, flat, palm down.

"Didn't I say we shouldn't see each other anymore?" She ground out.

Smack smack smack. He spanked the fleshy part of her butt, fast and hard, and all she could do was gasp each time his hand met her ass.

"Do I look like a quitter?" *Smack smack smack smack.* Each time his palm hit, blood rushed through her body, the pain turning instantly into pleasure.

He stopped and she squirmed on his lap, her pussy going damp. *Smack smack smack.* She pushed up a bit, lifting her ass, wanting him to continue. But he didn't.

"Don't become a quitter *now*!" she said.

But he pulled her underwear back up and set her on her feet. With a triumphant gleam in his eye, he kissed her quickly, opened the door, and left her there, staring after him.

The rest of the day she couldn't get the experience out of her head; not when she and Meg discussed the Spring Fling over lunch at Savor, not when she created the catering order for the event, not when she rode the bus home.

And later that night, she stood in front of her full-length mirror, her dress hiked up around her waist, gazing at her ass. Her right cheek was bright red, redder than it had been after the first time with him, after the hairbrush. She looked at her face and realized she was biting back a small, secretive smile.

The next day, Ruby wore the bra and panties.

Drinking coffee, working at her computer, digging through the prop room; she was constantly fighting the urge to pick the G-string out of her ass.

Despite her discomfort, carrying out his order turned her on. The feel of the silky thong between her ass cheeks was a constant reminder of what had happened when she disobeyed, and she couldn't stop thinking about how he'd pulled her into the closet and disciplined her. That morning she'd found excuses to walk up and down the hallway about ten times, hoping for a repeat, but as far as she knew, Mark hadn't left the studio the entire morning.

The band worked hard, long hours, and Ruby listened to the muffled rhythm of the music they were creating. Mark called himself a pianist, but he was obviously so much more. From her office, she listened to the bizarre instruments and electronic sounds coming from the studio. One day she watched as he took a mattress and a microphone into the bathroom and shut the door. When she asked him what he was doing, he distractedly told her it was the only way to get the distinct sound he wanted.

No, he wasn't just a pianist. He composed the songs, and each note she heard in his music seeped into her somehow; a constant reminder of who he was. And of who he was about to become.

The next big thing.

Pushing herself up from her desk, she went to the studio. Emmett sat at the editing bay, and when she entered he glanced over his shoulder and nodded a hello. Mark, Yvette, and Jake were on the other side of the glass, creating music. New, unique music like she'd never heard before. The three worked together in sync, oblivious to anything except their instruments and one another.

Mark perched on a stool, surrounded by a large keyboard with an older, smaller keyboard on top of that. A battered guitar case was propped next to him, and at his feet were various pedals that he tapped as he played. But it was so much more than simple electronic piano music coming from that machine. Old recordings, random beats, unfamiliar instruments; he seemed to have it all at his fingertips, and the result was totally exceptional, fresh and innovative.

He didn't look up from his composition. He had no idea she was there, watching him. Listening.

She put a hand to her heart, which had started to ache. Because she knew, all too well, what it was like to be with a man like this. A man obsessed with something greater than life, always searching for meaning through his art.

Why did she always fall for these types of men? Writers, photographers, musicians; each one thinking they were so special they needed to contribute to the culture-at-large and, of course, that was much more important than any relationship could ever be.

For once, she didn't want to be second to the art. She wanted to *be* the art. She wanted to be the center of someone's universe.

Maybe that's what she'd been looking for when she'd posed for Ash; maybe she thought that she could be both: the love and the art, all mixed into one bound, naked bundle.

Oh, how wrong she'd been.

Yvette looked up and caught her eye. Gone was the glare Ruby had witnessed that first night, but now Ruby saw something else, something worse. Sympathy.

Turning on her heel, Ruby walked out the door, knowing Mark would never even realize she'd been there.

The phone was ringing when she got home that afternoon. She ran into the kitchen and grabbed the receiver off the wall. "Hello?"

"Hey, Ruby Tuesday. Watcha doing?"

Dropping her bag onto the old Formica dining table, Ruby smiled. "Claire Bear! What's goin' on?"

She heard the clinking of dishes in the background. "Not much," Claire said. "I'm on a break and thought I'd see what's up with my big sis."

Ruby and Claire were closer than most sisters. Even when their mom had been around, she'd been distracted with their huge circle of friends, and Ruby had taken on the role of mother from the time Claire was born.

Ruby dropped into a chair. "Pretty good. I miss you."

"You too."

"When are you going to give up this acting business and come home?" But Ruby was kidding. More than anything, she just wanted Claire to be happy, even if it meant her thirty-four-year-old sister was a barista at Starbucks while she waited for her career to take off. But Claire was talented. It would happen, Ruby knew it would.

"Well, I do think I'm overdue for some Ruby time. I'm going to come up for a visit," Claire said.

"Oh, I would love that. When were you thinking?"

"I was thinking toward the end of the month. Would that work?"

Ruby pulled a calendar out of her handbag and flipped it open. "Oh, you have to come after this big event I'm doing, or I'll be too swamped to spend any quality time with you. Have you heard of the Dark Riders?"

"Um, yeah? The clubs in L.A. play that single all the time."

Ruby couldn't help the little smile playing around her lips. Every time she heard something positive about Mark's band she felt proud of him.

"Well, I'm planning a show and they're playing. Can you come after that?"

"Sure. So have you met them? That Mark St. Crow is fucking hot."

"Yeah, he is." She sighed. "He really fucking is."

"Ruby Tuesday. You *have* met him. And, if my instinct is correct, you've done more than just meet him."

Her sister knew her too well, could pick up on any little nuance in her voice. That thought wiped the smile off her face; the last thing she wanted was for Claire to know the nature of her relationship with Mark.

Ruby had managed to keep the bondage photographs a secret, and Ruby didn't want Claire to find out about them. Ever.

"Ruby? Are you gonna spill about this guy or what? My sister's dating one of the hottest guys around, and she won't tell her own sister. Very rude."

Ruby focused on a peeling piece of floral wallpaper. It was vintage, and she hated the thought of having it replaced. Everything in this building was original, which was why she loved the place so much. The history made it feel solid, grounded. All the things she'd never had growing up.

With her fingertip, she traced an abstract pattern on the gold-speckled tabletop. "Mark is nice, and if he was older, not a musician, lived in my time zone, and wasn't surrounded by beautiful women all the time, I might consider dating him."

"Oh, Ruby. First of all, you're gorgeous. And the beautiful people thing? Trust me. That gets real old real quick."

Ruby shrugged. "Maybe. Regardless, even if I did have a crush on him, it wouldn't matter. It would never work."

"You've been saying that your entire life."

"And it's never worked."

"Maybe that's because you go in telling yourself the relationship is doomed," Claire said.

"I dunno. All I know is that I'm thirty-seven and I keep picking the wrong guys." The gold pattern twisted and turned under her finger.

"You pick guys you know won't stick around."

"Not on purpose," Ruby said. "It just...happens."

"You're always looking for the perfect man, but honey, he doesn't exist."

"I don't want perfection. I just want a normal, steady relationship. Is that so much to ask?"

Claire laughed softly. "You want a fifties sitcom. God, remember when we watched reruns of those show every day after school?"

Yes, Ruby did remember. If her parents were sailing or home or at a party, it didn't matter. Because every day at three o'clock, she could escape into black-and-white perfection. Two reruns in a row. An hour of watching how normal people lived.

Or so she'd thought at the time.

"Anyway," Ruby said. "I hope you come visit."

"I will, soon. Love you."

"Love you, too." She hung up the phone but remained seated, staring at her cozy kitchen. If the Cleavers had lived in an apartment, it would have looked like hers. Bright, sunny yellow cabinets, white-tiled counter, and black-and-white laminate flooring straight from the 1950s.

Maybe this was it. Maybe this was where she'd spend the rest of her life. Maybe Claire was right and she was looking for a man who existed only on television.

She thought of James Cleaver. He seemed perfect, and yet he'd never made her heart thud. He'd never made her want to tell him her most secret fantasies.

And, at the opposite end of the spectrum, there was Mark. He was so immersed in his music he hadn't spoken to her all day. As he should be, his music was his job and she respected that. Still, she hated the way her heart hurt with the disappointment that he'd been distracted from her so easily.

Pushing herself up, she tried to drive the feeling away. She'd prepared herself for this, hadn't she? It was exactly the reason she'd resisted him in the first place. The nature of their relationship had ratcheted up their intimacy level too fast; zero to sixty-nine in under a week.

She pulled a half-empty bottle of chardonnay out of the fridge and poured herself a large glass. And as she drank it, alone in her kitchen, she told herself she wasn't going to settle for anything less than what Meg and Emmett had. The perfect couple, they were proof that what she wanted was possible.

Right?

Chapter
Thirteen

Meg was spying on her husband, and she didn't even care if she got caught.

They hadn't had sex in months, ten weeks to the day to be exact. Meg knew because the last time they'd fucked she'd been ovulating. She had it all marked on a little calendar, the possible baby-making days starred with a red pen.

They'd missed several baby-making days.

But she didn't care about that. What she cared about was that her husband wasn't interested in her anymore.

Looking back, she could see he'd been distancing himself from her for a while. The question was, what was she going to do about it?

Why, spy on him, of course. She'd briefly glimpsed the porn on his computer, but she thought maybe if she studied it, she could get a real idea of what he wanted. Which brought her here, to his office, to his desk, where she was sitting, waiting for his computer to boot up.

It finally did, and ignoring her damp palms, she clicked the history on his Internet browser.

And that was when she found it.

It wasn't the pornography itself that shocked her. No, it was the type of porn her husband appeared to be fond of.

She landed on one site, the links flashing, a garish neon sign in the dark:

Boy toys for you!
Naked men who clean!
XXX Men who give you what you need!

Meg wasn't a porn aficionada, but most of what she'd seen in her life featured fake-breasted women who spent a lot of time fondling each other and giving men blow jobs. But the sites Emmett had been browsing boasted naked men. Lots of them.

"Holy shit!" The screen came up with various images of young men surrounding cars. They held buckets and sponges and towels. They were all naked. Many had erections. Some had penises that just bobbed around as they cleaned windshields and bumpers.

She couldn't stop clicking; she'd never seen such things. Images flashed across the screen: Women lashing men with wet towels. Women forcing men to crawl on their knees as they served the women. One image featured a man tied to the bumper of a Nova, his face buried in the behind of a tall blonde. Meg's pussy went moist. She couldn't help it. The images of the naked subservient men made her squirm in her husband's chair.

She found a video and clicked the Play icon.

Two nude men washing a red, eighties-model Mustang came to life on the computer screen. Her pulse hammered as she watched a curvy woman with a sleek ponytail and a long leather flogger circle the men. Meg's nipples started to tingle when the woman smacked one of the men's naked asses. The woman on the screen did it again, and

Meg's cunt throbbed as she watched a red welt appear on the man's golden flesh.

Meg thought of the paddle she'd bought but hadn't had the balls to show Emmett, and she was envious of the woman on the screen. And when the men started pleasuring each other Meg closed the window on the browser with a fast click. Her skin was burning and her pussy was aching. She was disgusted at herself. She had just discovered that her husband had a fetish for male porn, and she was more turned on than she was angry.

What was *wrong* with her?

She pushed the chair back and left the office. As she walked up the stairs, she tried to ignore the way her thighs rubbed together and tingled the sensitive flesh between her legs.

She couldn't stop thinking about the way that woman had smacked the young man's ass. The image was burned into her brain. And she was turned on and jealous and hurt.

But at least she had figured out why her sex life had gone to shit. Her husband was gay.

On Saturday Ruby was working on catering invoices when a package arrived via courier. It was wrapped in brown paper and had no return address. Mark. She instinctively knew it was from him.

She hadn't spoken with him the day before, although he'd sent her a text message late last night that said: Sorry. Worked late. See you tomorrow?

She hadn't sent a message back.

Now she had butterflies as she walked through her apartment, took the package into the kitchen and placed it on the table, on top of the papers she'd strewn about as she'd worked.

Should she open it now?

Just then her phone buzzed and she picked it up. Open it up, the display said.

Open it up. And, as usual, she did.

The box was long and narrow, the type of package roses were shipped in. But when she lifted the lid off this box, she saw no roses inside. Her breath hitched. The dry scent of leather hit her, and she had to smile.

She began lifting items and placing them on her kitchen table: black leather, fur-lined handcuffs. A second set, but bigger: ankle cuffs. Some black nylon straps. And a vibrator. This she lifted and held in her palms. It was different from her little pink bullet; this was longer, wider, and the tip was angled. It was made out of a jelly-like material that was slightly squishy. She turned it over in her hands. Through the transparent material she could see the motor, but there didn't appear to be any way to turn it on.

The screen on her phone showed no new text messages. He knew she'd received the items, obviously, so now what was she supposed to do? She stood there, waiting, but instructions never arrived. Finally she returned the cuffs and other things to the box. What was he up to?

Back on the sofa, she opened her laptop and tried to focus on invoices. But now her entire body pulsed with anticipation, excitement. Her breasts felt heavy and her pussy was tingling. And he'd know this, of course he would. It would be part of what he wanted, to get her going, get her ready, aching.

Finally at seven-thirty her cell phone rang.

"I hope you didn't start without me," he said immediately.

She'd just taken a bath and was standing in her bedroom, wrapped in a towel. The air was chilly against her wet skin, but a flash of heat went through her at the sound of his voice. "How could I?" she asked. "The vibrator you sent must be faulty. It doesn't have an On button." She unwrapped the turban-style towel on her head and shook out her wet hair. "How was your session today?"

"Great, but exhausting. I don't want to think about it anymore."

"Oh. Okay." She tried not to be disappointed that he didn't want to share his day with her. *Don't go there. This is just sex, remember?* After her last phone conversation with James, she'd decided to allow herself this tryst with Mark. To have casual sex, to get it out of her system. Only then, she'd concluded, could she go on with her life, just as things had been.

"All I want to think about is you," Mark said.

His words made her heart stop, just for a second. This was bad, so very bad; every time he said stuff like that she knew it would be harder to get back to the normal life she craved.

But... there was that flutter in her belly again, telling her she was too weak to say no to him. The excitement was too good, too thrilling, and now anticipation coursed through her, erotically charging her.

"I'm in L.A. or I'd come see you, baby."

She paused. "L.A.?" He'd never even mentioned he was leaving.

"Some stupid private party—sorry, I didn't mean it that way."

"It's okay," she said, but for the first time she wondered what his band thought of him agreeing on their behalf to play the Spring Fling.

"We'll fly back first thing in the morning."

"You sound tired," she said.

"I'm beat. You know what's keeping me going?"

"No," she said, lifting a leg and resting her foot on the bed. She soaked up the last of the water off her calf with her towel.

"What's keeping me going is knowing that I'll be seeing you when I get back, knowing what I'm going to do to you. Knowing how you're going to submit for me."

Frozen, she listened to his words.

And then he said, "I can take you there right now, if you'll let me."

A shiver raced up her spine. "What do you mean?"

"Ruby, baby. You know exactly what I mean."

"Mark..."

"Baby, I can already hear the surrender in your voice."

"I don't know, Mark."

"Don't fight it, sweetheart."

Hadn't she been waiting all day for this? "Okay," she said, even as her gut twisted with nerves.

"Good girl."

His simple approval cemented the deal, no turning back now. And besides, he was three hundred miles away; what did she have to lose?

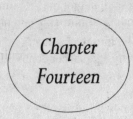

Chapter Fourteen

Where are you?" he asked.

"My bedroom." She hadn't blown her hair dry; it would be a frizzy mess tomorrow. She tucked a damp strand behind her ear. "I just got out of the bath."

"Fuck, are you already naked for me?"

"It wasn't for you, but yes. I'm naked."

"Baby, I can picture you so well. I can see you standing in your room, with that frilly little lamp of yours turned low. I can see your pale skin glowing like it did on the beach. Have I told you how much I love your body, Ruby?"

His words were like a hot whisper over her skin, melting her. "No."

"I do. Your breasts fit in my hands perfectly, your legs wrap around me so tight."

Her legs turned liquid and weak, but she didn't sit down. He hadn't given her permission for that yet.

"But you know what I noticed first about you?"

"No."

"Your hair. I really love your hair."

She thought he wouldn't think that if he saw it now, damp and a wild mess. "Really?"

"Yes. Now, where are the things I sent you?"

"In the kitchen, still in their box."

"Good. Now listen, Ruby. This is what I want you to do. I want you to go into the kitchen."

The air was chilly against her damp skin as she walked down the hall, teasing her nipples, making goose bumps sprinkle her arms.

"Are you there now?" he asked.

"Yes."

"Standing naked in your kitchen?"

"Yes," she said. "It's freezing."

He paused; she could hear him breathing, and then he said, "Good girl. Now I want you to take out each thing in that box, and, as you do, I want you to tell me what you're holding in your hands."

She approached the box, her pulse loud in her ears as she opened it. "I have a leather cuff...another cuff." She sounded breathless, like someone else. "Two more cuffs. And the vibrator."

"Ah, yes. The vibrator. But that's not just any vibrator, doll. It's a very special toy, one of the better results of modern communication technology."

She held the pink phallic-shaped implement in her hand, comprehension finally beginning to dawn on her. "No way."

"Yes, way—and by the way, I didn't give you permission to talk. Now, are you ready to behave?"

She sighed at the thrill that shot through her.

"Okay, then. Now, pull out a chair and sit down. Are you sitting?"

"Yes." The vinyl seat was sticky on her bare skin, but she kept that to herself. There would be time for disobedience later.

"Okay, baby. Now spread your legs for me. I need you to straddle that chair, I want your feet next to the legs, got it?"

"Yes," she said, not quite believing she was in her kitchen, naked, having phone sex with Mark St. Crow.

"Good girl. Now, tell me how you're feeling."

"Ridiculous. Horny."

"Honest enough." He laughed. "Isn't that what's so great about this, though? About you and me? Instant honesty through our dual perversions?"

"Is that what this is? Because I honestly can't believe what I've let you do to me...what I've told you."

"But you love it, don't you, baby?"

She hesitated, then shrugged. "Yes. But I'm afraid of what will happen when this is over. When you go. Will I ever be able to go back to normal?"

"Why would you want to?"

She pictured James Cleaver, her "perfect" man, representing everything she'd wanted her entire life. Stability, reliability, dependability. She'd thought she'd dodged a bullet with Ash, but now she was wondering if she'd just been scared of something. Scared of what she felt now, with Mark.

"I don't know anymore," she whispered. "You've got me all fucked up."

"Well, forget about it for now. Now, you're mine, right?"

"Yes."

"I want you to give yourself to me, to trust me. Do you trust me?"

"Yes." And she did as he said; she pushed all thoughts out of her head until it was only her and his voice, telling her what to do. Setting her free.

"Are you open for me now?"

"Yes." Wasn't she always?

"If I was there, I'd tie you to that chair. I'd bind your ankles wide apart, I'd have you spread open for me. Bound for me."

She hitched a breath, her heart hammered in her chest.

"I'd tie your wrists to the arms of the chair and you'd be at my mercy. I could do anything to you then, couldn't I, baby? I could take your breasts in my hands, pinch your nipples until you cried out. Couldn't I, Ruby?"

"Yes," she hissed, her breasts now heavy, throbbing.

"I could step between your legs, let you suck my cock."

She closed her eyes and licked her lips, remembering exactly what he tasted like, how his penis had beat with his pulse, in her mouth, on her tongue. She remembered how powerful that feeling had been, and her own sex responded by getting wetter; the air was cool, hitting her between the legs, and she squirmed in her seat.

"Oh, God...I...I wish you were here," she said.

His voice was soft. "So do I, baby. But for now you'll just have to obey me and let me imagine you there, spread wide and open for me. Tell me again who you belong to tonight?"

"You, Mark. I belong to you."

"Good girl. Now, I need you to take the larger cuffs and bind your ankles to the legs of that chair."

Her fingers trembled as she lifted a large leather band and unbuckled the strap. About three inches wide, made of black leather, each restraint was lined in soft, minklike fur. They smelled like leather, like Mark. Bending, she wrapped the cuff around her right ankle and locked the buckle. Then the other ankle and she was done. Bound.

"Are you finished, baby?"

"Yes."

"How does it feel?"

"Soft. Good," she said, satisfaction settling inside her.

"Good. Now I want you to take a picture with your cell phone and send it to me."

"What?" She'd promised herself she'd never pose nude again.

"Are you questioning me?"

But this self-bondage was nothing like what she'd done with Ash. Ash had been all about the art and beauty and composition. It had never been about her at all, had it?

With Mark, no matter how submissive a position she found herself in, she realized, in the end, it was about her pleasure, about *her*.

"Come on now, baby. I wouldn't put it past you to be faking the whole thing, being the unruly little spitfire you are. I need proof before we go any further."

"Fine. I'll do it."

"Good girl."

Holding her cell phone in front of her, she angled it as best she could to get her lower body in the frame. She pushed the button and waited for the *click* to tell her the picture had been recorded.

She studied the image. Was that really her? Legs open wide, bound to a chair with oversized black leather restraints, like some sort of prisoner?

Yeah, it was.

"Did you send it to me?"

She did.

A few seconds later she heard him inhale. "Oh, fuck,

baby. You're so gorgeous. You deserve your reward now. Get the vibrator."

She picked it up off the table, held it in her palms.

"Now tell me. Are you wet?"

"I am."

"That's good." Suddenly the vibrator started humming in her hands. "Feel that? I just love modern technology."

"Oh God, I think I do, too."

"Touch yourself now, baby. Touch your clit."

With her gaze on her sex, she pressed the humming vibrator to the throbbing nub at the top of her pussy. She jerked, gasped.

"That's it, touch yourself now, baby. Touch your clit, rub that vibrator around your beautiful pussy."

Sagging into the chair, her ankles pushed against their soft restraints, she did as he commanded. She was so slick, so turned on, the jellylike vibrator slid easily over her pussy.

He upped the power and she cried out. "Oh...fuck..." Knowing he held the power in his hands, despite the distance, turned her on even more, made her buck against the back of the chair as she held the buzzing instrument between her thighs.

"That's right, baby. Feels good, doesn't it?"

"Good...ah!" she gasped, nearly dropping the phone. "Oh, God...Mark."

The vibrator stopped buzzing, going still in her hands. She sat there panting, dazed. "What...?"

"You didn't think I'd just let you get off, did you? What fun would that be?"

"Mark!"

"This hurts me as much as it hurts you."

She had to bite her lip hard to keep her response inside. She was so close to coming, so fucking close. Her fingers curled, itching to help relieve herself.

"Don't you even think about touching yourself, doll."

"I'm going to get you back for this."

"Promises, promises. Now, are you going to behave?"

"Yes," she ground out.

The vibrator started humming again, this time softly. "Let's try this again. But first, tell me about your nipples."

"My nipples?"

"Yes, those things on your breasts."

"Funny."

"Are you talking back?" he asked.

"Of course not."

"Good. So why don't you pinch one of your nipples for me. Hard, like I would do it if I was there. I want to hear you cry out for me."

She took her hard nipple between her fingers and pinched. Inhaled sharply. The pain shot straight to her sex, and the throbbing between her legs intensified.

"Okay, that was good. Now, put the vibrator into your pussy."

Finally. She kicked at her restraints as she slid the vibrating toy into her vagina, closed her eyes as it filled her. Not as good as Mark's cock, but her pussy was hungry, needy, and her thighs trembled as she fucked herself. Still, she wished it was him there, his own body driving her pleasure.

"I can hear you breathing hard; you like this, don't you? You like being mine, under my control."

"Yes," she said, angling the vibrator deeper. "Oh, yes."

"Now, I want you to keep the vibrator inside you, but keep your hands off it. I want total control of your pleasure."

Her entire body was quivering, needing release, but she obeyed. She placed the thrumming instrument as deep as she could and let go. It hummed softly inside her, making her moan.

He turned up the power, and she had to grasp the arms of the chair to keep from touching her clit. So close...

"You're doing so well, baby. I wish I could reward you myself. I wish I could stand between your legs and show you how hard your obedience makes me. I'd take my cock in my hands, I'd let you watch as I stroked myself. For you."

Was he doing that now? Masturbating? Was he lying on a generic hotel bedspread, his long, sure fingers wrapped around his erection? Pumping himself, from his soft pubic hair to the head of his cock and back again?

The image upped her desire for him, but she dared not ask what he was doing; the last thing she wanted was him to stop the lovely toy vibrating in her pussy. Because her breaths were coming quick now; her body was on fire. So close to climax...but oh, how she needed something on her clit.

Her fingers would do nicely.

She writhed in her seat, gripping the chair's arms.

The vibrator humming inside her, he went on: "If I was there with you, I'd take your hair in my hand, wrap it around my palm and tug, just enough to make you squirm. Would you like that?"

"Yes...yes..." So close. Her clit was pulsing, begging. She looked down to that empty place between her legs. Her fingers trembled as the desire to touch herself coursed through her blood.

Slowly, she removed her hand from the arm of the chair and reached to her thigh, just touching the inside. God, her clit was so close, if she just reached over a little more...

"I have a thing for hair. I love to feel it on my skin. I love to wrap it around my dick and feel it across my balls."

His words were too much. She touched her clit and swallowed a cry of pleasure.

"If I were there I'd take my cock and bring it to your lips. I'd let you lick the cum off the tip."

"Yes, Mark..." She touched herself lightly, as if a soft pressure wouldn't count as much.

"Do you want to come?" he asked, and the vibrator became faster inside her, more insistent.

"Fuck, yes. Please."

Her clitoris pulsed, and she took the swollen piece of flesh in her fingers, pulled, pinched. Worked herself.

"With your hair in my fist, I'd hold you steady as you took me into your mouth. You wouldn't be able to move at all because I'd have you tied to the chair. You'd squirm, but you know you'd love it. Would you like to suck my cock, baby?"

"Oh, God. Yes, Mark...oh, *God*..."

She didn't register his prolonged pause until it was too late.

The vibrator went still. "Ruby?"

"W-what?" she gasped. Her entire body was shaking.

"Are you touching yourself?"

Fuck. *Fuck!* She froze. How had he known? She jerked her hand from her body, even though it was too late.

"Ruby? Did you disobey me?"

"No, I was just helping things along." She tried to laugh, but it sounded hollow. Desperate.

He sighed, and she could imagine him running his hand over his shiny scalp. "What were you doing? Tell me exactly what you were doing."

"I was touching my clit. I was..." She felt her cheeks begin to burn with embarrassment, but she kept going. "I was pinching myself there. Rubbing."

"Why? You didn't trust me to take you there?"

"I couldn't take it anymore. I needed to feel something!" Shocked at the sting in her eyes, she quickly wiped a tear away.

"You needed to feel something?"

"Yes."

The disappointment in his voice nearly killed her. "And you weren't?"

"No, Mark—it wasn't like that! Listen to me—"

"You know what happens when you don't follow directions. You get punished."

She sucked in a shaky breath. "Mark. I'm sorry."

"I bet you are. You're all hot, turned on. Ready to come. But now you're going to have to wait."

One quick pulse from the vibrator inside her made her cry out. But then it stopped: He'd hung up.

Sitting on the bed, Mark stared across the hotel room. One leg bent, his fingers tapped a steady beat on his knee.

Cutting Ruby off hadn't been easy. And he loved the disobedient side of her even as much as it frustrated him. But that unruly part of her was too much fun to mess with; he couldn't stop himself.

And he had to admit it bothered him that she hadn't waited for him, hadn't trusted him to take her where she needed to go.

A good sub needed to learn patience, that patience was, in fact, a virtue. Especially a sub who didn't want to spend an entire night on the edge of an orgasm.

Ah, but she wasn't the only one on edge, was she? After hanging up, Mark was left with a very painful erection. His cock was full, throbbing. His balls were tight. Listening to her through the phone, hearing her breathing become heavy as she got off, was a kind of torture. He wanted to be there, see her eyes glaze over. Smell her arousal, feel her tremble beneath his fingers.

His phone displayed the image of Ruby. He couldn't see her eyes, just those long legs, spread wide and cuffed to the metal-legged chair. And the ends of her hair, touching the tips of her breasts. It was no wonder Ash had used her as a model. She was gorgeous; made to be captured in all senses of the word.

And probably ready to kill him right about now. But she should have followed directions. That's what subs did. There were rules to be followed, and that was what made these types of relationships work.

He tried not to picture her, one of her elegant hands tugging at her clit, masturbating as she listened to him. He tried not to picture the way her skin would flush, the way her nipples would be hard little tips.

He tried not to picture those things. And failed.

His cock was about to explode.

Throwing his phone down, he jumped up and went to the bathroom. He pulled a familiar-looking bar of soap out of his toiletry bag and held it to his nose. He'd found a few extra bars in her bathroom and, impulsively, he'd stuck one in his pocket, thinking to take it with him to the store and buy her an entire case of the stuff. Something about the scent made him go crazy with desire for her.

And now, like some kind of desperate teenage boy, he held the bar to his face, inhaled the jasmine scent deep into his lungs. He was hard everywhere, and he reached to his crotch, cupping his erection through his jeans. He was so fucking hot for her he jumped at the contact. He yanked his T-shirt off, threw it on the floor. Unbuttoned his jeans and jerked them along with his boxers down his legs. Kicked them aside.

He was going to jack off. He couldn't remember the last time he'd done it—pussy was too easy to find to bother doing it himself. But right now? He didn't want any pussy but Ruby's.

He turned on the faucet. Then he unwrapped the soap and caressed the sleek bar until a foamy lather came alive in his wet hands. He took his time, letting the fragrance permeate the bathroom. It was like having a bit of her there, with him. And yeah; he was that desperate.

His hands slick with the creamy lather, he palmed his cock and slowly brought his fist up until he reached the head, already dripping cum. He turned to face the full-length mirror that hung on the back of the bathroom door. *This is what Ruby would see if she were here*. It would be her punishment. To watch him do this to himself. She would want to feel him so badly, but he would tell her no, would make her squirm for a while. Remind her who was in charge.

If she were bound before him, she would see the way the muscles in his shoulders moved as he slowly brought his fist down to the base of his erection. She would see the way his hips tilted forward as he stroked himself, up and down. She would see him tugging at his left nipple piercing until he grimaced. Helpless, she would watch as he masturbated before her. Her eyes, big, dark, and wanting.

His rhythm became faster. His breath hitched and he groaned, imagined her touching the vibrator to herself, the way she'd buck against the little device. He bent his knees slightly, his legs going tense as he stroked himself faster and harder. In the mirror he watched his hand's even rhythm.

He could recall precisely what it felt like to be inside Ruby, fucking her. So warm...and tight. He could almost feel the inside of her clenching around him as she climaxed. He remembered the way her inner walls had spasmed around his cock. He jerked one last time against his hand, grunting as everything in him tensed in one all-consuming moment, frozen. He felt his own hot cum hit him in the chest when he exploded.

Panting, he bent over and rested his elbows on the bathroom counter. When he caught his breath he looked up at his reflection above the sink and shook his head. *Idiot*. He'd hoped masturbating would clear his mind and release him a little from the hold Ruby had over him. But his forehead still looked creased and tense.

In the sink, soap bubbles popped softly. The light perfume managed to accost his senses, making his balls go tight once more.

Masturbating hadn't helped. He wanted her now, more than ever.

Chapter
Fifteen

This is nice." Yvette settled into the plush seat of the private jet and sipped her orange juice. "It almost makes it worth getting up at the ass crack of dawn to get back to S.F."

Next to her, Jake gazed around the elegant beige interior. "I guess we're good enough for a private jet, just not good enough to choose the time we fly. Whatever. It's better than coach."

The sun hadn't yet risen, and Mark flipped on the overhead light in order to see the notebook he was scribbling in. So close. He had the lyrics, but the melody was evading him, just out of reach. He wanted to nail it, and he wanted to do it now. For some reason it seemed important that this song make it onto this record.

"What are you working on, pet?" Yvette asked. "You've been totally distracted all morning."

He glanced across the aisle. "Just a new song."

"Give us a taste, brother," Jake said, picking up his ever-present drumsticks. "Give me a beat."

"Nah, it's not finished yet."

"Come on, Mark." Yvette tapped his knee with the tip of her pointy black boot. "Maybe we can help."

"Seriously, I just want to work it out first." Keeping his

head down, hoping they'd go away, he didn't notice Yvette leaning across the aisle.

"Does that say '*Ruby*'?"

"Fuck. Can't you just let me finish this?"

Jake gave a low whistle. "Dude. Have you ever written a love song before? I don't think so."

"No shit. He's too busy writing about going insane and things melting and other *heavy shit.*" Yvette sipped the orange juice, and Mark was starting to wonder if the drink was actually a mimosa.

He turned back to his notebook. "It's not a love song, not really."

"If it's about a woman, it's gotta be," Jake said.

"All I know is that this is the first time I've seen you so taken with a lass. Other than me, of course." Her voice was casual, but Mark heard the bite behind it.

He was too tired to argue. "I admit it. I like her. But she's made it obvious it's a temporary thing, which is cool with me."

"I'm sure it is." Yvette leaned forward, bracing her elbows on her knees. "Why do you think our Ruby is so intent on keeping things casual?"

Mark glanced up and when he spoke, his voice sounded tense. "I'm not exactly relationship material. She doesn't want to get hurt. The usual."

"Maybe, but it's not usually the girl making that decision." Yvette frowned and stared silently at him, the deep whir of the jet's engines humming through the cabin. Then she leaned back, sipped her drink. "And how does our stallion feel about this filly bucking him out of the corral?"

He tapped his pencil on the notebook. "We leave in

what? Two weeks? I'll just see how it plays out, I guess. I mean, she's just a girl." He tried to keep his voice casual, but there was an ache in his heart even he couldn't ignore.

"Just a girl," she repeated.

"You're right, Yvette," Mark said. "The last thing we need is a distraction like this, not now."

"Like what?" Jake asked. "It's just a girl. Remember?" He looked up. "What do you mean?"

"If she's just a girl, it's not a big deal. Shouldn't affect the music." But Jake's raised brow indicated that he was waiting for Mark to argue.

"Would you two stop making so much out of this?"

Jake threw up his hands. "Dude. We're not."

"Good," he said, turning back to his notebook. For some reason he thought if he could just finish this song, he could get both the music and Ruby out of his system. As it was, both were frustrating pieces he couldn't quite work out.

The doorbell woke Ruby up. "What the hell?" she muttered, glancing at the clock. It was 8:30 a.m.; who would be ringing her doorbell this early on a Sunday?

She wrapped her robe around her T-shirt, slipped into her fuzzy pink slippers, and padded to the door. "This better be good," she said into the call box.

"I usually am."

"Mark?" She jerked back as if the box were on fire. Then, she took a deep breath and pushed the call button again. "What are you doing here? I thought you were in L.A."

"I came to finish what I started last night. If you're willing to behave, that is."

Instantly, her body came to life. After they'd hung up last night, she'd been too annoyed to finish herself off. Instead she'd gone to bed frustrated and had slept fitfully, dreaming about sex. And with each dream she'd woken just before climaxing.

And now the source of all that frustration wanted to come up and complete the job?

"I can't believe you didn't call back last night."

"I told you. It hurt me as much as it hurt you. Now, let me up."

"You are such a..."

"Sexy beast?"

"I was thinking asshat," she said and pushed the button, opening up. Again. Too bad he was such an irresistible asshat.

She left the door open so he could let himself into her flat. She refused to greet him until she'd brushed her teeth, gone to the bathroom, and combed her hair. When she was finished, she found him in her kitchen, looking through the cupboards.

"Coffee filters?" he said as he shut a drawer.

"Make yourself at home." She pulled a box off a shelf and handed it to him. "Here."

He grunted a thank-you.

She said, "It's eight-thirty."

"I know. Why do you think I need coffee so badly?"

She tightened the belt of her robe and leaned her hip against the counter. "Tell me about L.A. About this private party."

He put a filter in the coffeepot and, from the container on her counter, poured a huge pile of her best French roast directly into the cone. "It was just a show. The usual."

"That's all? I'm an event planner, remember? I live for this stuff!"

"Do you? You love your job that much?"

"Most of the time. So tell me what it was like."

He glanced up. "I dunno. It was a big party for some movie studio. Dinner and champagne. Fancy."

"So," she said. Getting information out of him was like pulling teeth. "What songs did you play?"

"The usual."

After a minute she realized that was all he was going to say about the party. She pulled two mugs from a cabinet. "Well. Thanks for last night," she said sarcastically.

He gave her that lopsided grin, the one responsible for the flutters in her belly. "Maybe I was too harsh. But I'm very proud of you for not masturbating without me allowing it."

Glaring, she put her hands on her hips. "What makes you think I didn't?"

"Oh, baby. You're wound so tight I'm waiting for your head to explode. I know you didn't get yourself off. But, I think all that waiting has taught you a valuable lesson. Now, you deserve a reward for your good behavior."

"Are you serious? You just show up here on a Sunday morning and expect me to get on my knees and thank you?"

He winked. "You don't have to thank me, but I'd love to see you on your knees."

"You're...you're..." She threw up her hands. "Words fail me."

Calmly, he filled both mugs with steaming black coffee. "Am I right? Did you finish, Ruby?"

She crossed her arms in front of her chest and said, "Finish what?" But she knew what he was talking about.

He looked at her, and his eyes were serious despite his nonchalant tone, his casual stance. "Yourself. Did you hang up and masturbate? Did you climax without me?"

"No." She didn't add that without him, she hadn't even wanted to try.

He stepped closer until she was backed up against the counter. Everything about him was slow, unhurried, a total contrast to the sharp edginess coursing through her body.

"I did," he said. "And I thought about you the entire time."

Desire raged through her as she pictured him stroking himself, getting off. Thinking of her.

And it somehow made her defiant. "I have more will-power than you."

"Is that so?" he said, even closer now, and then he placed a hot kiss at that place just under her ear, that spot that made her close her eyes and sigh when she felt the tip of his tongue on her skin. "So now, if I said I wanted to take you and lay you down on your kitchen table and do all kinds of naughty things to you, you would say no?"

"Yes." He was close enough that the heat from his body mixed with her own, his long arms enclosing her as he leaned on the counter. She could just feel his cock, hard through the material of her T-shirt, robe, and his jeans. "Yes," she whispered. "I could definitely say no."

"Mmm-hmm," he murmured as he ran his lips down her neck, in front of her throat. "You could. But will you?"

Her legs were trembling now, and her eyelids were drifting shut. "Why do you do this to me?" she asked.

"I wish I knew." He pressed against her, his body hot and hard against hers.

She reached under his T-shirt and felt the muscles of his abdomen clench as she ran her hand over his warm skin. His jeans were slung low on his hips, and she felt his stomach, where he had just the tiniest amount of hair below his belly button. Then she ran her hands up, across the smooth ridges of his rib cage until she got to his nipple, gently scraping a silver hoop with her fingertip.

"Did it hurt? When you had them pierced?"

"Not especially."

"You're so tough, then?"

"I can handle pain."

Kissing him, she gave the ring a gentle pull. He tensed and his cock jumped against her. Something in his kiss turned harsher as she played with his nipple ring, and she pushed at him, tugging and stroking until he pulled back and she saw that his eyes were very dark, almost black.

"Where are the things I sent you?" he asked, his voice husky.

"Over there." She nodded to the corner, to the box that was now closed up tight. Next to it she saw a leather case that hadn't been there before.

"Take off your clothes."

She nodded; wasn't she supposed to be mad? Didn't matter. He'd broken that barrier with an easy smile. Yeah, she was that lost in him. Now, her fingers trembled as she untied her belt, slid off her bathrobe. She watched him move to rummage around in the box. His T-shirt rode up when he bent over, exposing the smooth skin at the base of his spine. He was such a combination of lean elegance and dominant male. It unnerved her.

Standing, he turned with two cuffs and the nylon tethers in his hands. He looked her over. "T-shirt, panties. Take them off."

She pulled the shirt over her head and his gaze dropped to her panties. As he watched, she pulled them down her legs.

"Beautiful." He placed the items on the table, then came to her. "So beautiful, my Ruby." Then he picked her up and carried her across the kitchen to place her on the table. Kissing her, he eased her down until she was flat on her back. The table was not large, and she bent her knees and let her legs hang over the edge.

"Mark . . . ?"

He took her left leg in his hands and placed a kiss on her ankle. "Just let go, Ruby."

He had rope; it must have been in the case he'd brought. Quickly, he tied her left calf to one of the table legs, wrapping the rope from her ankle to just under her knee, where he finished with a knot. He repeated the process with her right calf.

She hadn't felt rope on her body since Ash, but he'd never done anything so quickly, so practically. Ruby found she loved the swiftness of how Mark moved. For once, she felt as if she was more important than the rope itself, and the feeling made her float even higher.

Spreading her arms as wide as her legs, he used the restraints and tethers to bind her wrists to the table. She caught glimpses of him as he moved; the sharp line of his jaw, the mole at the base of his neck. He was beautiful, but somehow his dominance was what she noticed. She noticed his utter control.

And then she was stretched open, her legs and her arms bound to the four corners of the table. Open for him, totally.

He stood back, looked her over. "You know what? I just realized I haven't had breakfast."

She twisted her head toward him. "P-pardon me?"

He grinned wickedly and then she heard the door to her refrigerator open, the clamor of him pulling items out of it.

"Mark? What are you doing?" Her body was shaking from waiting and wanting.

Back in her line of vision, he shook his head. "Only vanilla ice cream? That's kind of ironic." He slid a spoonful of Ben & Jerry's into his mouth, then scooped up some more.

"Is this your idea of torture? Because I'm getting ready to kill you."

"The more disobedient you are, the longer you wait." He placed the back of the cold spoon against her nipple and she bucked on the table. "Fuck, that's cold!"

"In a good way, right?" He turned the spoon over so the frozen dessert rolled onto her breast. "Mmm. You look good enough to eat." He bent forward and took the ice cream, along with her nipple, into his mouth.

Gasping, she turned her head to the side and bit her lip. He licked, sucked, tugged. Spooned more ice cream onto her other breast and did it again. Soon she was writhing on the table, the metal hinges of the tethers clanking against the metal legs.

Her belly quivered as he kissed her between her breasts,

down her rib cage, and over her right hip bone. Then he was between her legs, nibbling the inside of her thigh.

Freezing-cold ice cream hit her clit and she cried out when his mouth followed, warm and wet, the contrast causing her to arch against his tongue, his lips. He spread her pussy wide, licking her, sucking her, playing her like she was one of his instruments. And, like one of his instruments, she made noises each time he did it just right. Little cries of pleasure; little gasps of joy.

Then his fingers were tracing her, sliding through her labia and past her vagina to her anus. She stilled when she felt a pressure there. But then his mouth was on her clit again, sucking, teasing, controlling her pleasure, and when he pushed his finger into her ass her eyes flew open, but she didn't stop him.

He pushed deeper, using his mouth to keep her on edge, using his fingers to intensify the sensations. She was going to come, come so hard...

"I didn't say you could come."

She bit the inside of her cheek, thought of her shopping list, her credit card bill, anything to control the orgasm hovering at her very core.

He continued to work her, and just when she didn't think she could control herself one second longer, he pulled back, slid out of her. Standing, he pulled his shirt off and threw it on the floor. Now he wore only jeans that fell to his hip bones and nothing else. She loved his body. His muscles looked taut and strong with controlled power.

Her chest rose and fell in heavy, deep breaths as she watched him. She could have watched forever, but he silently left the room and she waited. It was a power play, a move to remind her who was in charge.

As if she didn't know it already. She was naked, sticky, chained to a table, had just given up her anal virginity, and it wasn't quite ten on a Sunday morning.

Yeah. She'd say she was pretty much his.

This time when he came back, he was totally naked and held something in his hand. Something dark and black, but she couldn't quite make it out. And anyway, she was too busy looking at his body to notice much else. An entirely fresh wave of lust washed over her as she scanned his long legs, his strong thighs with a light dusting of dark hair. His concave belly, beneath which his cock rose, hard and beautiful. She licked her lips.

"I figured a girl like you would have a little toy in her nightstand, so I went looking for it. But, much to my pleasure, look what I found instead." He held up the black mini-flogger she'd purchased at Bindings.

He stood next to the table and lightly dragged the feather strands across her stomach. She shivered; the light touch of the feathers and leather on her skin was just as luscious as she'd imagined.

Sighing, she closed her eyes as he continued to drag the strands over her body. Her ribs, her breasts, her neck. It felt so good, soothing even.

Then, with a flick of his wrist, the leather softly smacked her breast. She cried out.

"You like that, don't you?"

She blinked, nodded.

He did it again, struck her nipples until the peaks were throbbing, sore, and alive. He seemed to be in touch with the flow of her endorphins because he started using more force, flicking her harder, until she was moaning, jerking, pleading.

He slapped her once right between her legs, hitting her swollen pussy, and she screamed and begged him to continue.

But he shook his head. "I'd rather fuck you now." His fingers found her pussy, and he flicked her clit. "Would you like that?"

"Just do it," she said, barely able to speak.

He took his cock in his fist and pumped a few times. Long strokes. Leisurely. Then he rolled a condom onto his erection.

"I want you to tell me how much you want me to fuck you."

"This much," she said, jerking her arms, which were still spread wide, beside her.

He laughed, then dipped out of her vision for a moment before straightening. She watched as he placed two items on the table. A bottle of lube and a small, curvy blue dildo.

"You liked my finger in your ass, didn't you?"

Blushing, she nodded.

"I'm going to put this in your ass, and I'm going to leave it there when I fuck you." He took the plug and squeezed a generous amount of lube over it. Then he bent over her, his legs between her open thighs, resting against the table.

He kissed her and she felt the lubricated dildo touch her clit, her labia, and then lower, poking at her ass. Still kissing her, he pushed it inside.

He climbed onto the table and knelt between her spread legs. Watching her face, he used his hand to guide his cock into her pussy, stroking her wet folds until she bucked, inviting him, begging him. He pushed into her wetness, and the dual penetration made everything he did to her more intense, more stimulating. She was instantly on edge and as he moved, pulling out and then driving into her, she heard her own voice, screaming for him to fuck her.

Screaming, moaning, crying...She couldn't have held off her orgasm now even if he'd demanded her to.

Luckily, he didn't, and soon he was coming as well, jerking one last time inside her, a groan erupting from his throat as if it were being ripped out. His cock pulsed in powerful waves, and she very nearly came again.

His brow was damp when he dropped his head into the crook of her neck. She wanted to touch him, feel his head in her hands, but she couldn't; he hadn't released her yet. Anyway, her limbs were boneless; she was helpless, nearly breathless.

His body was hot and slick when he sagged on top of her, as if he needed to catch his breath. She didn't mind his weight, but when he pushed away, looked at her and kissed her forehead, she smiled up at him.

"I need a nap," he said.

"It's not even noon."

"Does it matter?"

She had to think about it for a second before she replied. Then she shook her head from side to side, not caring that her hair was a mess around her face. "You know what? It doesn't matter." She grinned wider. "Yeah. Let's go to bed."

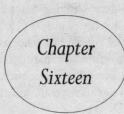

Chapter

Sixteen

Ruby, baby. Wake up."

She turned toward the soft whisper at her ear. "Mmm?"

"Get dressed. It's past three, and I want you to show me your town." He was sitting on the bed beside her, wearing jeans and nothing else, the afternoon sun streamed through the window, highlighting a spatter of freckles on his upper chest she'd never noticed before.

She reached toward him. "Are you sure you don't want to come back to bed?" As she turned, she let the covers fall, exposing the peaked nipple of her left breast.

His eyes raked over her. "You're such a temptress. But I'm leaving soon, and I want to see San Francisco." He leaned down and kissed her softly. "Also, it's not like we need a bed to fuck in." He winked. "Just wear a skirt."

His words woke her up, and she pulled the covers over her chest. "Right. Okay." Somehow, without the edge of passion, his language sounded coarse, vulgar.

Ignoring the feeling, she reached out and took his hand. Stroking his knuckles, she gave him her best sultry look. "I promise to do whatever you want. But first, come back to bed." She licked her lips, trying to look sexy. She wanted more of what they'd done in her kitchen, and she wasn't too proud to ask for it.

But then his cell rang, and he took his hand back to pull the phone out of his back pocket. "It's Yvette. Hang on," he said, walking out the door.

Staring after him, she watched him leave the room. Then she pushed herself out of bed, listening to the deep hum of his voice as he spoke. So. At least he didn't try to hide his priorities. It occurred to Ruby that if Mark did actually live closer, she would break it off now. Obviously, the band came first. Music, Yvette, his career; it was all the same to him, and, as she believed and he'd never denied, there wasn't room in his life for anything else.

But she wasn't going to make a big deal out of it because she knew what they had was temporary; she knew this fling was about to end. But it was too good, too addicting to give it up now. Like the strawberry dessert at the Ritz, she wouldn't be happy until she'd had every last bite.

She shook the whole line of thought from her mind. Mark wanted to see San Francisco, and she would have fun obliging him. She thought of all the places she could take him. Alcatraz, Fisherman's Wharf, the Presidio. Coit Tower, Lombard Street, North Beach, Chinatown. When was the last time Ruby had seen any of the city's famous landmarks? She couldn't remember. But she was keyed up about the idea of visiting those places again. With Mark. And she knew exactly where she wanted to go first.

She washed her face and tied back her hair. Too eager to get going, she skipped any makeup and went to her closet. She didn't even bother looking at pants. If he wanted to *fuck*, God help her, she wanted to be ready.

She settled on a mini-floral-print fifties sundress and ballet flats. Grabbing a cardigan from a hanger, she headed to the kitchen where Mark was cleaning up the melted ice cream they'd abandoned earlier.

He dumped the carton into the garbage. "Wow. I'm impressed. I don't think I've ever met a woman who could get ready as fast as you can."

Shrugging, she dumped cold coffee from their neglected mugs into the sink. "It's an old habit, I guess. I never had time to primp when I was growing up."

"Because you were taking care of your sister."

"I guess. So, everything okay with Yvette?" she asked lightly.

He shrugged, but she saw a tension in his body that hadn't been there before. "Everything's fine."

It obviously wasn't, but she ignored the subject and pulled some bread off the counter. "You want something to eat? Coffee? Toast?"

"I'd love both."

She threw out the old coffee filter and added a fresh one, measured out the appropriate amount of grounds, and turned on the machine. Then she stuck four slices of bread in the toaster. They fell into a relaxed silence until she placed their afternoon breakfast on the table.

She watched him take a huge gulp of coffee. "So tell me more. What was it like growing up Mark St. Crow, musical prodigy?"

He rolled his eyes. "Considering I could barely play 'Mary Had a Little Lamb' on the piano until I was five, I'd hardly call myself a prodigy." He pointed a half-eaten piece of toast at her. "Not that I didn't try. I've been playing since before I can even remember. But that Mary and her lamb were so damn elusive."

Laughing, she just shook her head at him. "And your parents were supportive?"

"Yeah. Sometimes I think Dad's living vicariously through my career. You know, achieving what he couldn't because he had to settle down."

She nibbled her toast, wanting to hear more. "What do your parents think of your lifestyle? All this travel? The instability?"

"They're proud of how hard I work, but I don't think they quite get how tough life on the road is. It's not all sex and drugs and rock and roll. Well, it's not the last two things, anyway," he said with a wink.

"And what about you?" she asked gently, not wanting to scare him but needing an answer. "Don't you ever want to settle down? Have a family?"

He shifted in his seat. "And give up my glamorous life-style?" he said with a laugh. "No way."

"I'm serious. You can't live out of a suitcase forever."

"I'm only twenty-nine; I have plenty of time to get tied down."

She raised her brows. "You mean when you're old? Like in your late thirties?"

A tinge of red actually stained his cheeks. "I didn't mean it like that..."

"Don't worry, I know what you meant. You want to enjoy it while you can." She sipped her coffee. "And I think you should."

He looked surprised. "Really?"

"Why not? Like you said, you're young. Free. You have the world at your fingertips. Why shouldn't you enjoy it?"

"Right," he said. "Maybe one day I'll slow down, but not now."

The words hung in the air for a few minutes before Ruby asked, "Are your parents still together?"

"For better or worse. Despite everything, even after all these years, they're still pretty into each other. Every year at Christmas I catch them kissing under the mistletoe." He gave a mock shudder.

"That's so sweet! They sound perfect." Ruby had a flash of she and Mark sharing a comfortable holiday kiss and quickly shoved the disturbing image aside.

He laughed wryly. "Far from it. Sometimes I think they want to kill each other. Hell, Mom's packed his bags more than a few times."

She sat back. "Really?"

"You look shocked."

"Well...your childhood just sounds so ideal, so wonderful. You had mistletoe, for God's sake! But then you say your mom's kicked your dad out of the house—more than once. I don't know, it's just confusing to me."

"Why? It's pretty normal when you think about it. You take two people from two totally different backgrounds, give them a baby and tell them they have to live together for the rest of their lives. *Forever.*" He shrugged. "There's bound to be problems. And then the question becomes, what are you gonna do about it? Stay together, or get a divorce?"

She just stared at him. When he put it that way, it sounded so simple. So uncomplicated. And maybe for him it was.

"What did your dad do, to get himself booted?"

Mark swallowed his last bite of toast. "He didn't cheat

or anything, not that I know of. But he used to work a lot. He hated his job but needed it to pay the bills. And I know, on some level, he resented my mom getting pregnant and forcing him to settle down. That's how he saw it, anyway. So he'd come home from work and take his anger out on her."

He stared into his mug, swishing the coffee around. "He was never physically abusive or anything. He'd just come home pissed. If my mom didn't have dinner on the table, he'd be pissed. If I was playing rock instead of jazz, he'd be pissed. He was pretty much just pissed all the time. So, one day he came home and Mom had packed up his shit."

"Wow. Mark, I'm so sorry."

He shook his head. "Don't be. Dad went to counseling with her, moved back in. And then a few years later it happened again. And he came back again. It kind of became this five-year pattern."

"Your mom must be very tolerant."

He stared into the depths of his mug. "She is. But I know she feels guilty for making my dad quit his music to get a real job. Anyway, no marriage is perfect, that's for sure."

Ruby thought of all the "perfect" marriages she knew, and wondered if there actually was such a thing. Her benchmark couple, Meg and Emmett, seemed to be having issues. And Mark's textbook family was anything but her ideal family. But they were all still together. Hell, even her own fucked-up parents were still together.

"I always wanted the perfect marriage," she murmured.

He grinned. "How's that working out for you?"

"Shut up," she said jokingly. "I'm just now beginning

to see there may be no such thing." She drained her coffee and set her empty mug on the table.

"I know some lifestylers, total master/slave people. They live that way twenty-four seven. To most outsiders, these people would seem like complete freaks. But guess what? They are some of the happiest people I know."

She scoffed. "Are you saying only BDSM people are truly happy?"

"Not at all. I'm saying people who are true to themselves have a better chance."

"Does that mean if someone outed you as a dom, you'd roll with it? Let the tabloids have a field day?"

He shrugged. "It's not exactly a secret. I don't have any problem with those people who want to keep it in the closet, but I don't put any of my own energy into doing so. It's who I am."

"Well, I wouldn't be so happy about people finding out about what I do with you, I'll tell you that." The thought of Claire knowing what her sister did behind closed doors made Ruby cringe.

"Because you haven't accepted who you are yet. When you do that, you can make the right choice."

"This," she said, waving at the box in the corner, "is not who I am."

"Right. Because the perfect woman would never want to be tied up, spanked, paddled."

"Stop it."

"Flogged, bound, whipped." He put his coffee cup down.

"Mark..." She squirmed, the seat suddenly uncomfortable beneath her ass.

"Restrained."

She slapped her hands flat on the Formica. "I don't think that."

He leaned over the table, his elbows sliding sideways as he came forward. "Tell me something, baby. When was the last time you actually felt perfect?"

Her skin burned hot with nerves. She knew the answer; it slammed into her with the force newfound truth always does, like a bag of rocks. Heavy and bruising.

The only time she'd even glimpsed that feeling of perfection was during her times with Mark. When she gave him her power, when they exchanged that energy. And it wasn't perfection, necessarily, but fulfillment. Satisfaction. Completion. So many emotions, all rolled up into one.

She wondered if June Cleaver was secretly a domme behind closed doors. Maybe that explained why she was always so fucking happy.

The tinny strumming guitar music woke her. She glanced at the clock; it was past two in the morning and Mark wasn't sleeping next to her. Pushing the covers aside, she got out of bed.

She'd fallen asleep naked in his arms, and she grabbed a silk robe off a hook as she walked into the hallway. She followed the low hum of not just the guitar, but also a melodic voice. Mark's voice. He had a deep, husky tone that sent shivers straight up her spine.

She found him on the sofa, playing the old guitar her dad had left behind. He wore flannel pajama bottoms and glasses. The muscles in his long, strong arms flexed as he changed chords and strummed.

Mark must have tuned up the guitar. The thing had

been sitting around, unused, for twenty years. But Ruby had never been able to get rid of the old instrument. Even now, the pads of her fingers tingled as she remembered the hours she'd spent strumming the wiry strings, trying to coax out a melody.

Pausing just outside the living room, she leaned against the wall of the hallway and watched him. He was obviously working on a song, and she loved this insight into his creative process. So different from the way she worked: researching, planning, organizing. Every detail meticulously arranged.

But this. Just like the man himself, his process was spontaneous, organic. He'd brush his fingertips over the strings for a few notes, then reach over the guitar to scribble something on the pad of paper on her coffee table. She recognized the paper as scrap from her office, and she was, for some reason, glad that he'd helped himself. She wanted him to know he was welcome to any of her possessions. Her paper, her food. Her heart.

At that realization, pure panic rushed through her, and she put a hand to her chest, which had begun to pound like a drum. She couldn't breathe; her vision began to dim. How the hell had she let this happen? She had gone and fallen for a man who epitomized everything she did not want in a guy.

"Oh, *fuck*."

"Sorry, baby. Did I wake you?"

Her pulse hammered in her throat as she took a few shaky steps to the sofa. "Maybe, but it's okay. What are you working on?"

She focused on his naked torso, fighting back a crazy desire to lick his shoulder, tug on his nipple rings. To hug him and feel him in her arms. Only he could untwist the knot of anxiety in her belly.

And yet she was smiling because, even though it was temporary, he was here now. And she couldn't help but take pleasure in that little fact.

She sank into the sofa, leaning her back against the arm. "Do you mind if I stay?" she asked as she brought her knees to her chest.

He shook his head, his eyes sparkling in the dim light. "Not at all. In fact, I'm about done."

"What are you working on?"

"A new song. I woke up with a thought, and I couldn't get it out of my head. I had to try to work it out."

"I know exactly what you mean. It's like that for me, too. When I get an idea for an event I can't rest until I write it down."

"Exactly. It's like this beast within, scratching inside your head until you let it out."

She nodded. "Yeah, that's it." Still nodding. "Precisely." They stared at each other a minute before she said, "So. Wanna sing me your song?"

For a second, he looked uncertain, and it was the first time she'd ever seen this expression on him. "It's not finished."

"I don't care."

He met her gaze, and she saw vulnerability in his eyes. She touched his shoulder. "Really. I love everything you do. Please. Play for me."

"Okay. Sure." He turned back to the guitar and started to strum. The melody immediately pulled her in with its soft, melancholy notes. But then he started singing, and that was all she could hear. His voice, the words.

She listened, losing herself as he revealed a part of himself she'd never seen. And he was singing to her, *about* her. It was a love song, and when he chanted her name in the chorus he looked directly at her, and she felt her bones turn to liquid.

Ruby, mine.

A love song. For her.

Chapter Seventeen

So, I'm pretty sure my husband is gay. Or bi. Frankly, it's a toss-up right now. It could go either way. No pun intended."

Ruby nearly spit her latte across the table. "What?" she said after she'd swallowed.

Meg crossed her legs. Today she wore a black hat with dotted netting covering one eye, a vintage dress that looked very Jackie Onassis except it was paired with black fishnet tights and on her feet were old Doc Martens boots.

"I said, I think my husband is gay. I might as well just sign up for one of Oprah's desperate housewives shows."

It was Tuesday, and they were having a "meeting" at Savor. So far Ruby had been able to avoid going anywhere near the studio, and luckily Meg hadn't second-guessed her reasoning for meeting at the café instead of their office.

"Wait." Ruby tugged the hem of her dress. In total contrast to her friend, she wore a pink fifties sundress and red round-toed pumps. A cashmere cardigan rested on her shoulders, fastened at her neck with a vintage pin in the shape of a rose. "Back up. Emmett is not gay. Or bi!"

Meg calmly removed her sunglasses and placed them

on the table. "Really? Allow me to present my case. Exhibit A: He hasn't had sex with me in months, even when I try to get things going, if you know what I mean. Exhibit B: I found all kinds of gay porn on his computer. Exhibit C: He's out late every night. Exhibit D." She looked up, then back down at the table. "I don't have an exhibit D, but I'm sure there is one."

"Meg, none of those things mean he's having an affair."

A wistful look in her eye, Meg was staring at a baby in a stroller. Ruby knew Meg and Emmett had been trying to have kids, but she didn't want to ask Meg about it, not now.

When the stroller had passed, Meg looked back at Ruby. "Then what does it mean?"

Pausing, Ruby remembered Mark's words about people accepting who they were. "Meg. Is it possible there's something Emmett wants? Something he's afraid to ask you for?"

"Like what? He knows I'll do anything for him. With him."

"Are you sure he knows that?"

Meg shook her head. "Absolutely. I mean, I think so."

"What if... what if there was something Emmett wanted to do, something he was embarrassed to admit. Maybe he's looking for it in porn."

"Which brings me back to my point with the homosexual porn! He's gay."

Ruby touched her friend's hand. "Okay, let's just take a breather here. Tell me exactly what you saw, with the porn."

For the first time Ruby could remember, she saw her friend look uncomfortable. But, ever the trouper, Meg spoke anyway. "There were a lot of men...and some women. A few women. But the women were..."

She squeezed Meg's hand. "What? You can tell me."

Meg lowered her voice. "They were all the things Emmett doesn't like. They were bossy, overbearing. Humiliating, even."

"Oh, sweetie." She tried to look reassuring. "How do you know he doesn't like those things?"

Meg looked taken aback. "He's told me so."

"Okay, but what someone likes in real life doesn't always transfer to the bedroom." Ruby was beginning to think she was a perfect example. After all, she loved being submissive in the bedroom, but none of her business associates would ever describe her as such.

"And," Ruby continued, "just a couple of weeks ago you yourself were asking me about spankings. If I were to jump to any conclusions based on what you've said, I'd say it's not you that needs a good flogging. Maybe it's him."

Meg froze. "What are you saying? You think my husband wants to be dominated?"

Ruby raised a brow. She'd started to suspect Meg had a dominant streak, and now she wanted to make sure her friend was comfortable discussing the possibility with Ruby. "Would that bother you?" she asked.

"No, of course not. It's just...I never would have guessed he might like it. I mean...I bought that paddle for him to use on me, if he wanted to."

"But would that be okay with you? If Emmett was the one who wanted to get spanked?"

"Yes!" Meg said loudly. "I mean, yeah, sure."

"Me thinks she doth protest too much," Ruby said, grinning.

"Actually," Meg said with a wink, "I didn't protest at all."

Ruby gave her friend a playful nudge. "You dirty birdie."

Meg leaned back and smiled. "Hey, I can't let you have all the fun, can I?"

They sipped their coffee and after a few minutes Meg looked up. "I just wish he wasn't hiding this from me."

Mark's words echoed in Ruby's mind. "Sometimes a person has to accept who they are before they can share it with someone else."

"True."

They drifted into their own thoughts. The fact was, Mark was right. She did like being spanked. She did like to be kinky. Ash had been the start of it, but it was Mark who'd fleshed out that part of her. Now, she seriously doubted she could just let it go when things with Mark inevitably fizzled.

"You're thinking about Mark, aren't you?" Meg asked.

"How did you know?"

Meg crossed her legs. "Just a hunch."

"He was gone when I woke up this morning. All I found was a note saying the band needed him." Ruby tried to sound as if she didn't care.

"I guess that's the way it is when you date a rock star."

"We're not dating," Ruby said.

"No?"

"No way. It's temporary. In fact, I'm going out with James after the fling."

"Finally!" Meg exclaimed. "It's about damn time."

"Yeah," Ruby mumbled. She should be ecstatic. So why

did the thought of kissing another man, having another man touch her like Mark had, make her stomach churn?

Still, she refused to bury this craving just because Mark wasn't around.

But she couldn't help but wonder: Did she like to be spanked? Or did she just like to be spanked by Mark St. Crow?

"I'll order for you."

Mark watched as Ruby put down her menu. When they'd gone for Thai food on Sunday night, it had been a normal dinner. They'd talked, they'd laughed. They hadn't been kinky. He couldn't remember when he'd spent so much normal time with anyone who wasn't in his band or part of his DNA.

And yet he'd been pensive ever since the conversation about settling down. If she'd come right out and demanded that he put her first, it would have made it so easy to walk away. But it was more than obvious that settling down with "someone like him" was the last thing on Ruby's mind, which should have been a good thing. It should have freed Mark to enjoy his time with her before he walked away.

So why hadn't it? The very fact that she wasn't asking him for anything made him want to give her everything.

Now they were having a late lunch near Ghirardelli Square. It was three, and at this in-between time of day on a Thursday, they were the only patrons in the restaurant.

Twisting in the booth to face her, he took a fallen lock of her hair in his hand and played with the silky strands. *Just think about today.* She'd put her hair up in some kind of clip thing, and it was simple for him to unclasp it. She watched his face as he combed out her hair with his fingers, her lids lowering slightly each time he tugged gently. She was so fucking reactive, so trusting of him, so...

Perfect.

He wrapped a silky lock around his finger. She looked at him, ready for any signal he'd give her. It was that trust that floored him, made his blood rush hot. When she looked at him like that he knew it would be easy to lose control, to forget he was in charge.

Leaning toward her, he nipped her earlobe, addicted to that gasp she made when he did it just right. He kissed her temple as he twisted her hair tight. When he pulled back he was satisfied to see the flush on her skin, the sharp rise and fall of her chest.

And he was hard. His cock was throbbing underneath the table. He wanted to take her, right there in the booth. He wanted to feel her pussy, wet and tight around his cock; he wanted to take her nipple into his mouth and taste her skin. He wanted to bite her, listen to her scream his name as she came.

He swallowed. "I love that you wore a skirt today. Did you do that for me, doll?"

She looked up through those dark lashes of hers, flirty. "Maybe."

"Good girl."

His blood was pounding. Every muscle in his body was tense, strained. He'd topped a lot of girls, but he'd never fought this hard to keep it together.

"Cakebread 2006 Sauvignon Blanc. Would you like to taste, sir?"

Mark slowly turned toward the waiter; he'd totally

missed the man's approach. He cleared his throat. "My guest would like to taste the wine."

"As you wish." He poured a tiny amount of the golden liquid into an oversized wineglass. Ruby took a sip and nodded her approval.

After the waiter had filled both their glasses and left, Mark turned back to her. She was looking at him expectantly. Her eyes wide and full of want. For him.

His balls tightened, and he wondered if he had it in him to wait.

With a deep breath he picked up the small bag of chocolate they'd bought earlier at Ghirardelli Square. She'd brought him to the square on Sunday, during their mini San Francisco tour, and it was easy to tell that it was Ruby's favorite spot in the city. The scent of chocolate swirled through the air, and Ruby had closed her eyes in ecstasy, a look Mark wanted to see on her face more often.

Now, he felt her gaze on his hands as he took out a bar of chocolate and unwrapped it. He broke off a piece and brought it to her lips.

Her eyes were wide as he slowly pushed the piece of chocolate into her mouth. He followed the chocolate with his finger, sliding into her mouth until the pad of his finger rested on her tongue. He could feel the chocolate melting, warm and silky against his skin.

She started to suck.

Lust blasted through him, landing deep in his gut, where it throbbed like a bass drum.

"Pretend it's my cock in your mouth. Show me what you'd do."

The pink flush that stained her cheeks made him burn. Her gaze locked onto his as she drew his entire finger into her mouth, slid him over her tongue, sucking him until the base of his knuckles hit her lips.

The chocolate was gone now, melted. Kind of like his restraint was threatening to do. He was so fucking hard, his erection throbbed painfully, every muscle in his body tight. She continued to suck him, taste him. Her eyes were dark and glittery, and he knew she was getting off on it. Knew she was wet for him.

He wanted to feel that wetness; he wanted to bend her over the table and bury himself inside her.

Instead he drew his finger out of her mouth and traced a soft line across her bottom lip. He cupped her face, and she twisted to kiss his palm. When she met his gaze her eyes glistened with something so true it made him ache.

"Will I see you again?" she whispered. "After you're done recording here?" She seemed to be holding her breath, waiting for his answer.

He touched the side of her mouth with his thumb. "I can't make any promises. It wouldn't be fair."

She exhaled. "Good."

"Good?"

She nodded. "Then you can leave and not say good-bye, like I asked. Because there's a chance you'll be back. Someday."

Their gazes locked until the waiter appeared, and they broke apart as he placed two plates of food on the table.

Some kind of intense silence hung over them as they began to eat. He was sure she felt it, too, this connection between them. They were in a restaurant, and yet it seemed the rest of the world didn't exist.

After they'd finished half their meals he topped off her wineglass. He then broke off another piece of chocolate and placed it on her tongue.

He took a sip of wine but didn't swallow. Then he leaned in and kissed her, letting the wine spill into her mouth. Her body slackened as she swallowed, and he pulled back to look into her eyes.

Her lids fluttered open slowly. He sucked in a breath. She was so fucking turned on, he could see it in the deep blue of her eyes; he could see everything there.

And it was too much. There was a sense of urgency thrumming through his veins, and he couldn't ignore it. He wasn't sure if it was the time restraint or just being with her that did him in, and at the moment it really didn't matter. All that mattered was being inside Ruby making her his. Now.

Running the pad of his finger over the back of her hand, he felt her tremble. "Ruby. I want you to go into the bathroom and get yourself ready for me."

Her gaze darted around the room quickly before landing back on his.

"Go on now, baby. I want you."

"You want me to what?"

"Any way I can have you. Now, hurry."

Her mouth twitched in a hidden smile. "Yes, Mark."

Yes, Mark. Every time she said that the throbbing in his cock jumped up a notch. And his hammering heart did, too.

"Go into the bathroom and lift up your skirt. Take off your panties. Then touch yourself, masturbate until you are about to come. But don't."

She narrowed her eyes, and he saw how badly she

wanted to come. Needed to come. He watched the flush on her cheeks spread to her upper chest, saw her glance dart down the hallway to where the restrooms were. She didn't need much more encouragement.

"Go."

One last glance at him and she slid out of the booth, taking her purse with her. He watched her walk away.

Running a hand over his scalp, he tried to be patient. He imagined Ruby in the bathroom, her skirt hiked up to her waist, her hand between her legs. She'd be wet, on edge within minutes. He'd made sure of it.

She wasn't the only one on edge.

He took another few sips of wine; they hadn't even finished half a bottle, but he didn't care about the wine. He just wanted to be with Ruby. With her. Inside her.

Instead he stared out the window at the sailboats bobbing on the bay. Waited for his erection to subside so he could actually walk through the dining room without scaring people.

The bill hadn't arrived, but he threw a wad of cash on the table and stood. His heart thudded as he made his way down a carpeted hallway. There were two unisex bathrooms, and he knocked softly on the first door.

"Ruby?" he murmured.

A second later the door popped open. He stepped inside and turned the lock. Her back was to him, and she was bent over, her legs spread wide. Her beautiful pussy glistened, waiting. For him.

"Goddamn, Ruby. You're…" He trailed off. She was too good for words.

Her hair hung loose around her face as she glanced over her shoulder. "I did what you said, Mark. I masturbated, but I didn't let myself come. I waited for you, but I can't wait much longer."

He jerked a condom out of his pocket and tugged his jeans down. "I'm here, I'm right here." Wrapping his hands around her hips, he pulled her to him. He entered her in a smooth, slippery motion that made her cry out. With her head thrown back, her hair draped nearly to her waist. He wrapped the length in his fist, tugged gently, and she moaned.

He withdrew and slid in, again and again, until she was begging, crying out, meeting his thrusts with a jarring force, as if she couldn't get it deep enough, hard enough.

"Yeah, baby. Perfect; you're perfect. Just like that."

She shuddered, and he wasn't in control anymore, not of her, not of himself. He slid in one final time, losing himself totally in his own climax.

He caught his breath and pulled out of her. His hands shook as he stripped the condom off and threw it into the trash can. Yanking up his boxers and his jeans, he turned to her.

"Ruby, I'm sorry."

She was still hanging over the sink, her skirt pulled up to reveal her smooth ass. Grinning, she glanced back at him, a glossy, satisfied look in her eyes. "What are you sorry for?"

He removed his glasses and rubbed them with the hem of his T-shirt. "I rushed things...I just couldn't hold back."

Straightening, she turned to face him and pulled down her skirt. "I don't *want* you to hold back."

He shook his head. "You don't understand."

Reaching out, she touched his shoulder. "I do. You don't have to be in control every second, all the time."

He met her gaze. "What are you talking about?"

She crossed her arms over her chest. "Now it's my turn to give you the psychological profile. This control thing of yours? It's how you stay disconnected."

"I'm not disconnected." How could she say that? He'd never felt so connected to anyone in his life.

She laughed wryly. "Are you kidding? Ever since that day you opened up in my kitchen, you've been distant. I asked you about the future and it scared you."

He just stared at her, knowing she was right. Because when he saw Ruby, he saw a future, and it made everything inside him clench whenever he thought about it.

She went on. "You say this controlling dom persona is who you are, but I'm wondering if it's just a pretense."

"I know a few girls who can vouch that this *dom persona* is no act, doll."

"See? You can't even settle on an endearment. 'Baby, sweetheart, doll.' It's all the same."

His body stiff, he took a step closer to her. "I've never claimed to be some kind of saint."

She met him head-on. "Oh, that's for sure. And isn't that the beauty of being a dom? It's the perfect excuse to love 'em and leave 'em. Shit, you even have a verbal contract before you do the deed, don't you? It's called *negotiating*, and you're damn good at it."

"You're wrong." But her words hit home. Because the thing was, when he was with her, it was easy to let go. There were no parents to pacify, no music to write, no manager pushing for a better hook.

And Ruby. She was different. For the first time in a

long time, he could let his guard down. Be himself. She didn't care if he was in control or not. She didn't care if he was in a band. She just seemed to like him for who he was: Mark St. Crow, a band geek from Akron with a fetish for spanking women.

Which meant he could really fall for her.

He felt his cell phone vibrating in his back pocket. Glad for the distraction, he pulled it out and flipped it open.

"Yeah," he said into the phone.

"Where the fuck are you?" Yvette demanded.

He turned away from Ruby's vulnerable eyes. "Out. What's up?"

"Oh, I'm just kicking back with a reporter from the *San Francisco Review*. You know? The biggest entertainment paper in northern California? The one who's supposed to be interviewing us *right fucking now*?"

"Shit!" Mark hit the wall with the side of his fist. "What time am I supposed to be there?"

"An hour ago."

"Goddamn it. Okay, stall him. Tell him I hit traffic, anything."

"I did. But you have fifteen minutes to get here, so move your ass. *Now*."

He clicked his phone shut and faced Ruby, who was looking at him as if she'd expected this all along. The disappointment in her gaze made his entire chest ache. And yet, something in him was glad for the reason to bolt. "Listen," he said. "Can we finish this conversation later? Right now I need to get over to the studio."

She nodded. "Go. It's your job. I understand." He knew she wasn't just saying the words; she was a business-woman, who did understand.

He tucked in his T-shirt. "I'll get you a cab."

"It's okay." She waved away his protest. "Seriously," she said, pulling a hairbrush out of her purse. "I'd rather not leave the bathroom with you anyway. Who knows who might see us?"

"Crap." He hadn't even thought of that. She'd turned to the mirror, and he kissed the back of her head. "I'll call you later."

Meeting his eyes in their reflection, she smiled. But it was a shaky smile, and her eyes looked closed off. She was shutting him out. "It's probably best if you don't, actually."

"Why?"

Her eyes were sad, and it was so much worse than if she'd been pissed. She waved her hand around the bathroom. "This is why. I can't do this. We both know your music has to come first. It *should* come first, and even though I know you have to focus on your music, I can't help wishing that I was just as important to you. But I'm not—no one can be. So please, just go. It's for the best."

He stared at her and, just for a second, he wondered if maybe she was right. Because at that moment he wanted to ignore the interview and stay with Ruby. For the first time in his life, he considered putting something—*someone*—before his music.

Silently, he turned on his heel and walked out the door.

*Chapter
Eighteen*

She was lacing her boots when the call bell rang. Who would be stopping by at nine-thirty on a Saturday morning? Not Mark. She hadn't heard from him since they'd parted ways at Ghirardelli Square, and she didn't expect to. It was probably some kids walking by the building who thought it was clever to push buttons as they meandered up the block.

Ignoring the ringing, she pulled a sweater over her head, having decided to spend the day at Golden Gate Park. The grounds always calmed her, and for some reason she felt the need to lose herself in the spring gardens.

She trotted down the stairs and pushed through her building's front door. The sun was shockingly bright, and she began digging through her purse, looking for her sunglasses. They were always buried at the bottom—

"So you're home."

Her mouth went dry. She knew that voice, but it couldn't be…

She looked up and her stomach dropped. "Ash? W–what are you doing here?"

Her gaze skimmed over him. It had been over a year since she'd seen him, but of course he looked as gorgeous as ever. Thin, with shaggy blond hair and a light

beard stubble that gave him that perfect artsy photographer look. It was even more irritating that the whole thing
came so naturally to him. He simply forgot to cut his hair,
and he couldn't be bothered to shave. He'd been in the
Navy, and he'd always said it was a great pleasure to not
have to worry about his appearance after he was dis-
charged. And that was all he'd ever said about his military
experience. Whatever the reason, the look worked well
for him, and the stack of broken hearts he left behind was
proof enough of that.

His eyes bored into hers, like they always had. "I came
to talk with you."

She smoothed her bangs, tucked a lock of hair behind
her ear. For some reason he'd always made her self-
conscious, more aware of her appearance than she normally was. "Good, because I wanted to talk to you, too."

He quirked a brow. "Oh? About what?"

"The photographs you sold. I thought we agreed that
you wouldn't do that." She tried to keep the hurt out of
her voice.

Scanning her face, his brow narrowed. "Which
photographs?"

It was as she'd thought. He'd simply forgotten. She
shrugged. "Never mind."

Ash reached out and touched her arm. "No, you're
upset. Which photographs?"

"There were a few you took of me when we were, um,
together. I wanted them, but you said they were your
favorite pieces—so I let you keep them if you promised
never to sell them."

Shaking his head, he let out a deep breath. "Oh, fuck.
Yeah, my intern—"

"You have an *intern*?" She couldn't help laughing at the thought of Ash being in charge of shaping young minds.

He grinned, too. "Don't laugh. I'm teaching a class at SFSU this semester, and it's part of the deal. Anyway, my intern was taking a bunch of my work to various galleries, and he must have dropped those off by mistake. I'll get them back, I promise."

What twist of fate had landed those pieces in Mark's hands? She shook her head. "No, it's fine. I'm just glad you didn't purposefully sell them."

"Are you sure? Because I can call the gallery right now."

"No. It's fine." She didn't mention that the pieces had already been sold. "Just make sure no other nude photos of me are out there, will you?"

"Yeah, of course."

"So, what did you want to talk to me about?" she asked.

He leaned against the building and stared at her. "I wanted to apologize for not showing up at Emmett's party a few weeks ago."

She blinked. "Really?"

"You look surprised," he said.

"I am. You've never apologized for anything a day in your life."

"I know how hard you work, Ruby, and I'm sorry I flaked. I got distracted with a shoot."

"Not surprising," she said with a laugh.

"I said I'm sorry, and I mean it."

She put a finger to his lips. "If only you were this apologetic when you were cheating on me."

He flinched. "I told you. That was a big misunder-standing."

Sighing, she raised her gaze to meet his. "Ash. I haven't seen you in over a year. Yeah, you flaked, but there's nothing new about that. So, tell me. What's going on?"

"Ruby, here's the thing." He lifted her hand, drew a circle around her wrist. Except, in bondage terms, her arm was a column to him, a thing to be tied. "I want you to model for me."

"What?"

"Model for me again."

He always had such an intense way of looking at her. She used to think it was sexy, and she was surprised to discover the look did absolutely nothing for her anymore.

"I have this idea for a scene, and I really think you would be the best model."

"Why me?"

His green eyes gave her body a quick once-over, an assessment she knew was purely an automatic response. "Yours is still my favorite form to photograph. Your body. Your ass." He grinned. "Your body was made to be photographed, and you, Ruby, were made to be bound."

She couldn't help the flicker that went through her at his words. And yet her mind went to Mark, and she thought about the way he'd bound her with his belt. It would seem crude to a purist like Ash, but now Ruby found she preferred the raw, open energy she had with Mark to Ash's methodical technique.

And yet...

"I'll think about it." She remembered exactly how the soft rope had felt on her skin. She recalled the way Ash had so skillfully restrained her with his beautiful knot work. Hours and hours they'd spent together as he silently and expertly covered her in his complex artistry. There was so much trust involved in that.

"Ash, can I ask you something?"

His stare was unwavering. "'Course."

"Did you stay with me for so long because you loved me, or was it because of how I looked in your photographs?"

He looked uncharacteristically tense, took too long to answer. He ran a hand over his head, and she saw that his long fingers trembled slightly. "I wish I knew, Ruby. I . . . It's hard for me to tell the difference."

She saw the raw honesty in his eyes, and for the first time, she was worried about the infallible artist.

She remembered the way he'd go into an almost trancelike state when he bound her. Moving like he was one with his rope, with a total grace she'd found beautiful. He'd always check her skin, assess her comfort level; he was good and responsible.

But he had a way of disconnecting from her as he carried out his task. Something she'd never realized until she experienced the electric connection she had with Mark. Maybe that lack of connection was actually getting to Ash.

Reaching out, she touched his arm. "Thank you for being honest with me."

She noticed lines around his eyes that hadn't been there before and realized he was thinner than she'd ever seen him. Everything about him seemed strained.

"Oh, pardon me!"

The door to Ruby's building flew open, crashing into Ash's shoulder. He whipped around to see who had burst through the door. "What the—oh . . ."

Ruby's red-haired downstairs neighbor, Joy, stared at

them, her hand over her mouth. "Oh my God! I am so sorry. Are you okay?"

He looked more than fine. With an intense expression that Ruby recognized, he was staring at Joy. Finally, he shook the look off his face. "Yeah, thanks. Are you?"

"I'm not the one who got slammed with a two-ton door." Joy's eyes were full of concern. Well, they would be. Ruby's neighbor was one of the nicest people she knew; her name described her perfectly.

Her petite neighbor continued to stare at Ash. Most women did. "You're sure you're okay?"

Ruby observed as Ash continued a stilted conversation with Joy. Interesting. Her neighbor was beautiful, but to put it frankly, she wasn't Ash's type. Just over five feet tall, she was shorter than Ruby and had actual breasts. And hips. Curves. And yet Ash studied her with a look Ruby knew very well. She rolled her eyes inwardly. Maybe he hadn't changed after all.

"Okay, well...I guess I'll be going." Joy gave a little wave, her gaze still locked on Ash's. "Bye."

After Joy had gone, Ruby turned back to Ash and noticed the way he clenched his jaw. "Ash, are you okay?"

He stared over her shoulder for a moment. "Yeah...I'm fine. I'll be better if I can get this shot done. Would you help me?"

He wouldn't rest until he saw his vision developing in a dark room, and for the first time ever, Ruby felt sorry for him.

"I'll think about it, all right?" The fact was, being bound did sound appealing, and it wasn't as if she had any reason to say no. If it wasn't as exciting as with Mark, at least it was familiar.

He nodded. "That would be great. You let me know."

After a quick hug good-bye, she continued up the street toward Clement. Keeping her head down, she walked briskly up the hill. It felt good to get that little meeting over with. She'd seen her ex, called him on his shit, and lived to tell about it.

And it hadn't been awful. In fact, it hadn't been awful at all.

Meg tapped her fingers on the arm of the black Eames chair that had been their first splurge as a married couple. She watched the door, waiting for Emmett to walk through it. She didn't care when he got home, she was waiting up. She had plans for him, for them. For their marriage. She wasn't giving up.

She felt like a stupid girl. How could she have missed all the signs? Like that time in the kitchen. It was months ago, and she'd been making breakfast when she'd suddenly felt frisky. She'd ordered him to fuck her right there, on the counter. And he had. With aplomb.

She'd watched the porn again and realized Ruby was right. The point of those movies was women dominating men.

Meg could do that. Fuck, she *longed* to do it.

She tapped a long leather paddle on her vinyl thigh-high boots. The sharp slap echoed in the loft, and her pulse jumped in anticipation. Just putting on the outfit, dressing up like a domme, had turned her on. The ritual of it, getting ready, was all part of the scene, and that's exactly what she was doing: setting up a scene, a fantasy. Her husband's fantasy.

Hopefully, she'd gotten it right.

An electric thrill bolted through her. She hadn't felt this charged up since...

She couldn't even remember when.

Ten minutes later she heard keys in the door. Her heart fluttered with a sudden attack of nerves, but she straightened her back and crossed her legs. The vinyl was sticky so she had to really work to get her limbs in exactly the right position—tough but sexy. She hoped to God she could pull this off.

Emmett opened the door and stepped into the hall. His gaze fell on her, and his metal briefcase dropped to the floor and landed with a heavy thud.

His eyes went wide as he took in her appearance in jerky glances. He couldn't stop looking at her, and he looked more shocked than happy or turned on. She began to get self-conscious; why didn't he say anything? Maybe the vinyl bustier was overkill? Or the fishnets? Or the paddle in her hand...

She tried to kick the flogger under the table, but the action only drew his eyes to it.

Running a hand through his hair, Emmett came toward her, slowly, as if he was afraid of her.

"Um, Meg. What's going on here?"

She pushed herself to standing. "No questions. I want you to take off your clothes and service me." She felt her cheeks burn. And the look he was giving her, as if she was insane, wasn't helping.

With a quirked brow he sat on the sofa and crossed his arms over his chest. "Service you?"

"Yes. You know...service me." Humiliation coursed through her. This was not going anything like she'd planned. Why wasn't he stripping? Why wasn't he obeying her?

"Meg." He patted the seat next to him. "Come here and tell me what's going on."

She remained where she stood. "I'm just trying to give you what you want! See, I finally figured it out. You want to be dominated." Her voice turned into a whisper. "I was just hoping you wanted to be dominated by me."

His eyes went soft. "Sweetheart, come here."

She hesitated.

"Now."

Shouldn't she be the one doing the ordering? Tears in her eyes, she dropped onto the sofa beside him, her vinyl boots squeaking and creaking as she sat.

He took the paddle out of her hand and inspected it. "Do you know how to use one of these things?"

Her cheeks burned. "I had a little lesson at the sex shop..."

His eyes got big again, but then he took her hand and kissed her fingertips. "Listen. I really appreciate the effort, and I gotta tell you, you're partly right."

She jerked her head up. "I am?"

"I do love it when you take charge."

"But why..." She gulped and her throat was painfully tight. "Why don't you want to have sex with me anymore?"

He cradled the side of her face in the palm of one warm hand. "Oh, sweetheart. You don't know how wrong you are."

She laughed hoarsely. "It's been almost three months since we, you know, made love. Don't you want me anymore?"

"Listen. This has nothing to do with me being attracted to you. I am. But you just seemed so obsessed with making a baby it wasn't about sex anymore. It was about me being a sperm donor."

She thought of her calendar and all its little red x marks. Baby-making days. "I thought you wanted kids."

"I do. But I want you more. I want *us* more. I don't want sex to be a chore."

"So you turned to porn?"

"I wanted to tell you this fantasy, but you were so pre-occupied with getting pregnant, there never seemed to be an opportunity."

Tears ran down her cheeks. "Oh, Emmett. I'm sorry. You should have said something."

He shrugged. "We were trying to start a family, and it seemed your number one priority. I didn't know how. I didn't want to let you down. Also, it's kinda hard for a guy to tell his wife he wants her to be controlling when it comes to sex. It's emasculating."

She thought about how emasculated he must feel sitting next to her, next to his wife who was dressed in full-on fem-domme regalia, who had invested $400 in sex toys but had no idea how to use them.

Glancing at the jam-packed coffee table, she scanned the items she'd purchased that day. Edible massage oil, candles, and handcuffs. Nipple clamps and a vibrating cock ring. A ball gag.

"Oh, God. Emmett, I'm so, so sorry—"

"Don't be. I'm glad you did this. We needed to talk." Grinning, he leaned in to kiss her. He took his time, slowly licking her lips before pushing his tongue inside her mouth. Instantly her sex started to throb. Her body had always been so responsive to him. That had never changed.

He pulled back slightly. "But you know what?"

"Mmm?" she murmured against his lips.

"I gotta tell you that just sitting here next to you has made me so fucking hard, and it's made me think of this one fantasy I've been having lately."

Her breath hitched. She wanted him to tell her so badly she had goose bumps on her arms. "What is it? What's your fantasy?"

He held up the paddle in his hand. "You don't need this." He grinned. "Not now, anyway."

Her pussy dampened, and a wonderful shiver raced up her spine. "Tell me, Emmett. Please."

He reached inside her thighs and touched the zipper of her left boot. "Maybe I should show you. How does that sound?"

"Yes. Please."

He spread her legs and knelt between them. Unzipping the thigh-high boots, he placed soft kisses on the insides of her thigh, at the edge of her newly exposed fishnet stockings. Her trembling legs fell apart.

After the first boot was off he unzipped the other one and pulled it off her leg. Her foot wrapped in his hand, he looked up. "You're beautiful, you know."

"Stop it."

"My beautiful wife." He pressed his thumb on the arch of her foot. Hard. "You've had a hard day, miss. On your feet too much. I need to massage your poor feet now."

Holy shit. Her husband had a foot fetish, too? She blinked but caught herself. "Oh, yes. You do. And call me ma'am."

He raised a brow but then, "Yes, ma'am. Tell me how you like your massage."

She slipped easily into the role. "First, take off my stockings."

He slowly peeled one, then the other down her legs. She saw the way his breathing went off rhythm when she spread her legs a bit more, giving him a peek of what she had on under the short skirt, which was exactly nothing.

She tried to look stern and it was surprisingly easy. "Now, take off your clothes."

He stood and stripped before her, removing his high-tops, his sweater, his T-shirt, his jeans. Her gaze fell on his erection, strong and hard and telling her everything she needed to know. He was loving this as much as she was.

She picked up the bottle of vanilla-scented massage oil and handed it to him. "Massage my feet."

"Yes, ma'am."

He dropped to the ground and lifted her leg. One hand encircled her ankle and the other started kneading her arch. Her tension drained away in a heavenly drift as he rubbed her heel, her arch, her toes. Her nipples tingled, strained beneath the vinyl bustier. She lifted her right breast out of the cup and beaded a nipple between her fingertips. She had no idea her feet were such a responsive erogenous zone.

He looked up, and his gaze landed on her exposed breast. His eyes went dark in the candlelight, his erection leaked a drop of white cream out of the tip. A powerful, erotic thrill hummed through her, making her nerves tingle. Because she was in charge now, and the rush of it took over.

He was naked, on his knees. Before her.

"Kiss my feet. Now." Just saying the words made her sex clench.

She saw him exhale before he brought one of her toes to his lips. He kissed the tip of her toe, and then he pulled her deeper into his mouth, using his tongue to lick her even as his hand found a tender spot just under the ball of her foot. The sudden combination of his mouth and his hand sent her arching off the sofa, moaning.

Her toes still in his mouth, his warm tongue licked her, sucked her, teased her. It could have been her pussy he was making love to, and her sex throbbed, slick and wet.

She felt his hand trail up the inside of her leg, higher and higher, until he brushed the edge of his fingers against her labia.

Resting her other foot on the edge of the sofa, she opened herself to him fully. "Touch me. Use your fingers."

He continued to play with her foot as he slid his finger into her pussy.

"Yes, harder . . ." She clutched the sofa cushion with her left hand and used her other to tug at her nipple. Soon she was moaning aloud for him, watching the way he loved her foot, shocked at how the image made her skin burn all over.

But he was starting to move his own hips now, moving as if he was looking for something to fill. Her pussy would do.

"Emmett, come here and fuck me."

He raised both her feet to rest on his shoulders and pulled her hips toward him. In one move he was inside her, fucking her. "Harder. Faster." She couldn't believe the words were coming out of her mouth; she couldn't believe how much it turned her on to say them.

"Yes, ma'am," he said, smiling. He thrust into her again and again until his own groans joined hers. And then he turned his face to the side and took her other foot, the one that hadn't been kissed yet, and brought a toe into his mouth.

Their gazes locked as he sucked and fucked her. She couldn't believe they were doing this. That she and her husband were doing this taboo thing, that the intimacy of it, the deep connection of the experience, sent her over the edge.

She exploded. The climax tore through her, and she knew he wasn't far behind. She knew his signals, the way his lids lowered and his grip on her tightened. She knew her husband's movements like she knew her own face.

But this man, this man who'd been harboring his secret desires for so long, was a stranger. This new Emmett wanted to be dominated and wanted to suck her toes. This new Emmett was probably open to letting her try out her new paddle.

This new Emmett loved her.

"You look happy."

Meg dropped a pile of willow branches onto Ruby's desk. "I took your advice."

Ruby eyed the sticks. "We need more. I want this party to look like a spring wonderland."

"I am so glad you talked James out of that rock-and-roll theme."

"So am I. But the party is one week from tomorrow, and we have so much to do! Anyway, what advice did you take?"

Meg grinned. "I got kinky with Emmett."

"I take it things went well."

"Yup."

"So, your husband's not gay?"

"Or bi," Meg said.

"I told you," Ruby said with a smile.

Meg dropped into the chair opposite Ruby's desk. "How about you? How are things with you and the rock god?"

Music thudded through the walls, a constant, reverberating reminder of his presence. She picked up a stick and snapped off a sharp edge. "Well, last time I saw him was Thursday. We'd just had sex in a public bathroom, and he had to rush off to some interview."

Meg looked incredulous. "Are you joking?"

"Sadly, no. But it was for his job. I know better than anyone what sacrifices need to be made to build a successful career."

"Still, leaving you like that? It's kinda jacked up."

"Whatever. It's for the best. I told him not to call me again. After the Spring Fling is over, he'll be out of my life." A life that, Ruby had to admit, sounded extremely boring without Mark in it. She never knew when he was going to show up, when he was going to pull her into a broom closet or ring her doorbell. It was enlightening how much she liked that sort of spontaneity.

"Anyway." Ruby stood and pulled a can of glitter spray paint off a shelf. "It's not like he made me any promises."

"And you're okay with that?"

She shook the spray can, the sound pinging around the office. "I don't have any choice, and, anyway, he's the worst possible man for me. He's young; he leads an unpredictable life; he's constantly leaving. He's everything I don't want in a relationship."

"You sound scared."

"I am not! I don't think." She barely knew anything about herself anymore.

Meg came around and put her hand on Ruby's shoulder. "You know, I've known you a long time. And whenever you get close to someone, it freaks you out and you push them away."

"That's not true. Ash cheated on me! What was I supposed to do?"

"You'd mentally separated yourself from him long before that happened, honey."

Ruby shrugged. "Whatever. It really doesn't matter, does it?"

"Of course it matters. Let me ask you something. Do you think you could ever have a normal relationship again? I mean, a non-kinky one? 'Cause I gotta tell you. I know I'm new to all this, but I really can't imagine going back now."

"A few weeks ago, that answer would have been yes," Ruby said. "To be honest, now I'm not so sure."

Meg smirked. "You do seem to end up with kinky guys."

"Twice. It's happened *twice*. And I'm not ruling out the kink, I'm just saying that I don't know if I need it." Maybe if she said it enough, she'd begin to believe it.

"So. If James Cleaver asked you to marry him, you would? Even if he's the most vanilla man on the planet?"

"Definitely." Ruby picked up a large twig and headed for the door. "I mean, theoretically speaking, of course. I barely know him. But stability is more important than anything else."

"Even love?"

The repetitive beat of Mark's latest tune thrummed down the hall, vibrating through the door handle into her palm. "Not everyone falls in love, Meg. And if they do, it's often with the wrong person, or it's just *wrong*. Period. My parents were in love, and look at them. They abandoned their kids to go sail the world. Their love didn't help their family. Where did their love leave everybody else?"

Meg's gaze softened. "That was then, sweetie. You're an adult now. A gorgeous woman who is finally coming into her own sexuality. Do you really want to give up now just because you're scared of getting hurt?"

"What do you propose I do about it? Start hosting sex parties in my flat?"

Meg's eyes sparkled. "Not exactly."

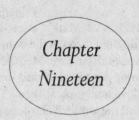

*Chapter
Nineteen*

This is going to be so much fun!"

"I still can't believe Emmett is okay with this," Ruby said as the cab pulled up outside a nondescript building.

Meg paid the driver and followed her onto the sidewalk. "Don't worry about Emmett—he encouraged me!" She teetered on her stilettos and grabbed Ruby's arm for support. "He wants me to have a flogging lesson."

"I created a monster," Ruby muttered.

Meg winked. "Two of them, actually."

So now, here they were, dressed like hookers, staring at the address listed on the flyer. Although Meg had talked her into coming, Ruby couldn't help but feel a little bit excited about venturing into her first fetish party.

It was being held in a brick building in the SOMA District. Decrepit warehouses mingled with sparkling new high-rise condos, creating a place where yuppies could feel cool because they lived in such an edgy neighborhood.

And so they tolerated things like raves and fetish parties, which was why Meg and Ruby currently found themselves staring at a large wooden door on Harrison Street. After a second a man emerged from the warehouse. He wore a suit straight out of Brooks Brothers, but tattoos covered his hands and neck. Eyeing Ruby and Meg, he pulled a cigarette from his shirt pocket and lit it. He took a deep drag. "You gals goin' in?" As he spoke, the man exhaled a surprising amount of smoke through his mouth and nostrils.

"Absolutely," Meg said.

The man perched on a stool that had been placed outside the door. "I don't think I've ever seen you two at one of these parties before."

"It's our first time." Ruby tugged at the hem of her miniskirt.

"Cool." He moved on to smoke rings. "So what are your roles?"

They just stared at him. "Pardon?"

Another deep drag. "Bottom, top, or switch?" More smoke rings.

"Top. Definitely." Meg nodded.

But Ruby felt her cheeks heat.

"I'm a bottom."

Deep inhale. "You sure?"

"Why?"

Deep exhale of smoke. "No reason." He held out a hand. "I'm Rich. I manage these things."

She shook his hand. His palm was warm, his grip surprisingly gentle. "This is Meg, and I'm Ruby."

He closed his eyes and took another deep drag off his cigarette. Then, with his lids still shut, he began to sing "Ruby Tuesday."

It wasn't as if she'd never heard the Rolling Stones song before, but somehow it sounded new coming from the burly bouncer. The words struck something deep inside her, but she couldn't put her finger on exactly what it was.

He opened his eyes. "Ruby." He fell silent, as if singing

the rest of the song in his head. Then, "House rules. Don't intrude on anyone's scene. In case you don't know, a scene is anywhere someone is actively playing. If someone asks you to join him or her in a scene, feel free. You'll find cleaning supplies at stations set up at various locations inside. Please sterilize any equipment you use. Safe sex is up to you, but you'll find condoms located throughout the premises."

Ruby put a hand to her belly. The thought of sex with a person who wasn't Mark made her stomach turn. She coughed. "Um, we don't plan on having sex with anyone." She was just here to support Meg and check out her options. Meg had been right—it was time to move on and embrace her sexuality.

He sucked deeply on his cigarette. "Well, in case you change your mind, you know the rules. If anyone gets too close to you, you just come and get me and I'll take care of it."

"Thank you." She eyed the man's tattooed hands. They looked quite capable of taking care of any troublemakers.

"That'll be twenty dollars."

"It's on me." Meg reached into her purse and handed him the money. After pocketing the bills, Rich slid off the stool and held the door open. "In you go, girls. Have fun."

Ruby's heart hammered as they stepped inside. After checking their coats, she and Meg began to wander through the mazelike setup. The lights were very low, and electronic music played from hidden speakers.

The warehouse had been set up in such a way that partitioned-off sections were devoted to different themes. Each room seemed to be dedicated to a separate fantasy.

They passed a medieval torture chamber, a jail cell, a hotel bed. They passed a man chained to an X-shaped cross. He was on the receiving end of spanking being delivered with gusto by a brunette in garter belts who was an obvious transvestite.

"Oh, look!" Meg said, pointing at a sign. "Flogging lesson starting in ten minutes! Wanna go with me?"

"Do you mind if I take a look around instead?" Ruby's pulse had begun to buzz, the sexual energy of the place seeping into her system, rushing through her. She found herself curious to explore, to see everything in the club.

"Of course not. Just don't do anything I wouldn't do," Meg said with a wink and tottered off to learn how to whip her husband.

The music beat a steady rhythm, and Ruby found her confidence going up as she made her way through the crowd. She could do this. Chin lifted, she continued on through the space.

But she stopped when a particular scene caught her eye. A naked man lay strapped to a table. He was shorter than Mark, but his body was tight and muscular. His skin was olive-toned, and his hair was golden, everywhere. His prick sprang from a blond thatch of pubic hair.

A thin woman holding a candle walked around the man's supine form, watching him intently. Finally, she stopped at the head of the table and raised the candle high above the man's chest. Slowly, so slowly Ruby found herself holding her breath, the woman tilted the tall votive and let the hot wax spill onto the man's nipples. Ruby's own nipples tightened as she watched the man gasp and squirm. Ruby had never experienced anything like it herself, yet she could almost feel the molten heat on her own breasts. Her pussy throbbed as she imagined how the hot wax would feel hitting her body.

But strangely, it was the woman she envied. She imagined what it would be like to strap a man down, to make him gasp.

The woman walked around the table as she held the candle over the man's now-writhing body. She painted his ribs, his chest, and his stomach with the melting wax. The group of observers watched quietly, all eyes fixated on the way the domme could bring her subject to such an obvious state of arousal with a simple candle.

Ruby felt her own sex dampen as sweat beaded under her breasts. Thinking of Mark, she wondered if he'd ever done anything like this. Or had it done to him.

She looked away. With a deep breath, she went on through the party, watching an assortment of sexual scenarios unfurl. She hadn't expected the party to be so shocking, so bold. To her left a man stood, stroking his exposed cock as he watched two women rub their breasts together. To her right a man wearing a G-string and a dog collar licked water out of a bowl. The place smelled like sex and lube and leather, and it thrilled her even as it scared her.

The next room looked quite tame at first glance. Two stunning women with sleek ponytails sat on a burgundy brocade sofa. Wearing matching short spandex dresses, they sipped wine and talked in quiet, whispered tones. The thing that made the little scene less than normal was the naked man on his hands and knees before them. On his back rested a tray weighted down with a bowl of grapes and a bottle of wine. The man was sideways to the crowd and Ruby could see his rather impressive erection.

But he didn't move at all. Staring straight ahead, he was like a statue. The women completely ignored him. To them, he was a piece of furniture.

Slap.

A shudder raced up her spine at the sound, the sound of a palm landing on someone's ass. Turning, she followed the rhythmic noise.

Her stomach was in knots. Nerves twisted in her gut even as a little thrill kept her sex wet. She kept walking, following those magic sounds of slapping skin.

She saw a curvy blonde woman in a G-string kneeling over a simple red bench. Her ass was pink, and the cause of this was obvious. Behind her a tall, gray-haired man held a long-handled leather paddle. He wasn't using it, though; he was using his other hand to spank her. His back was to the crowd, but she could read the experience in his authoritative stance.

He must be aware of the crowd, but he didn't show it, instead focusing fully on the woman who knelt before him. He hit the lower part of her ass, her upper thighs. Each time his hand came down on her skin, the woman jerked and gasped, the flesh beneath her skin tensing.

Ruby's pussy throbbed steadily as she watched him spank the woman one, two, three times, quickly, making Ruby recall the time when Mark had pulled her into the storage closet. The memory sent a jolt through her and she watched as the blonde woman clenched her hands together and tossed her head back. The look of pure euphoria on her face made Ruby's sex go even hotter, and each time the woman cried out, each time the man slapped her skin, Ruby felt her own pussy clench.

The man eased up, taking the paddle and slowly

tapping the blonde's shoulder in light, rhythmic slaps. Ruby gasped; she could nearly feel the leather on her own skin. The man continued, trailing a rhythm across the woman's upper back, slowly increasing pressure until she was visibly trembling.

The woman stuck her ass in the air, higher than before. She was begging for it. Begging to be hit with the paddle. Ruby knew exactly what the woman wanted. Ruby wanted it, too.

Just watching the scene before her took her there a little. She was already feeling that surrender, that need to escape. Ruby's heartbeat went a little erratic, her breath caught. She watched as the man ceased the spanking and started gently stroking the woman's back. She whispered something in his ear, and the man nodded. The woman looked over her shoulder and met Ruby's gaze. Something passed between them, some kind of connection, as if the woman saw the longing Ruby was sure she couldn't hide.

Then the man looked at her. She saw the authority in his eyes, in his demeanor. He reminded her of Mark in that way.

"Would you like to join us?" he asked.

Could she do this? Play with two strangers this way? Her palms were damp at the thought, and her heart raced. But then she looked back at the other woman and saw the euphoria in her eyes.

She wanted to feel that euphoria again. *Needed* to feel it.

But not like this. Not without Mark.

"I'm sorry..." She turned and pushed through the crowd.

The place was more crowded now, more noisy. She

heard someone cry out, from pain or pleasure—probably both. Unfamiliar faces walked through the warehouse, gazing at the various displays of kink.

Her gaze fell on an older, slightly frumpy-looking couple passing by, clothed in nothing more than a few draping, clamoring chains.

She had to get out.

What had earlier seemed like a maze was now easily navigated if she just stayed around the perimeter. Her boots thudded on the floor as she ran toward the room where she'd last seen Meg. She found her, a long-handled flogger in her hand. Meg stood about four feet from a man with his arms chained above his head, waving the leather tails at his back with a flick of her wrist, as if she were a kinky Zorro. But Meg immediately caught her eye, put down the flogger, and a second later was at Ruby's side.

"What's wrong?" Meg asked.

"Can we just go?" Ruby begged.

"Yeah, of course, sweetie." Meg retrieved their coats and, holding her hand, pushed through the front door. Fresh, moist air hit Ruby's face, and she sucked in deep lungfuls of it.

Then the scent of smoke reached her. Rich, the manager, was watching her, and then, without a word, he stepped into the street and hailed a taxi. He held open the door and Ruby slid inside after Meg.

"Thank you," she said to the doorman.

Looking down at her, he nodded and blew out a lungful of smoke. "Good-bye, Ruby Tuesday," he sang in tune.

The taxi door shut with a solid clunk.

They sat there for a second, the song echoing in Ruby's head. It was just a song, a familiar melody. And yet the words had new meaning to her. Was she changing with every day? She felt like it. She certainly wasn't the person she'd been two weeks ago.

"Where are you headed?"

Meg gave the driver Ruby's address and turned to her. "What happened?"

Ruby shook her head. "I am so fucked."

"What?" Meg took her hand. "What did you do?"

But Ruby could only smile ruefully. "It's not what I did, Meg. It's what I didn't do."

*Chapter
Twenty*

Mark was high.

It was Saturday, and they were in Michigan. At the last minute they'd been called in to play a music festival, filling in for a headline band whose singer had succumbed to "exhaustion," also known as rehab. Now, as he and Yvette hopped into the limo, pure energy rushed through his veins in crashing waves. His heart pounded loud in his chest, louder even than the crowd of five thousand people hoping for a third encore. He could still hear them. But the Riders were done for the night.

The show had gone well. It had gone especially well for Jake. The drummer had stayed behind with a pair of tall, beautiful locals.

They'd invited Mark, but he declined. Although he'd distanced himself from Ruby over the past week, he still felt her presence, and no other girl would substitute, not yet.

"I officially love Detroit." Yvette grabbed an already-opened champagne bottle out of a bucket of ice. Her long hair clung to her face in sweaty strands, and her black makeup was smeared around her sparkling green eyes. His best friend was as stunning now as she had been the first time he'd seen her all those years ago.

Looking back, Mark was glad they had never hooked

up. If they had, he doubted they would be as close as they were today. And he needed that closeness. With their world becoming crazier every day, their friendship was practically the only stability in his life.

And, he supposed, that was how it would always be.

He held a glass as Yvette poured him some champagne. "It was definitely a good show."

She took a slow sip and held his gaze. "I'm surprised you didn't hang around with Jake. There were a number of lovely ladies eager to show their appreciation."

"I guess I wasn't in the mood."

She just watched him with those ever-seeing eyes of hers.

He leaned back into the plush leather seat, hoping she'd let it drop. Mark's hand went to his jacket pocket, and he reached inside to palm his cell phone. His fingers itched to call Ruby, but he resisted. She'd sent him one e-mail with details on the preparty before the Spring Fling, but other than that they hadn't had any communication since last week. And no matter how many times he picked up his phone to call her, he couldn't do it. That look in her eyes when he'd had to leave for the interview haunted him. He never wanted to see it again.

"Does she know you're here?" Yvette asked with a raised brow.

"Nope. I didn't get around to telling her."

"You mean you avoided it. Why?"

"I was just busy, that's all," he said.

"And this is why I'm a lesbian."

"What are you talking about?"

She smirked. "Men. You're all just little boys, scared of your own feelings. Scared to commit."

"I'm not scared of anything."

"Of course not—'cause you're a *big, tough man*."

His body tensed and he leaned forward. "I don't get you. One minute you're telling me to not get distracted. The next you're giving me shit about commitment. Make up your mind."

"Well, in that regard I'm a female as well. I retain the right to change my mind on a dime."

"Fuckin' A."

"Exactly."

He threw himself back against the seat. "You're totally losing it."

"Could be. But here's the thing. Over these past few weeks I've seen a change in you. You've gone..." She gave a mock shudder. "Mushy."

"And this is a good thing?"

"Much to my dismay, it could be. See, I think you found a girl you really like. And I think she inspires you." Her gaze went soft. "I've seen the way she acts around you. I think she actually likes you, and not just because you're gonna be a star. She makes you happy."

Mark glanced out the window. "I think the problem is more of me making her happy."

"So why are you pushing her away?"

"I told you. She doesn't want to get hurt."

"And you're so sure you'd do that?"

He thought of his parents. Yeah, they'd made it work, and there had even been happy times. But there was always that quiet resentment between them.

And Mark thought of the band, of how with each success the stakes got higher. "I'm not sure I wouldn't hurt her. She deserves better."

Yvette reached out and touched his knee. "Honey, you're the best there is."

They pulled up in front of the hotel. Seconds later the driver opened the door for them, and Mark followed Yvette into the lobby. They didn't have bodyguards and generally hadn't needed any, but Yvette had a few crazies that came out of the woodwork every once in a while, and Mark always made sure he had her back.

Once in the elevator, she turned to him. "You want to come to my room for a drink?"

He considered it. Thinking about Ruby had made him feel restless, and he wasn't ready to wind down yet. But having a drink with Yvette didn't seem appealing for some reason. The only thing that sounded good was talking to Ruby.

He touched his cell phone, thinking he'd call her when he got to the room. Even though she'd told him not to call, it was fucked of him to leave the way he had. He owed her an apology.

The elevator stopped at the top floor, and they stepped into the hallway. "Nah. I think I'm gonna crash." He waited until Yvette's door clicked shut, and then he went a few doors down to his own room.

He paused outside the door. A muffled female voice seemed to be coming from inside his. And he could have sworn she was saying, "Help."

Sliding his card into the lock, he burst inside. The lights were low, but he could make out the form of a woman on his bed.

"What the fuck?" He flipped on the light.

"Mark! Help me!"

"What the hell is going on here?" A blonde woman

was tied spread-eagled to his bed. She was naked. She was gorgeous. And she looked vaguely familiar.

"Mark! I'm so glad you're here—"

"Shut up, bitch!"

He turned as a second woman emerged from the bathroom. She was a petite brunette wearing a black lace bra, garter belts attached to black stockings, and black panties. She carried a long-handled leather crop in one hand. She walked straight up to him. "Bad boy. You kept us waiting. Shame on you." She stood on her tiptoes and leaned in close. "I need help disciplining my naughty little girlfriend."

He was too stunned to respond. Instead he watched as the brunette stalked over to the bed. She wore the sluttiest high heels he'd ever seen—which was saying something—but she was a pro at strutting in them. Each step she took sent one hip out in a jaunty jerk. Left, right. Swish, sway. It was mesmerizing.

She smiled down at the girl tied to his bed and then slapped one of her nipples twice with the flogger. The girl cried out, but her eyes went wide.

His cock jerked at the sight.

He ran a hand over his scalp. "Who the fuck let you in here?"

The brunette just looked at him. "Mark. Don't tell me you've forgotten us. That would make me very sad. And very, very mad."

He let his gaze drop over her small form. Her breasts were disproportionately large and round. He raked his memory. They did look familiar. But where? When? There were just so many of them. So many and none of them memorable. Just sex. Bodies. Toys.

Grinning, the brunette knelt on the bed, next to her "prisoner." She reached right between the blonde's legs and, using two fingers, spread open her pussy. "Come on now, Mark. Don't tell me you forgot this cunt." Leaning down, she licked the woman's pussy in a long, slow lap. Then she slid two fingers inside the blonde, causing a piercing cry to erupt from her mouth.

He remembered that sound. It all came back in a rush. Last year, in this city. He'd been at a BDSM club and he'd found these two playing there. They had been beautiful; the blonde had been tied to a cross, her back to the crowd. He'd watched as the brunette flogged her sub until Mary had been crying out in pleasure. That unique, almost-annoying cry.

Mark had noticed that whenever Mary would clench her hands, her domme would stop and kiss her gently. It had been a beautiful thing, and from them Mark had learned a lot about watching the signs of a sub and knowing when they were reaching their limits.

After, they'd gone back to his room and spent the rest of the night using Mary as their willing plaything.

He was hard thinking about it. He remembered the way Mary had taken him into her mouth as her mistress—Beth, if he remembered correctly—had spanked her ass. He remembered the way each time he heard that *slap* of skin on skin, she'd taken him deeper and deeper.

He closed his eyes. "I remember, it just took me a minute." Suddenly needing a drink, he pulled a bottle of Jack from the minibar. Ah, you knew you were successful when the minibar was stocked with full-sized bottles of booze.

He poured a shot into a tumbler. "How could I forget

Detroit's kinkiest couple? But you didn't answer my question. How did you get into my room?"

Beth smiled sweetly. "Don't you remember? You told your manager to let us in anytime you were in town. We wanted to surprise you."

He laughed, the sound rough and cracked. "Yeah. You did."

Beth raised a brow at him. "So why are you still dressed?" Bending, she reached beside the bed and picked up a long-handled rubber paddle.

Setting his glass down, he took the paddle and drew the wide end across his hand. He looked at Mary, tied and naked before him. Her pussy was glistening, waiting. Her eyes were dilated and expectant. She was a professional, this one. A true pain slut, exactly how he liked them. He could really let go with her. He could turn her over and paddle her shoulders, her ass, her upper thighs. He could take a flogger and drag the long, leather strands across her open pussy until she cried out for him to smack her clit. And he knew from experience that was exactly what she'd do.

He slapped his palm with the paddle, and the girls both jumped at the sound. He grinned. "Now, ladies. Who wants a drink?"

It was 1:30 a.m., and Ruby couldn't sleep. Her head hurt, her heart hurt. She was a mess.

She was sitting at the kitchen table staring at her cell phone. She hadn't heard his voice since she'd called to make sure the Riders would be playing for the Spring Fling. She'd had an excuse to call him then, but now she just had a need. A need to hear his voice. Unfortunately, she'd gotten his voice mail and she hadn't left a message.

The need to see him burned inside her gut, and she was having a hell of a time putting that fire out.

He was just across the city. She didn't know for how much longer, but he was there now, and she wanted to see him.

She picked up the phone and dialed.

"Ruby?" He sounded breathless.

His voice was such a comforting relief that she started to cry when she heard it. Pausing, she waited for her throat to relax enough to speak.

"Ruby. What's wrong?"

"Oh, God." She started babbling because she had to talk about her experience at the sex club with someone who would understand. She told him everything, from the bouncer to the candle wax to the man who'd invited her to join him at the spanking bench.

"Oh, God. Mark, it was just so…" She trailed off when she heard noise behind him. Voices. She held her breath, filled with an odd premonition. "Am I calling at a bad time?"

"Oh, baby." There was something in his voice, a haggard strain she'd never heard before. "It's fine. Talk to me, Ruby."

"Where are you?"

"Detroit, actually. We got called in as a replacement band at the last minute."

"Oh." A chill went through her. "Detroit." He'd flown across the country and she hadn't even known. "Okay. So, are you at a party now?"

"Um, not really. No." She'd never heard him sound so

tense, and her stomach lurched with a sickening wave of nausea. The voices were murmuring in the background. Female voices.

She swallowed down her queasiness. "You ... you're busy. It's fine."

"Ruby," he strained out in the slow, measured way one would use when speaking to a person on the edge. "Give me two minutes. Two minutes, and I'll call you right back."

"You're with someone, aren't you?"

A long pause and then, "Yes."

A singsong voice came through the phone. "*Mark. Are you coming back to us?*"

Ruby couldn't think or breathe or speak. There was a vise clamped around her throat. Even as she told herself she had absolutely no right to be jealous or angry, her words came out in a tight screech. "Us? *Us?* As in *two*?"

His voice came at her in a low and intense hiss. "Didn't you just go to a fetish party, Ruby? Didn't you just call me because you had to tell me all about your experience and how hot you are now because some guy invited you to join him in a little play session?"

She squeezed her eyes shut. "It wasn't like that."

"What was it like then?"

He was agitated, angry, and the last thing she wanted to do was fight with him. There was a part of her that was still high from her experience at the party, and she just couldn't deal with it. Couldn't deal with anything, especially him and his *sluts*.

"What was it like?" he asked again, and in her mind she could see him clenching his teeth.

The experience had left her too raw, too open to lie

now. "I wanted it to be you," she whispered and hung up the phone.

"God*damn* it!" Mark threw his phone onto a side table where it skittered across the wood and landed with a thump against a lamp. Ruby wasn't answering. She'd been distraught; he shouldn't have argued with her when she was coming down off a high like that.

"Mark, you want another drink?" Mary pulled on her coat and tied the belt at her waist. "Before we go?"

He shook his head. "I don't think so."

Beth cocked her hip to the side, emphasizing her long, gorgeous legs. "You sure you want us to go? You seem upset, and we have just the girl for you to take your frustrations out on." She winked at him. "Our offer still stands. It's not too late to change your mind."

He'd just finished a drink with the girls, and they were on their way out. Despite how sexy they were, they didn't appeal to him. He'd figured one cocktail would be enough to send them on their way without too much argument, and he'd been right.

But now? He was tempted, so *fucking* tempted. He knew from experience that sex was a fan-fucking-tastic way to forget his problems.

The thought of some other man touching Ruby made his chest pound with cold jealousy and anger. He knew damn well he had absolutely no right to those feelings, but he couldn't stop them.

Playing with these two women would get his mind off things, chase all those fucked-up feelings away.

At least temporarily.

Beth took a step toward him. She rubbed her hands

up his chest and purred like a kitten. "You sure you don't want us to stay? Me on bottom. You on top, just like last time." She bit her lip in a practiced way. "I haven't let anyone top me since you, babe."

He doubted that very much, but he appreciated the effort. His gaze darted between the women, so beautiful, so sexy, and so available.

He shook his head. "I'm sorry, ladies. Not tonight."

After they'd gone he went to the window and pulled open the curtain. A million lights twinkled in the skyline. He stared until the bright colors blurred together.

Last year he'd had a great night of meaningless sex with two gorgeous women. And tonight he'd sent those same two women away. If he'd been here a few weeks earlier, he would have been fucking ecstatic to find them in his room.

Then why did he feel as if he'd just dodged a bullet? What had changed?

Of course, he knew. The answer came in the form of a wickedly smart, sexy raven-haired woman who smelled like jasmine and tasted like heaven.

So, yeah. He knew the answer. The question was: What was he going to do about it?

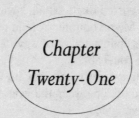

Chapter
Twenty-One

Ruby woke from a recurring nightmare.

It always started the same. She was back at the house at the beach. It was dark and she couldn't find her sister. She was in her nightgown, running through their small house, calling Claire's name. But she couldn't find her; not in their room, not in their mother's room, nowhere...

She jerked awake, her heart jackhammering in her chest.

It was ridiculous to feel guilty about a dream. Ruby tossed her covers aside and padded to the bathroom. She checked her reflection in the mirror. Her eyes were wide, scared. Her body felt empty.

Making her morning coffee, she couldn't shake the feeling that something was wrong. But as her mind slowly awakened she realized it wasn't really the dream that had her upset; it was the experience from last night. The party, the things she'd seen. The late-night call to Mark.

What the fuck had she been thinking? With her coffee, she went to the living room and plopped into her favorite chair. She took her cell phone out of her bathrobe pocket and dialed.

"It's nine a.m.," a gravelly voice answered. "This better be good."

"I had a bad dream."

"Aw, sis. The geyser dream? Or the locked door?"

"Locked door."

She heard the sounds of Claire stifling a yawn, moving in her bed. "It's okay, honey. It was just a dream."

She laughed shakily. "You'd think I would be used to these by now. I mean, it's been what? Twenty-some years?"

"You're too uptight. You never allowed yourself any room to get pissed or frustrated. I'm not surprised it all comes out in your dreams."

"Thanks, Freud."

"I'm just sayin'."

"I guess." She blew on her coffee. "Claire, can I ask you something?"

"Shoot."

"Do you think I failed you? Be honest; I can take it."

She heard a quick intake of breath. "What? Are you kidding? Growing up, I thought you were better than any mother I knew. And way cooler, too."

"Mom did her best."

"Mom's a flake and you know it. You're the one I always looked up to. Even now, you're still my role model."

"I'm no role model, far from it." What would Claire think of her perfect sister if she knew where Ruby had been last night? She didn't want to know.

After they'd disconnected, Ruby stared at the phone. Ten missed calls, all from Mark. She wasn't even sure why she was avoiding him. Partly from anger, but was she mad at herself or Mark? Or both?

She threw the phone aside and went to her bathroom,

suddenly in need of a soothing, warm soak. She loved her bathtub. It was a claw-foot that was probably as old as the Victorian building in which she lived. It had been a rusty old beast when she moved in, but one weekend she'd holed herself up and painted the exterior a shiny black to match the black-and-white tiled floor.

She turned on the ancient brass faucets and squirted a healthy dose of jasmine bubble bath into the water. She slid off her robe and nightie, and once the tub was full she sank into the warm water. Breathing in the pungent jasmine scent of the bubble bath, she immediately began to relax.

Steam filled the small space, fogging up mirrors and windows. She'd wanted the water extra hot this morning, and it felt good, cleansing. Closing her eyes, she steadied her breathing, listened to the flow of water from the faucet as her heart started to slow its nervous pace.

For the first time since last night she was calm enough to really think. And she couldn't get the images of what she'd seen at the fetish party out of her head. When she went to bed last night, she was too upset to allow herself any pleasure from the experience.

She turned off the water and suddenly the room was quiet. So silent she could hear the murmur of her neighbor's television and the traffic on Clement Street. The sounds of normal San Franciscans going about their normal Sunday routines.

But nothing felt normal to Ruby this Sunday. Because she couldn't get the erotic images out of her head.

And, with a start, she realized she didn't want to.

When she closed her eyes she saw the woman with the candle wax. Out of nowhere, she had a picture of Mark tied to a bed, covered in hot wax. She imagined what it would be like to slowly tilt a votive until the molten wax spilled out of the candle and onto his nipples, onto the piercings he had there. He'd jerk at the shock of the heat, like the man last night, but his erection would tell her how much he enjoyed it.

For the second time in twenty-four hours, she contemplated what it would be like to dominate someone. She sank under the water, washing the question out of her head. The last thing she wanted was another *curiosity* creeping up.

But she couldn't help that just the thought turned her on, and when she emerged she let her legs fall open, let the water caress her now-throbbing pussy. Her juices provided enough lubrication to withstand the bathwater and she slid one finger, then a second, into her vagina. She gasped, her legs twitching as she plunged her fingers deeper.

She continued fucking herself, finding a rhythm, gasping aloud, losing herself in the pleasure of it.

And she imagined Mark was there, watching her. Instructing her. Despite her little fantasy, she couldn't deny how much she wanted to have him rule her. She craved it like an addict craves alcohol; that exhilarating freedom of giving him her power. How liberating it was to trust him fully.

She pinched her nipples hard enough to make her gasp, hard enough to make her sex throb. She moved her hand to her clit, touched a finger to that swollen tip. She pretended it was Mark St. Crow. Telling her what to do with her hands, her fingers. *Rub your clit harder, harder—don't stop. That's a good girl.*

Her knees splashed in the water as she thrust them open. Her legs strained against the sides of the tub as she bucked against her hand, hearing his imaginary voice in her head. *Open up, baby. Fuck yourself for me. I want to see you come for me. Fuck yourself, baby, like it was my cock inside you. Fuck yourself, baby…Harder, harder, harder…*

She cried out, her entire body going still against her palm. Her eyes popped open, and she focused on a crack in the ceiling as she came. Her core spasmed in nonrhythmic bursts; she momentarily stopped breathing.

She tried to drag the feeling out because it was so lovely there, floating in that tingly haze. Mark's imagined voice still hung in her head, but as her breathing slowed and her body sank back against the ceramic tub, the words began to fade. It was like being awakened too soon from a magnificent dream. She wanted to go back to that place. But the reality was slowly returning.

When the tremors subsided Ruby noticed that the sun coming through her frosted-glass window seemed brighter; the noises outside came through the walls louder. Standing in the tub, she grabbed a towel. She loved her flat, but for some reason it seemed stifling today. She wanted to be outside, to see the open sky. She didn't want to be alone with her thoughts.

After she was dry, she went to her room to get dressed. Twenty minutes later she was outside and on her way to the park.

She nearly ran into the tall, thin man as he came around the corner of her street. And when she jerked her head up to see Mark gazing down at her, she forgot everything and felt her smile turn up to full blast. She couldn't help it.

"Mark! What are you doing here?" she asked, staring up at him.

He seemed to scan her entirely in the sweep of a single gaze. "I was worried about you."

"So you just came to San Francisco? What about your band?"

His stare was unwavering, slowly drawing her in. "We needed to come back here today anyway. To finish recording."

"Right. Recording." Seeing him brought back all her raw feelings from the night before, had her head twisted in confusion. Angry and jealous, excited and scared; her heart beat madly as so many emotions rushed through her.

He dropped his bag, reached out and took her into his arms. She buried her face in his neck, inhaled his woodsy scent. He was long and hard, warm against her body, and it was heaven.

Lust hit her. Bone-melting, liquid desire for this man made her entire body go weak.

She felt his voice vibrating right into her body. "Listen. Let's just be together right now. No promises, no explanations. Whatever happens, I'm here *now*."

She nodded silently, her nose brushing the warm skin of his neck. He was here. He had gotten on a plane and come to her. No matter what he'd done while away, he was here. In San Francisco. He'd come to check on her, and that was something.

At the moment, it was everything.

She pulled back and looked up at him. "Do you have the day free?"

He nodded, his eyes dark liquid behind his glasses.

Butterflies were going crazy in her stomach. "What do you want to do?"

He glanced at his bag and back at her. "I have a few ideas."

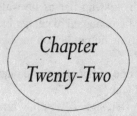

Chapter
Twenty-Two

The minute the door shut behind her he backed her against it, overwhelming her with his strength. His hands were everywhere, his lips hot and insistent as he kissed her mouth, her neck, behind her ear. He was pulling off her cardigan and sliding it down her shoulders, pausing to hold her arms beside her.

"Nothing happened last night," he said, and his voice sounded hoarse. "With those girls."

"I don't care," she said, but her heart felt lighter hearing him say the words.

He kissed her again and again, as if he couldn't get enough of her. His tongue searched hers, slowly tasting, licking, sucking. She felt the kiss in her knees, her breasts, between her legs.

"I lied," she said, pulling his shirt up and over his head. "I do care. I'm glad you weren't with anyone else. Neither was I. I never wanted to be!"

"I know. I figured that out as soon as you hung up on me." He started unbuttoning her shirtdress, and soon that was being pushed off her body as well. Then she was standing in just her bra and underwear and flats.

Laughing, she jumped onto him, wrapping her legs around his strong back.

He caught her, kissing her as he walked to the bedroom. Somehow he managed to get her bra off in the hallway, and by the time he put her on the bed her hair was a total wreck.

He pulled off one of her shoes and placed a kiss on her ankle. "I missed you."

"Oh, Mark," she sighed, resting on her elbows. "I always miss you when you go."

Removing her other flat, he kissed that ankle as well. "I never realized it would be so hard. To leave someone, I mean."

For a second she pictured herself and Claire, waving good-bye to their parents as they sailed away. She pushed aside the memory. "Take off your pants," she said, smiling.

"Take off your panties."

As she slid them down her legs he removed his boots and jeans and boxers. Then he climbed on top of her and gave her that cocky grin. "You are so much more agreeable about taking off your panties now than when I first met you."

"I told you. You make me lose my mind."

"Glad to oblige," he said, sinking between her legs.

She paused, cupping his strong jaw in her hand. "I don't even know you."

"What do you mean?"

"I don't know your middle name or where you're from. I don't know if you have any siblings. I don't even know if you sleep on the right or left side of the bed." So far they'd never slept together, one being, one body, all through the night.

"Rufus. Akron, Ohio. No siblings. Right side."

She blinked. "Rufus? Seriously?"

His hand was on her hip, and his grip tightened. "Don't laugh. It's an old family name."

"It's...interesting." She was trying so hard not to laugh her mouth hurt.

But it was him that chuckled, the sound reverberating from his chest and into hers. "I know," he said. "That's why you have to swear, right now, that you will never, ever, tell anyone that bit of information."

She quirked a brow. "And if I don't promise?"

He leaned down, his face looming over hers. He'd taken off his glasses, and now she could see the gold flecks in his brown eyes. "I'll have to punish you, of course."

His cock was already hard, pressing at her thigh. She wiggled until he was settled between her legs, just where she wanted him. She felt the metal of his piercings scraping her nipples.

The hot flesh of his erection felt heavenly against her pussy and she closed her eyes. "You feel so good, your skin on mine."

"I want to feel you; I want to feel my cock in your body," he said, kissing the crook of her neck, his warm breath making her shiver.

"I want that, too," she whispered.

Her pussy was so wet, and he was so hot, hard. She moved just a fraction, just to feel him on her clit. One more tilt and he'd be inside her.

"Condoms," she said. "Bedside drawer."

He rolled off, leaving her panting. But then he was back, between her legs, and she imagined it was his own skin she felt, not polyurethane, as he slid the head of his cock from her clit to her entrance and back again.

Teasing, sliding, he had her moaning within minutes. Then he entered her and she arched under him, his name on her lips.

He made love to her in a slow rhythm, caught her gaze with his. Now, there was no top or bottom, no dominance or submission, just Mark and Ruby, their uninhibited groans of pleasure mingling, the sounds of his body sliding into hers. There was the soft look in his eyes as he pulled out and slid back in, so slowly she couldn't breathe. There was Ruby, unable to tear her gaze from his as she reached up to rake her fingernails across the small of his back, encouraging him deeper, deeper.

They came like that. Silent, sweaty, and still. And after, when he lay on top of her, his heart beating against her own, Ruby realized it wasn't the D/s thing that had her freaked out, it was this. Raw, vanilla fucking. There were rules through submission, expectations. It had seemed so risky at the time, but nothing was as scary as this, as the feel of Mark's damp breath under her ear, or the way she loved lazily tracing patterns on the slick skin of his back. He soothed her as no one ever had.

These moments were what she wanted. *This* was real.

And fleeting. Soon, he'd be gone, on tour, performing. Living in New York. She always knew he would go. She just hoped he would obey her wish and leave without saying good-bye.

When her doorbell rang on Friday night, she knew it was Mark. Earlier, he'd asked her to wait for him until he'd finished recording and she'd been anxiously waiting ever since. The next night was the Spring Fling, and so far they hadn't discussed anything past that point.

Now, unsure, she answered the door with a smile plastered on her face.

He burst inside, and suddenly her apartment seemed to come alive from his energy. Yanking her to him, he kissed her, hard, and when he pulled back, his eyes were bright.

"We finished. The record will need some post-production of course, but we're done! And this album kicks fucking ass."

She pulled her sweater tighter around her shoulders. "That's wonderful," she said, trying to sound enthusiastic. But the fact was, she found it hard to be happy, not when they'd never discussed what would happen when he was done here.

"The guys are all celebrating, but I wanted to spend the night with you. Here." He thrust a bag at her. "You'll wear this tonight."

Blinking, she pulled out yards of shimmery cobalt fabric. "Oh my God, Mark. Another present?" It was a wrap dress with a low neckline, and she recognized the designer as a name she'd seen only in *Vogue* magazine. "Mark! You've given me too much as it is. I can't accept this."

Casually, his glance dropped to the necklace at her throat. "You can. And you will."

When he looked at her like that, like he owned her, her insides quivered. She got wet. She got off on it. And fuck it, at this point she couldn't deny him anything. Or deny herself.

He stepped closer and kissed her, slowly. "Get dressed. I wanna go out." He gave her a few more instructions before sending her off to get ready.

She had no idea what he had in store for her, but

anticipation tingled through her veins. Because whatever he wanted, she knew she'd give it to him. She'd give him everything.

Minutes later, standing in her bra and panties, Ruby looked at her reflection in the bathroom mirror. Her skin was flushed pink and her eyes sparkled. Mark wasn't even in the room, yet excitement coursed through her. He'd been very precise in how he wanted her to appear, and she wanted to please him.

She'd laid out her makeup in an organized row on the bathroom counter. Black eyeliner, black mascara, plum blush, and red lipstick. Although she'd never prepared herself like this for anyone, it seemed very ritualistic, almost sacrificial.

What a strange word to use to describe what she was about to do. Sacrifice. But it seemed appropriate; the description fit. After all, she was giving herself fully to a man she was certain would break her heart.

That didn't matter. What mattered was now; knowing he was in the other room sent a shiver of something wonderful up her spine. Knowing he was waiting for her made her heart palpitate with eagerness. He'd been dominating her from the very minute he'd stepped through her doorway, and she'd loved every fucking minute of it.

Tapping his foot impatiently, Mark stared out Ruby's bay window as he waited for her to get ready. He barely took in the view, he was too keyed up from what he'd just finished. The record had turned out fucking amazing; it was everything he'd wanted. He didn't care if critics liked it or if it got played on the radio. What mattered was that they'd made a great album.

All he'd ever wanted to do was play music for a living. Everything else was icing on the cake. He'd been banging on the keys of his parents' battered upright as soon as he was able to hoist himself onto the wooden bench. Nothing else had ever interested him like music did.

His father had been thrilled that his only child had shown an interest in playing the piano. After a few beers, Dad would begin to reminisce about the good old days. The days before he'd gotten married. The days before he'd given up touring for the responsibilities of fatherhood.

Maybe things were different in the seventies. Maybe life on the road was more exciting in the height of the sex and drugs and rock-and-roll era. Because sometimes Mark didn't quite get his father's nostalgia. Yeah, playing for a crowd was a huge rush. But Mark was always glad on the last day of a tour, standing onstage knowing he'd be back home the next day. He loved his loft in New York, could never wait to get back to the familiarity of his own bed, his own baby grand, his own life.

He loved his life in New York, just as Ruby loved hers in San Francisco.

"Mark?"

He turned from the window to see her standing in the living room. The sight of her made his pulse jackhammer. She became more beautiful by the second. The vivid color of the dress made her eyes shine brightly, echoing the cobalt shades she wore. She'd put on her makeup exactly as he'd instructed, so her eyes were rimmed with black, emphasizing her striking gaze and pale skin.

The stretchy blue dress wrapped around her body exactly as he'd imagined it would, emphasizing her lean torso and feminine curves. Her hair hung past her shoulders in thick temptation. He clenched his hands at his sides to keep from going to her and wrapping those silky locks around his fists. He remembered the phone conversation when he'd described exactly what he wanted to do to her, how he wanted to feel her hair moving across his stomach, his hips, his cock.

He went hard. *Get a grip. You have all fucking night.*

He pulled off his glasses and polished them on his shirt. "You look perfect, Ruby."

He didn't want to wait. The impulse to take her right then nearly overcame him. And the way she beamed at his compliment made it that much harder to resist.

He wanted her. And no matter how hard she resisted, he knew she wanted him, too. And once she figured out how much, he was sure she'd stop fighting him. So tonight, he planned on showing her exactly how good it could be.

Ruby slid into the back of the limo. Mark had been silent since he'd given her the compliment earlier, but there was a heightened energy radiating off him that made her nerves tingle. He hadn't told her where they were going; he hadn't told her anything. But the dark look in his eyes promised her all she needed to know.

He got in and the limo began to move. She inhaled that familiar scent of him: woodsy, earthy, leather. She wanted to smell his scent all the time. Remembering how her new flogger reminded her of Mark, she thought she might start sleeping with it, like a teddy bear.

"Why are you grinning?"

Looking up, she touched his cheek. Should she tell him her ridiculous idea?

He wrapped his hand around hers in a light but firm grasp. A reminder that all of her was his tonight, even her very thoughts.

Blushing, she shook her head. "I was just thinking about something; it was silly."

"Tell me."

Oh God. Swallowing, she lifted her chin. "I just love the way you smell."

His gaze on her was steady. "Yeah?"

"Yes." Her heart hammered as she spoke. Why was this so hard? "It's like this leather scent; it's so...nearly suffocating, but I like it." She shook her head at herself. "I find myself inhaling you, trying to keep the scent in my head. Is that crazy?"

He lifted a strand of her hair and wrapped it around his index finger. In the dim interior light, his eyes were liquid and dark behind his glasses. "No, it's not crazy at all."

Her lids fluttered shut when he tugged gently on her hair, and she loved the corresponding flurry in her rib cage, the little pulse between her legs.

And for some reason she kept speaking. "So." She laughed nervously. "You know that flogger I have? I bought it because it smelled like you; that's why I wanted it. And I was just thinking that I wanted to sleep with it next to me, like a stuffed animal."

"You are fucking cute when you blush."

She shook her head. "I am not."

"Are, too," he murmured. His gaze lingered on hers a moment longer before he gently pulled her hair toward him. A second later his lips were on hers, licking her, tasting her. She melted into the kiss, held on to his smooth scalp as he pushed his tongue deeper into her mouth. The entire world faded away as they continued this simple act, and when he finally pulled back she was panting. Her nipples tingled and her heartbeat was unsteady. He affected her as much with a simple kiss as he did when he had her restrained and on her knees.

"Untie your dress."

With trembling fingers she reached to her waist and pulled the sash apart. The fabric immediately gaped open, revealing the black lace bra she wore underneath.

His fingers were warm as he reached into the cup of her bra to pull out her right breast. She gasped as he tugged on her nipple, pulling the tip to a hard point. She noticed something shiny in his other hand then. Something he was bringing up to her breast. Two little metal clamps with a screw on one side, held together by about six inches of chain.

He pulled out her other breast and toyed with her, tugging her flesh until that nipple was a tight bead in his fingertips.

Glancing at the items in his hand and back to her breasts, he said, "I'm going to screw these onto your nipples, Ruby. You're going to wear them for me. All night."

He pulled her nipple through the clamp and began to adjust the screw. Tighter and tighter, he didn't stop until she gasped. After he'd screwed the second one on, he gave the chain a tug.

She cried out, the sensation shooting through her, directly to her pussy. He reached behind her, unclasped her bra, and threw it aside. Then he pulled her dress back over her shoulders.

Tying the belt, she looked at her chest and saw that the

clamps and chain were obvious lumps beneath the fabric. "People are going to see them."

The limo came to a stop, and he turned to give her that crooked grin. "Where we're going, doll, no one will care."

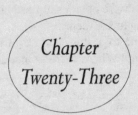

*Chapter
Twenty-Three*

The place looked normal from the outside. Just another club in an industrial area of San Francisco. But as soon as Mark ushered her through the door, his hand at the small of her back, she realized where they were. A sex club.

The entrance was a small room, sectioned off by a black curtain. There was a counter, behind which a beautiful blonde sat reading a magazine. The way she nodded at Mark and let him in with an easy silence told Ruby he'd been here before.

They went around the curtain, and Ruby saw that this place was nothing like the fetish party she'd gone to with Meg. The first thing she noticed was that it wasn't crowded. A few people mingled, standing or seated, around the low-light perimeter, and she felt their eyes on her as they passed.

She'd heard rumors of a very exclusive, private dungeon in San Francisco, and she realized she'd just been granted access.

A man walked by them, holding a leash. The leash was attached to a studded leather collar that was fastened around a naked woman's throat. As they passed, the woman kept her eyes lowered. Somehow, watching the couple sent a little pulse to Ruby's sex. Did she ever want to be owned like that? By Mark? She supposed she'd never know.

There was a hushed air of secrecy here, and none of the flagrant, unashamed eroticism she'd witnessed at the fetish party. Instead of fantasy themes, there seemed to be one purpose to this place: extreme domination and submission. Mark took her hand and led her deeper inside, to a corner, where he positioned her facing away from a dark wall. "Tell me something, Ruby. At that fetish party, did you enjoy watching? Did it make you wet?"

Tremors ran through her body, causing her nipples to throb in their metal clamps. Frightened yet turned on, she nodded.

He leaned closer. "Did you want to participate? Did you want to be watched?"

"Yes," she whispered, her skin burning.

"But you said you wished I'd been with you. Is that true? Do you want everyone to see what I do to you?"

She could barely breathe. If she said yes, it would mean pushing herself further than she'd ever thought possible. And yet, she hadn't been able to stop fantasizing about it, about having Mark do wicked things to her while people watched.

He closed in on her, backed her against the dark wall. His eyes on hers, he took her wrists and pinned them above her head with one of his hands. Then he placed his palm on her chest and, using his thumb, gently toyed with the lock at her throat.

Her eyelids fluttered closed as everything in her shut down under his touch. A river of desire flooded her, turning her limbs to liquid.

"I hate the thought of another man touching you—hell,

even *looking* at you. Ever since you told me you went to that party, all I've been able to think about is making you mine. I know you can't stop thinking about what you saw there, but I want you to experience it with me. Only me."

She thought he'd already pushed her as far as she could go, but she'd been wrong. Each time he dug out one of her desires, a new one seemed to pop up. And now... all she wanted was to fulfill the fantasy she'd been ignoring ever since that night at the fetish party.

"Are you mine tonight, Ruby? Truly?"

His gaze held hers until finally she nodded.

Something flashed in his eyes. Relief? But then it was gone, and he released her arms to take her hands in his. "Now, you truly belong to me. No one will even talk to you tonight unless they ask my permission first. So I need you to follow the rules."

"Yes, Mark." How easily she fell into her role.

"I'm going to take off your dress now. I want everyone to see how beautiful my woman is." He untied her dress and slid it down her shoulders, her arms, until he held it in his hands. "And now, give me your panties and your shoes."

She had no desire to hesitate. Electric energy coursed through her; anticipation ruled her. She wanted this, wanted it with him.

After she'd removed the rest of her clothing, a woman in a leather skirt and underbust corset appeared, and Mark handed her the dress before she scurried away, taking Ruby's clothing with her.

Ruby stood then, naked except for her nipple clamps, for anyone to see. Her blood ran hot through her veins, and her nipples were hard peaks in the metal, her pussy moist. She realized she liked this, liked being his pet to show off.

"Hands behind your back."

She clasped her hands at the base of her spine, causing her chest to jut forward; the chain swinging between the valley of her breasts.

"Good girl." With a possessive hand on the back of her neck, he moved her along.

There was a floor-to-ceiling chain-link fence around the center of the room, and they stopped at a gate. A short, stocky man dressed in leather pants came forward, nodded at Mark, and let them inside.

She followed Mark to a table where an array of leather gear was displayed. Just looking at the floggers and whips and paddles released something in her, something that made her nipples swell within the clamps and then turned that sting into lust.

Mark nodded toward a large X-shaped wooden cross, similar to the one she'd seen at the fetish party. "That's a Saint Andrew's cross. I want you to go over there, stand facing the cross, and wait for me."

Nodding, she went to that part of the room. This close, the cross seemed huge, overbearing. But the endorphins had been released, and she felt juice from her pussy on the inside of her thighs.

They were the only ones in the chained-off area, but she felt eyes on her. Knowing she was being watched only turned her on more. When Mark came to her holding four sets of leather cuffs, she shook her hair back off her face as if she was proud.

Maybe she was. Maybe, just tonight, she could be proud that he'd chosen her. She felt young, beautiful, as he spread her feet wide and encircled both her ankles with the thick leather cuffs. He secured the cuffs to the O-rings bolted on the cross near her feet, then did the same with each of her arms. Soon she was spread wide, revealed, for all the world to see. Once again, open.

Looking over her shoulder, she saw Mark grinning at her. "You'll do. Now look forward."

She did, and it was then that she felt the leather on her back. The strands of a soft leather flogger, dragging over her back, soothing her. The tautness in her shoulders started to subside, and she hung her head as he continued to caress her, draining any remnant of nervousness out of her body.

He increased the pressure, the light strokes becoming harder, more forceful. But she was beyond feeling any pain. All she felt was pleasure, pure and hot. And when the strands of the flogger hit her with a loud smack she cried out. It stung, but in the best way possible.

He came around once and took her chin in his hand, kissed her lips.

"You're smiling," he said, and she nodded. She was too high to speak.

Tenderness flashed in his eyes as he held her gaze, and it seemed there was no one in the room but them. But then he was gone, and she felt the strands of the flogger again, landing on her everywhere: her shoulder blades, the middle of her upper back, her thighs, her ass. The inside of her legs. She was spread so wide he could whip her there, and she felt the wind of the flogger on her damp sex.

Yes, she thought, leaning into the restraints. *Hit me there, touch me there, please...*

He pressed against her back, his body hard and hot against her naked flesh. She felt his breath on her neck when he pulled her hair aside. "Everyone in this place is watching you. Everyone is watching the way I turn you on, the way you squirm under my touch. Does it make you wet? To be watched?"

"Yes," she breathed.

His hand came around her and spanned her belly. If her feet weren't bound, she would have clamped her thighs shut to ease the ache within.

But he moved his hand, lower and lower...was he really going to touch her here? In public?

He was.

She gasped when she felt his thumb on her clit, rubbing her in tight circles, making her so wet, so needy, she bit her lip to keep from crying out.

"It's okay, I want to hear you. Everyone wants to hear you." His thumb still on her clit, he slid across her pussy with the rest of his hand. Opening her up, pushing into her. Fingering her right there, in front of a crowd.

Her back burned lusciously from the flogging he'd given her, and her nipples stung in the clamps. Her body was trembling everywhere from lust. "Mark...Oh, God! It's so good," she cried, her voice husky.

"I know, sweetheart." With his free hand he reached around and gave the chain hanging between her breasts a sharp tug.

She screamed. She cried out, again and again, knowing people could see her, hear her. Mark pulled the chain at her nipples again, and this time he didn't let up, the pleasure searing through her in a rush. His hand between her legs worked her faster, harder, deeper, and he whispered into her ear, "That's it, baby; come for me. Come now."

An enormous shudder tore through her as she climaxed, for everyone to see.

Mark released her quickly. His heart hammered as he carried her trembling body. She clung to him, silent. He'd found a small but private room with a sofa and once seated, he held her, rocked her as if he were calming a child. Finally, she looked up, her eyes such a deep shade of blue they were almost black. She smiled. "That was amazing."

He gently unscrewed the clamps on her nipples. She gave a light moan as he released her, and he massaged flesh he knew would be sore. She sighed against his chest, and his cock immediately started throbbing.

Fuck, how he wanted her. Touching her like this, seeing her sink into her world of pleasure, made his cock so fucking hard. Made him shift underneath her and take deep breaths to try to control himself.

He kissed her forehead. "You were beautiful out there. Everyone envied me."

"Really? I made you happy?"

"Of course."

Sliding out of his lap, she knelt in front of him. "I want to make you even happier."

He nodded. She was irresistible, unlike any woman he'd ever met. His blood rushed through him as she unbuttoned his jeans and boxers and slid them down his legs, and then she took his cock in her hands, drew him into her wet, warm mouth so deep, he groaned out her name. She sucked him, stroked his balls, and didn't seem to mind the palm of his hand on her hair; tugging, guiding.

"That's perfect, Ruby, just like that..." But when he was about to come she stopped and looked up. "I want to feel you inside me, Mark."

"Then come here, baby."

She pulled a condom out of a bowl next to the sofa and opened it, slid it onto his cock. Then she straddled him, guiding his dick into her pussy in one smooth, sure motion. She threw her head back as she rocked against him, her eyes dark, her mouth open as her breathing came faster and faster.

He gripped her thighs, her body tense under his hands as she used the muscles in her legs to ride him. This she did with total freedom; pinching her own nipples, working her own clit. It was as if the earlier public display had released her somehow, as if she had no inhibitions left in her at all.

He watched her face as she came. Her eyes closed, her mouth spread in a wide smile. It was so beautiful he followed quickly, jerking her to him so he could pump into her body, letting the little contractions of her inner walls milk every last drop from him.

She collapsed on top of him and he held her like that, until both of their breathing returned to normal.

He had to convince her that they could make this work. Suddenly his career, the band, seemed so much less important than keeping this connection with the girl in his arms.

"Listen, Ruby. We have to talk."

She said against his chest, "I'm exhausted, I can't think."

"But there are things—"

She yawned. "It's been a tiring night. Can we just go home?" She snuggled deeper against him. "I know we need to talk. After tonight, I can't ignore my feelings for you any longer..."

She went quiet, and after a minute he realized she'd dozed off. He kissed her forehead and picked her up. They could talk later, in the morning. Really, he just needed to assure her that he could balance his career and a relationship with her. And he needed to reassure her that she was a strong enough person to deal with it.

She was barely conscious as he got her clothes, dressed her, led her to the limo and took her home. And she was still asleep when they arrived, so he dug the keys out of her bag and carried her into the apartment. In her room, he stripped off her clothes and laid her under the covers. She murmured a thank-you but was snoring softly within seconds.

He stifled a laugh. He'd just discovered one of her imperfections.

Pulling off his clothes, he undressed and climbed in beside her, pulled her into his arms. Soon he joined her in a deep, dreamless sleep. But when the bright rays of the sun woke him in the morning, Ruby was gone.

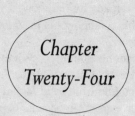

Chapter Twenty-Four

This place looks amazing."

Ruby looked up from where she'd been arranging a bunch of twigs. She wore one of her typical prim dresses—this time in a soft blue—and her hair was pulled back. The only thing that gave away her sensual side was the sexy shoes on her dainty feet.

Hugging the clipboard to her chest, she beamed at him.

It was the day of the Spring Fling, and Mark had stopped by to check the stage. That, and he wanted an excuse to see Ruby. She'd been out the door before he'd dragged his ass out of bed, so this was the first time he'd seen her since last night.

The event was being held in an old theater, a building originally built as a movie theater in the 1930s. There was a small stage, behind which red velvet draped from the floor to the ceiling. Round tables had been set up on the floor, and each table had been decorated with gold twigs and leaves. With the brightly colored linens and china, the place looked like something out of a movie.

She placed her clipboard on the stage and began arranging a vase of iridescent feathers. "So. Are you ready for tonight?" she asked as she played with the feathers.

"Yeah." He was ready for the show; it was afterward he was having trouble wrapping his head around. "Listen, I have some bad news."

She glanced over her shoulder. "What is it?"

He ran a hand over his face. This was even harder than he'd thought. "You know the band January Blues?"

She rolled her eyes. "Um, yeah. Even I've heard of them. They're huge."

"Yeah. They just dropped out of a European tour they're doing with two other bands, and we've been asked to replace them."

Her smile faltered but only for a second. "That's wonderful." She turned back to her arrangement. "When do you leave?"

"Tomorrow."

She froze but didn't look up. "Wow. Tomorrow. That's so...soon."

He put his hand on her shoulder. "I know." He squeezed her shoulder and felt how small she was, how fragile. "We can talk on the phone. E-mail. We can make it work."

Her body went tight under his hand. "Okay, sure."

He turned her around and met her watery gaze. "You remember how much you trusted me last night?"

She nodded.

"You need to do that now. You need to trust me. I won't let you down."

"*Mr. St. Crow?*"

It took him a minute to drag his gaze from hers. A man was jogging toward them. He looked a few years older than Mark. His brown hair was cut neatly, and he wore khaki pants and a blue button-down shirt. When he reached them, he held out his hand. "I'm James Cleaver."

Mark shook it. "Nice to meet you."

The man bounced on the balls of his feet. "My employees are ecstatic about tonight! We can't wait."

"Thanks for asking us to do the show," Mark managed.

"When I found out Ruby knew you personally, I just couldn't resist asking her if you'd play for us."

Mark glanced at Ruby. "I just can't say no to her. Her wish is my command."

"And, I'm looking forward to the cocktail party," James said. "And so are five of my most important clients." He turned to Mark. "God, she is really something, isn't she? I swear, she can pull off magic. I had CEOs begging to get an invite to this preparty!"

"What?" Mark shook his head. "What preparty?"

Smiling, Ruby stepped on the top of his foot with her heel. Hard.

"Mark's kidding. The band is going to be at your place at six sharp." She glared at him. "Right?"

Fuck. He'd totally forgotten he'd obligated the band to a schmooze fest before the show. He nodded. "Yeah, right. Of course we'll be there."

She glowered at him for another moment before giving James a huge smile. "Everything seems to be running smoothly, James. It's going to be a fabulous event."

James beamed at Ruby, and something in Mark went tight. He didn't like the way this guy was looking at Ruby, not one bit.

"Of course it's going smoothly," James said. "With you running the show, everything goes exactly as planned. Always does, gorgeous."

A pink flush tinged her cheeks. "Thank you."

Mark's gaze darted back and forth between the two: Ruby in her retro outfit; James in his neatly pressed pants and preppy shirt.

Mark's gut clenched as he realized this Cleaver guy epitomized everything Ruby had wanted her entire life; he could give her what she'd always wanted.

Because the one thing Mark knew without a doubt was that no other man could ever love Ruby the way Mark knew he could, if she would just give him the chance.

Now, she smiled at Mark but her eyes were cold. "You probably need to go pack for your tour. I'll see you tonight, Mark. At the show." She turned away to show the Cleaver guy something on her clipboard.

And just like that, Mark was dismissed.

Mark slammed the door behind him, causing Yvette to look up from her bowl of cereal. Jake paused his perusal of the issue of *Rolling Stone* he was reading and said, "'sup." He was lounging on the sofa, wearing Mickey Mouse pajama bottoms and not much else.

Mark stepped around their packed luggage, sitting in the living room of the loft they'd been living in for the past two weeks. He'd hardly seen the place. Most of his time had been spent at the studio or with Ruby. And now they were leaving.

Twenty-four hours from now they'd be in London. Far away from San Francisco, far away from Ruby.

"What's up, Doc?" Yvette asked and spooned in a mouthful of Lucky Charms. She wore a white tank top and boxers and looked like she had just woken up, even though it was past three.

He dropped into a chair opposite her. "Nothing. I'm just ready to split."

"Everything okay?" she asked as she chewed.

"I don't fucking know."

"It's that chick, isn't it?" Jake called from his spot on the couch. He shook his head. "I knew it was a love song."

"We never did hear it," Yvette said.

"And you never will."

"My, my. Someone's got his Underoos in a wad."

Mark grunted.

"Seriously," she said, her voice softer. "What's up?"

"I went to talk to Ruby today, to tell her that I wanted to try and give things a go."

Yvette gave a low whistle. "Wow. That's pretty serious."

"She was less than enthusiastic, especially when I told her we were leaving tomorrow."

"Really?" she asked.

"Yeah."

"Now, why would a healthy, red-blooded, hetero woman go and push away a hot guy like yourself?" She leaned forward. "Maybe she's gay."

"She's not gay. She has a crush on Mr. Cleaver." Mark cringed.

Yvette jerked back. "The Beaver's dad?"

"No, the dude who's putting on this gig tonight, but he may as well be the guy from the show."

"And so what did you do?" Yvette said between bites.

He shrugged. "What was I supposed to do? I left."

Yvette threw herself back in her chair. "You're kidding."

"Do I look like I'm kidding?"

"No, not really." She pushed away her empty bowl, sat back and rubbed her belly. "Mmm mmm good. Anyway, what are you going to do now?"

"I think she wants me to leave."

"That's mighty pussy of you, dude," Jake put in and went back to reading.

If looks could kill, Jake would be DOA.

Yvette drilled him with her gaze. "So, can you talk to her again before we leave?"

"Hell yeah, I am. But I'm not sure what to say to convince her, especially with Mr. Fucking Perfect sniffing around." And calling her *gorgeous*. Mark felt like he'd been sucker-punched.

"Listen," Yvette said. "You gotta try something. As it is, you're pretty useless."

"What are you talking about?" he demanded.

"Have you eaten today? Did you sleep last night?"

"What's that got to do with anything?" he muttered even as his stomach growled.

"We're about to embark on our first European tour. I can't go see Big Ben with a lovesick zombie! Now, we need to do something to woo this girl, at least long enough to get you through our crazy upcoming schedule."

"I told you, I'm going to talk to her later, when she's not so busy getting ready for tonight."

Yvette shook her head sadly. "Men," she said, rolling her eyes. "I respect any woman with the patience to put up with one of you. Now listen to me. I have a plan."

*Chapter
Twenty-Five*

Ruby punched the button to dial Mark's cell phone number again, and just like the twenty-three other times, he didn't answer.

"Ruby, we have time for one more drink, and then we need to go."

Ruby turned away from the floor-to-ceiling window of James Cleaver's loft. Behind him, a buffet table was elegantly set with an array of colorful appetizers. Holding delicate champagne glasses, people mingled. But what had started as excited conversation at the beginning of the night had turned into hushed, disappointed murmurs.

Mark hadn't shown up.

As she faced James, her throat was so tight she could barely speak. "I don't know where they are, James. Something must have happened."

Gently, he placed a hand on her shoulder. "I'm sure there was some sort of emergency. Don't worry about it."

But panic was racing through her, making her brow tingle with sweat. It was past seven; the Riders were over an hour late.

How could Mark do this to her?

A woman Ruby recognized as the recent benefactor of a huge Napa winery walked by. Ruby had been dying to make a good impression with her; the young heiress was known for throwing totally extravagant parties, and Ruby wanted a piece of the action. But after tonight, she seriously doubted that would be happening.

The room was full of potential high-end clients, and they were all looking at her, waiting for her to produce the Riders out of her ass.

"They're not coming," she wanted to say. *"And yeah, it's all my fault. It's all my fault because I trusted a fucking musician!"*

Instead Ruby smiled at the guests as James led her to a leather sofa. Sitting next to her, he said, "I know it's not your fault the band didn't show up."

"I take full responsibility for this, James. Consider this party compliments of Umbrella Events." She nearly cringed when she said the words; the catering bill was more than she'd earned all month. But she felt she owed it to James. After all, he'd paid for a preparty with the Riders, and she hadn't produced them.

He shook his head. "No way I'm letting you foot the bill. Besides, I'm still enjoying myself. Very much." He smiled, and even if it didn't melt her insides the way Mark's smile did, it was a nice smile nonetheless.

"Well, I'm just sorry about this, but rest assured. They'll be at the party tonight." Even if she had to track them down and drag their asses there herself.

"I'm not worried about it, gorgeous. I'm just enjoying sitting next to the most beautiful girl in the room." With a grin that was getting cuter by the second, he plucked two glasses from a passing server and handed her some champagne. "Now, don't worry. Everyone here will get their chance to meet the Riders later, right?"

Ruby nodded and tried to ignore the feeling of dread that was creeping through her body.

Later, at the venue, Ruby managed to avoid Mark. She was too angry to speak with him, or any of the band, so she went about her job, letting Meg deal with any stage issues that arose.

Now, Ruby watched from the upper balcony as the Riders finished their fourth song of the night. They'd arrived on time, and if the band held any resentment over playing the private party, they didn't show it. They performed with all the enthusiasm and passion she'd seen in them that first night, and the audience's excitement seemed to only rev them up.

From her second-floor perch, Ruby watched. She wasn't hiding, not exactly. But she didn't think she could handle talking to Mark. He was leaving in just a few hours, and she couldn't believe she'd been about to take him up on his offer of trying something long-distance. On one level she was glad he'd blown her off; it had only helped her dodge another bullet.

Now, the band was on a break and dessert was being served. Every seat was occupied, every wineglass was full. The excited cacophony of guests talking filled the space. Everyone was waiting eagerly for the Riders to get back onstage, and the anticipation was nearly palpable.

"You did a wonderful job."

She jerked her head to find James Cleaver standing beside her. She hadn't heard him approach.

"Thank you," she said. "I'm pleased with this part of the night, at least." The room looked like a modern spring wonderland. She'd gone through a case of spray paint, but it was worth it. Now, golden branches and white lights twinkled everywhere, from the ceiling and walls and floor. Little flowers were scattered throughout the entire space, and it was like walking through a storm of petals. The vintage backdrop of the theater gave a perfect, almost medieval charm to the whole thing. Everything was modern yet ethereal. Exactly what she'd had in mind from the start.

"Beautiful."

But when she turned to James, he was looking at her. "Are you seeing him?"

"Who? Mark?"

He nodded.

"No." *Not anymore.* Just then Mark, Yvette, and Jake walked back onto the stage, and she soon heard the disharmonious notes of them checking their instruments.

James stepped closer and took her hand. Why didn't he make her pulse jump as Mark did whenever he got this close? "Would you like to dance with me, Ruby?"

Such a gentleman. How could she say no?

Why did she want to? She wasn't going to let Mark ruin her night. In fact, let him see her having fun. Maybe the cocky bastard would see that he wasn't the center of the universe.

"Let's go," she said.

He took her hand and led her around the upper terrace, to the back of the theater where a large staircase wound down to the main floor.

As they walked to the front of the stage, the sound of one of Mark's unique compositions began to fill the room. Something in her blood immediately started to hum; it was funny how her body responded to his music. This tune sounded vaguely familiar, but she couldn't place it.

The crowd parted, and Ruby had to smile. If she wasn't so upset, she would have felt like a princess. She'd even dressed the part. She was wearing an emerald organza dress. It draped over one shoulder, falling to the floor in petals and petals of whispery fabric. It seemed to flow as she walked, and it was so beautiful, just wearing the dress made her feel elegant and sexy.

The gold twigs and colorful flowers seemed to float all around, and as she walked toward the stage she saw Mark was looking right at her. Her heart started to pound.

When they reached the dance floor they were the only couple on it. This was a slower song, and Mark's eyes burned into her as James took her in his arms and began to sway.

"I want to see you again, Ruby."

"Yes, of course," she murmured, wishing Mark would stop staring at her. She was getting hot everywhere, and with a burst of frustration she realized it had nothing to do with the man who held her in his arms.

"But I'm not sure what's going on with you and Mark St. Crow."

"He means nothing to me. Absolutely nothing." But her voice sounded weak, even to her.

James pulled back, and his eyes were full of sympathy as he said, "Are you sure?"

She glanced up to see Mark lean into a microphone. He wore a white T-shirt that showed off the strong body she'd gotten to know so well. The body she'd had between her thighs, just last night.

"Yes, I'm sure," she whispered. But her heart was

pounding in her ears, and just meeting Mark's gaze caused
her legs to tremble.

Then he started to sing.

She doesn't know what she does to me
I fell the second she teased me
Tie me in jasmine
Eyes that glitter like her ocean
Tying you in knots
You tie me in knots
But I don't wanna be free
If freedom means you'll ever say good-bye
Good-bye is not forever
Just a fleck of time

Her heart felt like it had jumped into her throat when he
hit the chorus, and instantly she recognized the song—it
was the one he'd been composing that night at her house.
Her gaze was locked on his as she listened.

All I'm asking for is time
A hundred years or more would suit me fine
Don't leave me in this darkness loving blind
I might leave, but I'll always come back, girl
Sweetheart, doll, baby
Fuck 'em
Always come back to my Ruby Mine
Good-bye is not forever
Just a fleck of time

Everyone was looking at her. James was looking at
her with an unreadable expression on his face. "He com-

pletely flaked off your preparty, Ruby. I like you too much not to warn you to be careful with that one."

She turned away from him. The crowd blurred as she ran down the center aisle and pushed through the huge double doors. Images slammed into her head—of Mark, of all the things they'd done. A few weeks ago she'd known exactly what she wanted. Now confusion made her head spin, made her heart race as she burst outside and onto the sidewalk.

"Spare a quarter?"

A man sat on the cement, an upside-down hat next to him along with a small piece of cardboard, upon which was written in a messy scrawl, *Change Appreciated*.

"I'm sorry," she said. "I don't have my purse."

"Then how about a pretty smile." He gave her a gap-toothed grin.

It was cold and she started to shiver. "Sorry," she said, walking away.

She heard the door open, slam shut, and then, "Ruby."

She stopped but didn't turn around. "Just leave me alone, Mark."

He was in front of her in an instant, standing close. Too close. She could smell him. His unique scent, his sweat. Leather.

When he grabbed her, his hand was warm and damp on her bare shoulder. "I'm leaving tomorrow, Ruby. Talk to me."

"I know you're leaving, trust me. That's the one thing I do know."

"What's wrong? Why were you dancing with that dickwad in front of me?"

She jerked back. "You made a fool of me tonight."

He truly looked confused. "You mean the song?"

"No! You didn't show for the preparty." Humiliatingly, she felt her eyes start to burn. "This is my career you're fucking with."

She saw his eyes flash with anger. At himself. "Oh, fuck." He ran a hand over his face. "Oh, baby—I'm so sorry."

"Sorry doesn't help the twenty people who showed up tonight hoping to meet the Riders because *I* promised them it would happen!"

He reached for her, but she jerked away. "Just tell me why, Mark. What was so important you left me like that and couldn't even bother to call?"

A few yards away, some guests were standing around, banned outside to smoke. Glancing at them, Mark said in a low voice, "Listen. I can explain. Let me take you somewhere private."

"You mean you want to ditch the rest of your set? Typical!"

"Fine. Just promise me we'll talk later so I can explain. *Promise me.*"

"When?" She slapped a tear from the corner of her eye. "You mean tomorrow? Oh, wait! You'll be gone."

"It doesn't have to be like this. Just come inside and talk to me. We can work it out if you'll just let me explain." He took a step toward her. "Trust me."

She jerked her chin up and ignored the plea she saw in his eyes. "I do trust you. With you, there's something I can always trust you to do."

His eyes went dark. "What's that?"

"I can *always* trust you to leave."

His jaw clenched, and she saw all the muscles in his arms bunch. For a second, she thought he might punch the brick wall behind them. He turned away, sucked in a breath, and then turned back to her. "Fine. I guess I'll just say good-b—"

"Chihuahua!"

He looked baffled. "What?"

"Chihuahua. Isn't that what I'm supposed to say when I can't take it anymore?"

"Yeah, but this isn't what I meant. That was for when you were in pain."

"I *am* in pain!" She lifted her chin, wiped away some more damn tears. "At the very beginning, you wanted to know my limits. I told you no good-byes. You're pushing me beyond my limits. So, Chihuahua."

"Your limits are fucked up."

"They may be, but they're *my* limits. R-remember?" She was really shaking now; her teeth had started to chatter.

His brown eyes turned black as he stared at her. She could see the struggle going on in his mind, but, in the end, he finally took a step back. "Fine."

"Fine."

He looked ready to say more but finally just shook his head and walked away. She didn't turn around until she heard the door to the theater slam shut.

Beside the door, the homeless man shook his head. "Don't be scared."

"What are you t-talking about?"

"You, my dear. You're scared of love."

"That is not t-true." And why was she arguing with a delusional old man? But she didn't want to go back inside the theater, not yet. She might run into Mark, and, if she did, she knew she'd break down and lose it totally. She refused to allow that to happen at one of her events.

"Anyway, he's bad news," she muttered.

"The good ones always are," the man said. "I mean, Janis Joplin was a real wildcat in the sack, but it was worth every bruise and scratch."

"Janis Joplin died of a drug overdose."

"Exactly," he said and gave a watery cough. "Imagine if I'd turned her down. I'd always have wondered what it would have been like." His expression turned wistful.

"That makes no sense." Did it? Her head was pounding. She put a finger to her temple and rubbed.

"Girl, you gotta take a chance! You gotta grab 'em by the horns!" He made a fist and swung his arm to illustrate his point. "And you need balls to get the horns, right? Everyone knows that!" His watery eyes gazed up at her, excited and expectant. "You got balls, don't you, girl?"

"I have something better. A brain." She unclasped the necklace around her neck and dropped it into the man's hat, where it disappeared into a pile of mismatched change. "Thanks for the advice."

Chapter
Twenty-Six

The next week Ruby was too busy to notice Mark's absence.

Almost.

An article had appeared in the Sunday Society section about James Cleaver's Spring Fling, and ever since, she'd been slammed with people wanting to hire Umbrella Events for weddings, grand openings, galas, and myriad other parties. If the mishap at the preparty was affecting her business, it wasn't noticed.

But no matter what she was doing, she always felt like there was something missing. And it didn't take a Jungian therapist to help her figure out exactly what that thing was.

"Call him!" Meg had said on Wednesday over breakfast at Savor. "Emmett says he had a really good reason for blowing off the cocktail party."

Ruby had to admit she was curious. "I don't know. What would I say?"

"That you miss him. That you can live with phone sex."

"Here ya go, girls." Bree placed a basket of croissants on the table. "I just wanted to thank you again for inviting me to see the Riders last weekend. Getting to meet Yvette after the show was...pretty fucking cool." She ran a hand over her spiky black hair.

"No problem," Meg said, crossing her legs. Today her tights were bright green, which went nicely with her short plaid minidress.

"So, what's going on today, ladies? More business stuff?"

Meg glanced at the server. "I'm just trying to figure out why Ruby has decided to go celibate."

Bree looked astounded. "Why the hell would anyone want to do that?"

"I have no idea," Meg said. "But our friend here is pushing two men away, and I'm not sure why."

Bree brought a chair around to their table. "I can understand the pushing-men-away thing, but the sex part? Not so much."

"You guys don't understand. The things I said to Mark the last time I saw him..." Ruby shook her head. "I was awful."

"That's what makeup sex is for," Bree said.

Meg's brows quirked above her sunglasses. "Okay, so you were a bitch to Mark, and now you're afraid to call him. But why haven't you gone out with James? You've been pining after him for months, but you have yet to take him up on his offer of a date. Why is that?"

Ruby slumped into her chair. "I don't know." She couldn't admit that after being with Mark, she just couldn't settle for anyone who didn't make her heart race like he had. Or grinned like he did. Or wielded a flogger like he had.

"I'm fucked up, aren't I?" she said, ripping apart the croissant and shoving a huge bite into her mouth.

Bree and Meg nodded.

"But you can do something about it," Meg said. "Go see Mark. Let him explain. Emmett wouldn't give me details, but he seems to think you'll forgive him."

Ruby shook her head. "We're too busy right now."

"Work can wait. I can handle everything."

"I know, but come on. I don't even know where he is. Germany or somewhere."

"Ya, ya," Bree said in a horrid German accent. "Go to Deutschland an' spank heez monkee."

Grinning, Ruby gave Bree a playful slap. "Stop it. Really. It'll be fine. Hell, he's probably forgotten all about me by now." The thought made her heart hurt.

"No way," Meg said. "He's totally into you. All you have to do is say the word."

She had said the word. It started with C and rhymed with wawa. "I'm sorry, Meg. I just can't take the instability of being with him. It just wasn't meant to be."

On Friday night the doorbell rang and Ruby's heart did a little leap. Would she ever hear the damn bell without thinking of Mark?

"Yes?" Ruby said into the call box.

"Surprise!"

"Claire? Is that you?"

"Yes, and I'm freezing in this damn fog. Let me in!"

Ruby buzzed her in, and a second later Claire was crushing her in a bear hug. "I'm so happy to see you!"

"You too!" Ruby said, pulling Claire even tighter. "I can't believe you're here!"

After a few minutes they pulled apart. Ruby eyed her sister's small bag. "Where's the rest of your luggage?"

"You're looking at it."

"God, I couldn't even fit a weekend's worth of shoes in that thing."

"I guess that's the one thing I learned from Mom. Remember what she always said?"

"If you don't use it every day, don't bring it!" They finished the last part together and burst into laughter.

Smiling, Ruby stood back and gave her sister the once-over. Designer jeans enclosed Claire's long, supermodel legs, and she wore a T-shirt with lots of sparkles. She was much taller than Ruby, but her four-inch brown boots added even more height, and Ruby had to tilt her head back just to make eye contact. The only physical characteristic the sisters shared was their blue eyes.

Ruby touched a lock of Claire's hair. "You have highlights."

"You can never be too blonde in Hollywood," she said.

Ruby laughed, smoothed back her ponytail. "Which is why I choose to live here in San Francisco, where anything goes."

"Well, San Francisco really is the best place to be an individual, I'll give you that."

Ruby lifted Claire's suitcase and walked to her bedroom, where she dropped it on the bed. "Make yourself at home. You want anything? Coffee? A glass of wine?"

Claire glanced at her watch. "It's almost five. How about some wine?"

"Sounds good. You freshen up, I'll go open a bottle. Meet you in the living room."

Ruby went about getting out the chardonnay and glasses. All week her house had seemed extra quiet, extra dead. Just her sister's presence cheered her up immensely.

In the living room, the sisters sat on the sofa facing each other, resting their backs against the arms of the couch.

"Cheers," Ruby said, holding up her glass.

"Cheers!"

"How's L.A., anyway? Any roles lately?" Ruby asked.

Claire shrugged. "Not really. But I tried out for a part in an indie film that could be awesome. It pays shit, but it would be great name recognition." Her eyes started twinkling. "Enough of that. What I really want to know is what's up with you and Mark St. Crow."

Ruby shrugged "Nothing's up. I haven't talked with him since last Saturday."

Just then Ruby's cell vibrated on the coffee table. Claire had never been known to respect her sister's privacy, and she set down her glass of wine to pick up the phone. "Oh, look! A text message. From *Rufus*." She looked up with one quirked brow. "Rufus, huh? It says, 'In Munich. Miss you.'"

"It does?" Her heart leaped. This was the first communication she'd had from Mark since he'd left.

"Rufus wants to know if you want to come to Germany. On him." Claire glanced up. "Come on him in Germany? Hell yeah, you do." She started typing.

"What?" Ruby set her glass on the coffee table and lunged for her sister.

But Claire had always been the more agile of the two, and she managed to avoid Ruby's grabbing hands.

"Rufus wants to know why you won't talk to him."

"Claire! Stop it right now!"

"If you don't tell me who Rufus is, I'm going to start having text-message sex on your behalf."

"You little...!" She rolled Claire onto the ground, but

her sister just sat on top of her, pinning her to the floor with her freakishly long legs.

"Oh my God! Rufus wants to know what kind of panties you're wearing!"

Ruby's face burned, and she glared up at her sister.

Claire talked as she typed. "Rufus, *if* that is your real name, this is Claire, Ruby's sister. Who are you?"

"I'm going to kill you," Ruby said, through clenched teeth.

"I'm shaking in my boots." Then a laugh burst out of Claire's throat. "I'm talking to Mark St. Crow!" she exclaimed, her eyes on the phone's screen. "Oh my God! Too cool. Love your code name, by the way. Rufus. Ha!"

"Seriously. Put the phone down. *Now*." Ruby hadn't been able to totally delete Mark's number from her cell phone, but she'd changed his name to Rufus. In some kind of strange attempt to forget him.

"In a minute." Claire typed some more. "Are you boinking my sister?" she asked the phone.

"Claire!"

Her evil sister gave her an innocent smile. "What? If you're not gonna give me any details, I'm going straight to the source."

Ruby reached up and grabbed her sister's hand, twisting her wrist until Claire screamed and jumped off her. "What the fuck? That hurt!"

"Good." Ruby picked up the phone Claire had dropped and turned it off. "You know I fight dirty."

"What's the big deal, anyway?" she asked, massaging her wrist.

Panting, Ruby pushed herself to her feet. "I'm in love with him. Are you happy now? I'm in love with Mark St. Crow!"

"You don't want to talk with him because you're in love with him? Okay. That totally makes sense. *Not*."

"Listen. You know how hard it is for me to say good-bye. With him, I'd be doing it all the time. He's totally unreliable. I can't live that way."

"Right. You're looking for Mr. Perfect."

"Not anymore. I've realized there is no such thing. But that doesn't mean I have to settle, does it?"

"Most people wouldn't consider Mark St. Crow settling material."

"Most people couldn't handle the lifestyle he leads. I mean, come on, Claire. Can you see me waiting for him to come home from tour? From parties and shows all over the world?" She shook her head. "And I refuse to give up my life to follow him. I refuse to..."

"Be like Mom?" Claire asked softly. She felt Claire's gaze on her for a second before her sister asked, "But does he make you happy?"

Ruby dropped back onto the sofa. "On occasion."

Claire crossed her arms over her chest and gave her a look. "On occasion?"

"Yeah, when he's not blowing me off or running away to some interview or jetting off on a last-minute tour, yeah. He makes me happy."

"So, when he's not living his life, things are good." She picked up her glass.

"It sounds so lame when you put it that way," Ruby said, shaking her head.

"I just think you have something with Rufus. I don't want to see you throw it away because you're scared. Now, I'm gonna go slip into something more comfortable, like my pajamas." She sauntered off toward the bedroom.

Ruby stared after her, her pulse racing. Claire was right. She was so afraid of taking a chance with Mark, but was this any better? Why did it feel like not trying to make something work with Mark was the bigger risk?

A loud scream snapped her attention back and she ran to the bedroom. "Claire? What's wrong?" Her heart thudded in her ears; it was too much like her dream.

But when she got to her room, she saw it wasn't a dream. This was Ruby's own personal nightmare.

Claire had Ruby's black bag of toys on her bed.

"Oh my God!" Ruby ran over and tried to pull the bag away from her sister.

"I don't think so," Claire said, holding on to a nylon strap. She pulled out the leather cuffs and then the flogger. "Wow. So my big sister is a total perv!"

Ruby's face burned with shame. "Claire, I can explain."

Claire kept going. A paddle, left by Mark, was next. "You know, there are rumors of Mark being into this kind of shit, but I never, not in a million years, would have thought my own sister was so dirty." She pulled out the blue butt plug. Luckily, Ruby had put it through the dishwasher before she stashed the thing.

Ruby collapsed on the bed and dropped her face into her hands. "I'm sorry, Claire. I'm so sorry. You must be disgusted by me."

Claire just shook her head. "I...I don't know what to think. I think I'm in shock."

Ruby's gaze landed on the remote-controlled vibrator. "So am I. I never thought I'd like...this."

"But you do?" Claire asked.

Ruby rubbed her eyes with the palms of her hands. "Yeah. I think so."

Claire's gaze softened. "Listen. This is a—" She stopped and laughed wryly. "A big surprise. But it's not like I'm going to disown you. It's not like, say, you're a Republican or something."

"It's just that you always say I'm your role model. What kind of role model likes to be tied up and spanked?" She flung herself back on the bed and squeezed her eyes shut. "Oh God! I can't believe I just said that! To my sister!"

She felt the bed dip and then Claire's hand on her own. "Okay, that was TMI. But Ruby, as long as you're happy, it's okay. Frankly, I'm kind of glad I discovered this little secret of yours."

Ruby opened her eyes and met Claire's gaze. "What? Why?"

Her sister shrugged. "I dunno. It makes you more real somehow. Less perfect."

"Oh, honey. I am anything but perfect."

"I'm glad you're starting to realize it," Claire teased. "Anyway, have you always been so kinky? Or did Mark turn you on to the dark side?"

Ruby thought about it a few seconds. "I guess I always was, but he's the one who really showed me it was part of who I am."

"That's cool. I'm glad you're able to accept it about yourself, sis."

"You know what?" Ruby asked, staring vacantly at the toys around her. "I don't think I had. Until now."

"You're welcome. Now, let's recap. You're pervy; Mark's pervy. You love him; he's obviously interested in you. So tell me, sis, what's the problem again?"

Ruby opened her mouth to speak, but no sound emerged. She had no answer.

*   *   *

Ruby had hired a taxi to take her sister to the airport and on Sunday morning they pulled up to the curb at the terminal. "I'm not going to cry," Ruby said.

"Neither am I." But there were tears spilling out of both women's eyes.

"Give me a hug." Ruby pulled her sister into her arms and held her tightly. "I'll miss you."

"You too."

"Bye, Claire Bear."

Claire pulled back, looking surprised. "You said good-bye."

Ruby started. "So?"

"Yeah. You haven't said good-bye to me since... well, you've never done it. Usually you just say, 'See you next Christmas' or something."

"I don't know, I guess it just came out." *Good-bye is not forever, just a fleck of time.* The words of Mark's song hummed their way into her brain.

Claire stared at her for a silent moment. "You know, you've changed since I saw you last."

"You think so?"

"Definitely. You seem less edgy, more comfortable." Claire chucked her on the shoulder. "Maybe it's all that kinky shit."

"Stop. Go or you'll be late."

"Okay. Bye, sis."

"Good-bye, Claire." She watched until the sliding doors of the airport terminal closed behind her sister. After, Ruby did what most women did when faced with a case of the blues. She went shopping. By noon she found herself in retail heaven, San Francisco's Union Square. But she preferred the smaller shops over the department stores, so she made her way to her favorite side street, Maiden Lane.

Maiden Lane was a cobblestoned pedestrian alley lined with eclectic boutiques, high-end salons, and restaurants. Not many tourists ventured down the narrow passage, and locals often enjoyed a cup of coffee or a glass of wine at one of the outdoor cafés.

As she meandered down the alley her gaze landed on a couple sipping wine. The man looked strikingly like Emmett, but it couldn't be him. This man was sitting much too close to his blonde companion and rubbing her hand in an obviously intimate way.

But it really looked like Emmett. He was even wearing red high-tops, which was Emmett's signature shoe.

But it couldn't be him. Could it?

Strolling on the opposite side of the street, she tried to remain inconspicuous, but it didn't matter. The couple was totally oblivious to everything going on around them. And then the woman took him by the collar, tugged him across the table, and kissed him.

A significant amount of time later, she released him. Grinning, the man leaned back in his chair. His face was now totally in Ruby's view, and it was like a blow to the chest.

It *was* Emmett. Ruby forced herself to keep walking. She couldn't confront him because she wanted to strangle him.

How could he do this to Meg?

Meg was happy; she'd told Ruby that things with Emmett were back on track. Perfect.

Her heart pounded behind her ears as she marched back to Market Street. How could he cheat like this, in broad daylight? Well, the bastard thought he'd never be seen on Maiden Lane, obviously. And it was just a fluke that Ruby had happened to be wandering by; she hadn't been downtown in months.

But she had seen him. And now she fought the desire to run back there and slap him across the face.

Taking a deep breath, she forced herself to calm down. It wasn't her place to confront Emmett. It would only make things worse. Her heart ached for her best friend; Meg's world was about to come crashing down around her.

Oh, how she wished she didn't have to tell Meg. But how could she not? Was she going to go to parties with the happy couple and pretend she didn't know Emmett was fucking some blonde behind Meg's back?

Ruby knew she had to say something. She could never live with herself if she kept this information inside. Meg needed to know her husband was having an affair.

On Powell Street, tears pricked at Ruby's eyes. All the buses that went downtown did so via an underground route, and now as Ruby descended the stairs beneath Powell and Market, the crowded subterranean station closed in on her, making it hard to breathe.

Trembling, she waited on the edge of the platform for the bus to arrive. Soon a warm, artificial breeze blew her hair softly into her face, heralding the arrival of the N Judah line. She squeezed her way inside the bus, miraculously finding a seat at the very back.

Oddly, the scene she'd just witnessed made her want to see Mark even more. She realized she'd been searching for some stupid idea of what she wanted, but it was a fantasy. Emmett had just proved that. Life was unstable, no doubt about it. Perfection happened only on television. And Mark was right, the only time she'd even come close to achieving a sublime state was in his arms, when she gave herself to him, mind, body, and soul.

That was where she needed to be looking for perfection.

And yeah, being kinky was part of who she was. Hell, even Claire had accepted that about her. There was nothing left to be afraid of. Except, she realized, never seeing Mark again.

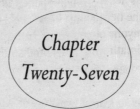

Chapter
Twenty-Seven

The limo dropped her off in front of the Four Seasons in Budapest.

Ruby didn't even know what day it was. When she'd gotten home from shopping she'd discovered a one-way ticket to Hungary that had been slipped under her door, compliments of Mark. It was a lucky coincidence because she'd already planned on tracking him down. She wanted to hear for herself why he'd blown off the pre-party, decide for herself if she could live with his behavior. She needed to hear him explain; she needed to take this chance.

So, here she was. They hadn't talked; she barely had time to toss a few things into a bag before rushing to the airport, where she'd had to make a mad dash to her gate. But she'd made the flight, just in time. Mark had sprung for a first-class seat, so she'd even been able to sleep a bit. There had been a driver waiting for her when she landed, and now, not even twenty-four hours after she'd arrived home to find the ticket, she entered the Four Seasons of Budapest, a little tired but jazzed up. In a few moments, she was going to see Mark.

She shouldn't be nervous; he'd been the one to send her the ticket. He knew she was here. So why were her palms sweaty? Why was her stomach twisting and turning? Why the hell should she be nervous to see a man who knew her far better than anyone else?

With a deep breath she willed her nerves to calm down. Her heels clicked on the marble floor as she crossed the lobby, and behind the reception desk, a scrawny man with a bad comb-over watched her approach.

"Do you speak English?" she asked hopefully. She hadn't had time to buy a Hungarian phrase book.

"A little," he said, and Ruby saw that he had kind eyes.

"Thank you! I'm looking for Mark St. Crow, please. Can you tell me what room he's in?"

The man looked regretful. "I'm sorry, ma'am. We have no registered guest under that name."

"But you didn't even look it up."

"Because I know we have no registered guest under that name."

Of course Mark wouldn't be registered under his own name. But how had he planned on her finding him? He hadn't left any instructions for when she arrived.

"You are welcome to wait in our lounge, ma'am. Just in case," the man said, waving to the side. Her gaze followed in the direction he pointed and landed on a dark-wood bar area, behind which dozens of liquor bottles sat on backlit shelves.

"Thank you," she said. A cocktail suddenly sounded wonderful. She needed something to help calm the unease that had been churning a rancid knot in her gut since yesterday.

She'd tried Meg once again after arriving home, but her friend still hadn't answered. Now, lack of sleep, a long travel day, and knowing she still had to talk to Meg about

Emmett were making that knot in her stomach twist even tighter.

"A chocolate martini, please." She settled onto a wooden stool and dug her cell phone out of her bag. She tried calling Mark, but it went straight to voice mail. Ignoring the nerves having a boxing match in her belly, she arranged her phone on the shiny wooden counter, where she could see it.

A few minutes later the bartender placed a chilled cocktail in front of her. Taking a deep sip, she savored the chocolaty drink, and of course it conjured up memories of that first night with Mark.

She still wondered how he'd instinctively known her, recognized what she needed, what she craved. How had he seen what had been a mystery even to herself? Well, he'd gone and unleashed something in her, something she could no longer suppress. If only he'd show up; she could start un-suppressing right then.

With the martini glass to her lips, she tilted another few drops onto her tongue. The tang of vodka mingled with the bittersweet chocolate, and she relished the combination as it slid down her throat.

Where was he? Obviously he knew when she was due to arrive. Was he even in the hotel? Maybe he was at a sound check, or whatever it was he did to prepare for a performance. He was a busy man. It was something she was going to have to get used to if they even had a chance.

She was about to order another drink when the sound of female laughter drew her attention. She looked to the hotel entrance, watched two young women enter the lobby. But she never registered what they looked like. Because, walking between them, with an arm draped over each of their shoulders, was Mark.

All the blood seemed to drain out of her body in a cold rush. Her throat went tight, capturing the shout that bubbled in her chest. Frozen, she watched as he led the women casually to the elevator and pushed a button.

His hand was in the hair of one of the girls, playing with it. Her own scalp tingled, remembering how his hands had felt there. She wanted to run to him; she wanted him to explain this horrible mistake.

But then they stepped inside the elevator, and she knew it wasn't a mistake. Because just before the door shut she saw him bend down, saw the way his mouth moved toward the girl whose hair he held. Saw the way her eyelids lowered as his lips got closer to hers.

And just before their lips touched the elevator doors closed, shutting off her view of them.

Yet she couldn't look away. Because it was wrong, it had to be. Maybe they were shooting a music video. Maybe the doors were going to open up again and Mark was going to emerge, laughing, and camera crews would appear and tell him they got the shot. And then he'd see her, his eyes would light up, and he'd come to her, take her in his arms and look at her in that way that melted her into a boneless mass whenever she was around him.

But when the elevator doors did finally open, it was only to let out a group of businessmen in navy blue suits.

Seeming to notice her distress, the bartender looked her way. "You need another one?" he asked.

"Y–yes, please. Several."

He just quirked a brow as if to say "*crazy American*" and pulled some vodka off the shelf behind him.

Why had Mark sent her the plane ticket? Had he wanted her to see this? Had he wanted to hurt her? Her mind was whirling; she couldn't think.

"You're a real tough cookie."

She looked up to find Yvette standing next to her. She wore tight jeans and a tank top with a picture of a lollipop that said, "It ain't gonna lick itself."

"What are you talking about?" Ruby asked.

Yvette ordered a beer before answering. "I mean, I don't know any other woman who could say no to the man who wrote a love song for her. But you did, you tough cookie."

Ruby gulped her martini before turning to Yvette. "Fat lot of good it did me. I just saw Mark headed upstairs with a couple of . . . *sluts*." She nodded. "That's right, I said it. *Sluts*."

Yvette cringed. "Yeah, I didn't mean that to happen. Bad timing, definitely."

Ruby turned and faced Yvette head-on. "Yvette. What's going on here?"

"I sent you the ticket." She put a finger to her lips and made a *sshh* sound. "But our boy doesn't know you're here. I wanted to surprise him."

"I'm gonna need another drink," Ruby said, waving for the bartender.

"Good call." Yvette slid onto the barstool next to Ruby. "See, I'm trying to be a good friend."

"By bringing me to Budapest to have my heart broken?" Ruby said incredulously.

"Not a friend to you. Although I'm sure you're quite nice. No, I was trying to be a friend to Mark. See, it was my fault we flaked on your preparty, so I was trying to make amends."

"Your fault?"

"I made him miss the party, but it was for his own good."

Ruby just stared and made a "Go on" motion with her hand.

"Oh. Okay. See, here's the thing. He's been absolutely miserable this last week. He's pining; he's moping. He's been shot through the heart, and you're to blame, baby; you give love a bad name!" She sang this last part as she played air guitar.

"You're insane."

"Why does everyone keep saying that?"

"Yvette," Ruby said as if speaking to a child. "Why did you buy me this ticket?"

"Because the reason we missed the party was because I made him perfect that song. Before the show the three of us got out our instruments and we just got lost in the music. It's really an amazing song, one of the best he's written."

Ruby was trying really hard not to lose it. Yvette was obviously a few cards short of a deck, but she seemed to have their best interests at heart. "Listen, I really appreciate the effort, but I think it's misplaced."

"Nah."

"How can you say that? He just went upstairs with two bimbos!"

"I think one's actually an astrophysicist. Or a stripper, I forget. Anyway, he's just dealing with things the only way he knows how. Girls. Domination. Sex."

The words caused a nauseous lurch in Ruby's stomach. "I don't care. He can do whatever he wants."

"He mentioned he told you about his family."

Blinking, she recovered from the quick change of subject. "A bit, yes."

Yvette ordered another beer, then turned to her. "He hardly ever talks about them."

Ruby paused. "Really?"

Ignoring the chilled glass the bartender provided, Yvette picked up the beer bottle and toyed with the label. "When he told me how much his dad resented his mom, it was when I first met him. And he was drunk."

"So? What does it matter?"

"You haven't known Mark long, but for him? That's opening up. Big-time." She tilted the beer bottle to her lips and took a deep swig.

Ruby's phone rang, making her heart jump. "Mark?" She snatched her phone off the bar, not even looking at the caller ID.

"No, it's Meg. I got your message. You're in Budapest? What's going on?"

Apologizing to Yvette, she excused herself and went to a table in the back of the bar, telling Meg how she'd been set up by Yvette. Then, taking a deep breath, she spewed out exactly what she'd seen Emmett doing on Maiden Lane.

"I'm so sorry, Meg," Ruby said when she'd finished recounting the story.

"Oh, Ruby. I'm the one who's sorry."

"It's not your fault!" Obviously, Meg was in shock and blaming herself.

"No, you don't understand. God, this is embarrassing." She heard her friend take a deep breath. "That was me."

"No, the woman I saw was blonde. I'm sorry, Meg—"

"I was wearing a wig. God, it was such a bad wig, too. I can't believe you didn't know it was me."

Ruby shook her head as if Meg could see her. "I don't understand."

Meg laughed nervously. "Okay, you remember how I told you that Emmett and I were having problems... sexual problems?"

"Yes, of course."

"Well, we've kind of been experimenting to get past all of that."

"Oh." Ruby's face warmed as realization dawned on her. "*Oh!*"

"Yeah, and that day I was just... playing a role. That day was 'the sexy businesswoman takes a lover' role. He was my male prostitute."

"Wow," Ruby said, nodding. "I'm impressed with your creativity."

"Hey, it finally convinced me to get glasses. To, you know, look smart." Meg laughed, and after a second she said, "Oh, Ruby. I'm so sorry. It must have been awful for you to think that Emmett was cheating."

She felt her eyes water. "It really was, but I'm so happy I was wrong."

"Me too. But I promise things are better than ever, and guess what? I'm pregnant!"

Ruby squealed. "Oh my God! Congratulations!"

"Thank you. Now, Ruby. Yvette is Mark's oldest, best friend. Trust her. Go to Mark."

After she'd said good-bye, she flipped her phone shut. She wanted to go home, but her ticket had been one-way. She needed to find a computer and book a return flight, but she just didn't have the energy quite yet. So she went back to join Yvette, who was now using her beer bottle as a pretend microphone and humming a Bon Jovi tune.

Ruby snapped her fingers twice in front of Yvette's face.

"Sorry," she said, taking a swig from her beer. "The eighties are back, ya know."

"So I hear."

"Anyway, he won't go through with it. Shagging those chicks, I mean."

"How do you know?"

She plopped the empty bottle on the counter. "Because I know *him*, and he only wants you. You know," she said, pointing a finger at Ruby, "loving you scares the shit out of him. He thinks if he commits to a woman it'll be the end of his career. Of the band. And he doesn't want to turn into his father."

Ruby laughed wryly. "God, we spend so much time trying not to become our parents, we totally lose sight of who we actually want to become."

"Cheers to that, sister!" Yvette saluted her with the beer bottle.

She studied the gorgeous woman for a moment. "What about you? You're willing to risk him having a relationship with someone who lives so far away? Someone who will demand his attention? Because I promise I'll be demanding."

Yvette's gaze sharpened. "I love Mark. I want to see him happy. You make him happy, happier than I have ever seen him. So I'm willing to take the chance. I'm willing to encourage *him* to take that chance."

Shaking her head, Ruby took in her words. "But—"

"No buts." She snatched a pen and a napkin from behind the bar and scribbled a number onto the crinkly paper. "Now, you scurry on up to room 2025 and rescue that man from himself."

Her heart started thumping in her chest. Yvette's words were pumping her up, making her want to go to Mark. But could she really barge in on him like that?

"Listen, Ruby. Mark is probably the best man I know, and, frankly, if I swung that way I'd have nailed him down long ago for myself. But he's still just a man, and sometimes men need their asses kicked." She pushed the napkin toward Ruby. "So I encourage you to go forth and kick some ass. Everything else will fall into place."

Ruby's fingers shook as she looked at the napkin.

"Go."

Ruby hopped off the barstool. She had no control over the future. What she did have control over was the present, and she wasn't going to let Mark go just because he was scared.

"Thank you, Yvette."

She smiled. "No problem. Just make sure you have him in the lobby by eight. I kinda need him for the show later." Grinning, Yvette swigged her beer.

She gave Yvette a quick hug and hurried to the elevator. As she rode up to the twentieth floor she thought that even if Mark had done something with those women she'd forgive him. Because despite all they'd done together, he'd never promised her anything. They had made no commitments, no promises. Cringing, she realized she'd made sure of that.

But, if they were going to try to make it work, that would have to change.

Finally the elevator doors opened and she burst into the hallway. But her dash to Mark's door slowed when she caught sight of two familiar women walking toward the elevator. She pretended to study a rather hideous landscape painting but watched the girls out the corner of her eye.

Red Miniskirt twisted a blonde curl. "I can't believe he asked us to leave."

Black Miniskirt smacked her gum. "I know. I've always heard Mark St. Crow was a real animal."

The rest of their words faded away as Ruby's heart swelled with relief. Yvette had been right. He hadn't been able to go through with it. She jogged silently down the carpeted hallway. She didn't need the napkin to tell her where she was going, and seconds later she was pounding on his door.

And then that door was opening and he was there, looking down at her, brown eyes wide with shock behind his glasses.

"Ruby! What are you doing here?"

She stepped inside and closed the door behind her. Meeting his gaze, she swallowed. "Yvette made me."

He looked confused and then horrified by what she must have seen leaving his room. "Nothing happened," he said fiercely.

"I know that, you idiot. And I know why you blew off the party. Not that I'm over it, but I'm willing to punish you later. Now, just hold me."

He yanked her to him, hugging her so tight she could barely breathe. Closing her eyes, she let him hold her, wanting to stay in his arms forever.

"I love you, Mark, and I'm sorry about those things I said the night of the party."

He pulled back, his eyes a warm brown as they bored into hers. But still he remained silent.

"I hope you can forgive me," she whispered, tears running down her cheeks.

"You had every right to be mad." His expression turned downright sheepish, and he pulled something from his pocket. It was the necklace she'd dropped outside the theater into the homeless man's hat.

She put her hand to her mouth. "Where did you get this?"

"A little birdie brought it to me." He clasped the necklace around her neck. "I love you, too, baby, and I'm not letting you go. Ever again." And then he kissed her. But this time it wasn't the Mark she knew. This man was urgent, clumsy even as he started pulling off their clothes. His fingers seemed unsteady as he undid her bra, slid her panties down her legs. That slight show of vulnerability caused her to quiver everywhere, made her toes curl. Made her love him even more.

It took him longer than usual to rip the condom open; he finally used his teeth, spitting a tiny silver piece on the floor after it eventually gave way. She watched him roll the sheath onto his erection, vowing to get on the pill as soon as she could. Her chest ached from the want to feel that part of him inside her, skin-to-skin.

The thought had her pussy dripping, making her slick and sticky and so ready for him.

He backed her against the door. "You're mine, Ruby Scott." He said the words into her hair, against her lips. "I want you to tell me that you're mine."

"I will, but we need to talk—ah!"

Her words were cut off when he lifted her, wrapped her

legs around his waist, and pressed the length of his cock to her damp pussy.

She gasped. "We can talk later."

"Mine." He plunged into her, her back sliding a few inches up the door as he did so. With her nipple between his fingers he twisted until she cried out; the sharp pain shot right through her, and she ground down onto him to soften the ache.

She felt his sweat, soaking into her skin in hot drips. His back was slick under her fingers and she couldn't get a grip, but it didn't matter. She didn't need to worry about falling; he held her securely in his arms.

Using the door for support, he made love to her as he whispered things he'd never told her before, hotly against her ear.

"Baby, you smell so fucking amazing. I never told you this, but I took a bar of soap from your bathroom, and I—" He pulled out, drove in again. "I use it when I masturbate. That scent gets me so goddamn hard. You get me so goddamn hard."

"Oh, God...yes." She was on fire, every inch of her burning up.

"I love you so much, Ruby..." The words sent a frisson of lust through her, landing between her legs.

He twisted her nipple again, sending her to the very edge of climax. "Mark, I'm going to..."

He pulled out, thrust again. Later, they could take their time, but now she needed him to let go, to show her uninhibitedly how much he wanted her.

"Fuck me, Mark. Make me come for you."

"Yes, come for me now, baby. Come for the man who loves you, the man you belong to."

"Yes," she cried, exploding into a million blissful pieces. "I belong to you, Mark."

"Oh, Ruby," he whispered. "Ruby mine." He drove into her one last time, his pelvis to hers, his heart to hers. She felt him inside her, his cock jumping in tiny jerks as he came.

As he sank against her, she ran her hand over his smooth scalp. That first night at Meg's she'd wondered how his head would feel beneath her fingertips. The answer was, it felt like home.

He pulled back. Sometime during their frenzy he'd lost his glasses. Now his eyes were dark and warm as he searched her gaze.

He carried her to the bed and tenderly placed her under the covers. Lying next to him, she silently stroked his chest, his stomach, his angular hip bones. The hotel was quiet this high up, and the feel of his fingers combing through her hair combined with the rhythmic sound of his breathing nearly put her to sleep.

"Oh, shit," she said after a while, glancing at the clock. "It's seven forty-five. I promised Yvette I'd have you back in the lobby by eight."

Groaning, he held her tighter. "Crap. I wish I didn't have a show tonight. Will you come?"

She raised her heavy lids to meet his gaze. "Of course. I would love to see you play," she said, suppressing a yawn.

"I forgot you've been traveling." Placing a soft kiss on her temple, he chuckled. "There will be plenty more shows. Just stay here tonight, rest up. I'll be back soon."

"No, I really want to go." She pushed herself up.

Kissing her, he didn't stop until she was lying back

down. "Seriously. Stay here and get some rest." He nipped her earlobe. "You're going to need it later."

"Okay," she said. "And when you get back we need to talk. About things..."

She was asleep before he walked out the door.

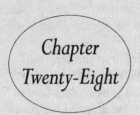

Chapter
Twenty-Eight

Mark opened the door to his hotel room and blinked. What looked like a thousand candles gleamed at him from every corner of the room. And on the small sofa was Ruby, wearing the red lingerie he'd bought for her all those weeks ago. Her nipples were hard peaks under the lacy bra, and the skimpy panties showed off her gorgeous legs. Her skin gleamed like white silk in the candlelight, and her hair fell in a dark, shining mass around her shoulders.

And she was his.

"You have them," she said.

"Have what?" He threw his jacket onto a chair, trying to get a grip. Lust was a river raging through his blood, and he was trying to gain control of himself.

"Those." Ruby glanced at two photographs leaning against a wall in the corner. They were the pictures he'd bought that day in San Francisco, the pictures of Ruby.

He shrugged. "Of course I do. I take them everywhere I go." He crossed the room and went to his suitcase. "Along with these." Pulling a scrap of pink silk out of the bag, he grinned.

Her eyes went wide. "Mark! Those are the panties I locked in the loaner car!"

"Yeah. You should have seen the mechanic's face when I had him unlock the glove box and I pulled these out."

"Oh my God. I'm so embarrassed."

"Don't be. The guy was impressed."

"Anyway." She patted a spot next to her, indicating for him to come sit. He dropped the panties and was beside her in seconds, kissing her, holding her.

Pulling back, she said, "Mark, we need to talk."

Silently, he waited.

She took his hand in hers and stroked her thumb across his skin, much as he'd done to her a hundred times. "I want to try and make this work."

"Me too, baby." He cupped the side of her face with his palm. "So fucking much."

"But the way we started was so much, so intense... I'm afraid you think I'll always be submissive."

"I don't understand."

She smiled. "Here's the thing. You helped me uncover my sexuality."

"And it was damn fun." He leaned in for another kiss, but she dodged.

"Focus, please. I feel like, because of how we started, you have the upper hand. So far, it's only been me showing my vulnerabilities. Me letting you be the one in charge. Me being submissive."

"I don't think of you as a submissive woman, Ruby, not outside the bedroom." He nuzzled her ear. "And sometimes not inside, either."

"I'm sure you don't think you do, but *I* need to be sure. And before we go any further, I also need to know you trust me enough to show me your own vulnerabilities."

He brushed a lock of hair out of her eyes. "If only you could see what I see."

"A woman willing to do anything for you? Anything at all?"

"A woman who *chooses* to let me be in control *for* her. A woman strong enough to give up that power."

"But—"

"Do you think I'm the kind of man who is attracted to weak women?"

She shook her head.

"Because let me tell you something. I was attracted to you the minute I saw you across a crowded room, bossing people around." He smiled. "Even before our eyes met. I saw you licking your martini glass, and I was hard. I saw your smile, and my heart actually beat faster. Then I heard your laugh, and I was toast. Fucking toast, Ruby."

She was staring at him, her cheeks flushed, her breathing fast. "But—"

"The first time we talked you had me reciting music titles. You were the boss, remember?"

He wrapped a strand of her hair around his finger. "When you submit I see such an amazing power in you, in your eyes. In your smile."

Her eyes searched his, looking for the genuineness in his words.

"It's true," he said. "When you give yourself to me, you glow with strength. It's because you know that, with just one word, I'll stop. You are comfortable in that power. And it's a beautiful thing."

Her eyes had gone dark; her chest was flushed red. His words were getting to her. And fuck it, they were getting to him, too.

He leaned in until his mouth brushed hers. "You are so much stronger than you give yourself credit for."

"I know that now," she said against his lips. "Which is why I need you to let me do something. To you. With you."

"Whatever you want, baby. Whatever you want."

She kissed him back, more forcefully now, and his entire world became his sweet Ruby. Her tongue licking his lips, her mouth opening so she could push her way inside his. Her hands on his head, clutching him to her in a tight grasp.

She pressed him against the back of the sofa, all the while kissing him, holding him. Controlling him. She climbed onto him, straddling his hips, rubbing herself against his jeans.

When she pulled back he saw a glow in her eyes that hadn't been there when he'd arrived. And there was something else, a spark that was unfamiliar and yet so easy to read.

He slid his glasses off, placed them on the side table and leaned back. "Show me what you want, baby."

She grinned. "I intend to."

"Go on, then. Kiss me again and show me—*really* show me."

She hesitated only a second before she leaned down once more. This time when she kissed him it was more forceful, more demanding. Shoving her tongue across his lips, she tasted him, played with him until her body was rubbing against his, until she was grinding against his cock, making little noises into his mouth.

He tilted his hips under her, rubbing his erection against her pussy, using the barrier of their clothing as a kind of leverage, letting her know how much he enjoyed what she was doing, encouraging her to keep it up.

It worked.

He felt the moment she let go totally, the moment she let herself take charge of him. Their teeth clashed, their noses bumped against each other. The kiss wasn't delicate or pretty, and yet there was a raw beauty in the total abandon of her touch.

After a sharp nip to his lip, she held him steady as she licked him, teased him. Like teenagers, they dry-fucked until his cock was full and throbbing, until he had to fist the sofa cushions to keep from taking over. His hands pulsed with the need to feel her hair in his grasp, to take control of her.

But he wanted her to be in charge. He wanted her to see that she chose when she wanted to give him control; that they belonged to each other equally.

When she pushed away from him her eyes were bright and alive, her breathing rapid. He took a deep breath, blew it out. "Baby, you want to switch." It wasn't a question.

She blinked a few times. "Have you ever let a woman have control over you? Do you think you could?" She whispered the words into his ear.

His cock was pounding, even as his mind was resisting. "Every good dom needs to give up control sometimes. It's been a while, though."

"Do you think you can do it? Can you let me take charge?" She ground against his cock, and he groaned.

"Baby, I think you already have."

"Good. Now tell me what I need to do."

"Whatever you want. All I know is that you're definitely going to have to tie me up if you want me to keep my hands off you."

He could feel her thighs trembling around him. "How will I know if I'm doing it wrong?"

He stroked the side of her face. "The only thing you could do wrong is walk away."

"That's not going to happen." She kissed his palm and then pulled up his shirt and tugged it off. Her gaze fell on his nipple rings. She bent down and took a ring in her mouth, sucked it, along with his nipple, across her teeth. It stung and he sucked in a breath.

She looked up in concern. But he moved his cock against her, showing her how fucking turned on he was. With a grin, she did the same with his other nipple.

Then he was holding her head, letting her tease him, letting himself go.

"And you want this, right?" she asked.

He leaned back, spread his arms wide against the sofa. "I want this, and I want you."

For once his Ruby would be in control. Of everything. Of him.

Fuck.

He drew in a deep breath and blew it out. "Go on now, baby. Just do it. Before I change my mind."

She climbed off him and held out her hand. "Come with me."

Chapter
Twenty-Nine

As Ruby led Mark to the bed her blood pounded in her ears. Yes, it was nerves. But she couldn't deny the buzz of excitement that thrummed through her as well. Ever since she'd seen that woman pouring candle wax onto the olive-skinned man, Ruby had been fantasizing about doing the same. To Mark.

Was there any fantasy she couldn't live out with Mark? She smiled, and her already-wet pussy began throbbing even harder. And when she turned to him, saw the way he watched her, the way he waited for her instruction, the kick of power shot through her, elevated her senses in an alarming jolt. The physical and mental combination was thrilling, heady.

"Take off your boots and jeans."

Quietly, he obeyed. She eyed his lean torso, his sinewy arms. He had the most beautiful body; just looking at him caused desire to pool deep inside her.

Mark was such a dominant man. In all aspects of his life, inside or outside the bedroom, he was in charge, powerful. And now? To know he was holding that power in check for her was more thrilling than anything she'd ever experienced.

He sat on the bed and she pushed him onto his back.

She smiled. It must be absolute torture for him to let go like this, but he was doing it. Doing it for her. Straddling him, she sat on his cock, her pussy aching as she rubbed against him through her underwear and his boxers. She pulled his arms above his head and pinned him like he had done to her their first night together. "Are you mine tonight?" she asked, repeating what he'd asked her so many times.

He nodded.

She stretched his arms as she slid her pussy down his cock, using his erection as a hard tool on which to rub her clit.

"Say it," she said. "Say you're mine."

"Ruby, baby. I'm yours."

"Good. Now, stay here. I'll be right back. I want you to get undressed and lay in the middle of the bed." The words sounded funny coming out of her mouth, but she shoved her self-consciousness away.

He nodded again, his eyes darker than she'd ever seen them.

As she flitted around the hotel room, collecting the things she needed, his words rang in her ears. *He's really going to let me do this. He wants me to do this.*

She went into the bathroom and shut the door, organizing the items she'd collected. When she looked up, she saw a different woman in the mirror. There was an uninhibited air about her that had been missing before. Her hair was a mess and she didn't care. She was wearing a G-string and a frivolous bra. She had a man at her disposal. Who was this woman?

It was her.

Smiling, she opened the door, just a crack. Without

looking inside the bedroom, she called out, "Close your eyes. Are they closed?"

"Yes." His voice sounded tight, gravelly. Oh, yeah. This must be downright torturous for him.

And it was about to get worse.

She entered the bedroom and nearly dropped everything in her arms. Because looking at him, lying on the bed, totally nude and waiting, stunned her.

He was long and hard, everywhere. His arms were at his sides, his fists clenched. His erection lay on his pelvis, stretching nearly to his belly button. It took every last ounce of her willpower to keep from stripping down and pouncing on him right then. Easing the ache between her legs with his beautiful cock.

But no. He was giving her this, and she wanted to take the gift.

"Keep your eyes closed."

He grunted in response.

It was truly amazing what a five-star hotel would provide its guests when asked. Now, she placed five tea-light candles, a box of matches, a jar of jasmine oil, two bars of Belgian chocolate, three Hungarian silk scarves, and a large bowl of ice on the nightstand. As she looked around the luxurious suite, at the opulent bed with a gorgeous, naked man on it, she thought maybe it wouldn't be so hard to adjust to the rock-star lifestyle after all.

"Open your eyes," she said.

She felt his hot gaze on her skin, taking in her lingerie, her saucy stance; the way she raised her chin to look down on him. His eyes flashed with desire, and she nearly jumped from the excitement of it. Because she'd never felt like this before. So powerful, so in charge. So in control.

It was thrilling.

Picking up the scarves, she climbed onto the bed and straddled him, her pussy resting on the hard planes of his stomach.

She took his jaw in her hand and leaned down as if to kiss him. But at the last minute she pushed him away to put her tongue on his skin, licking him from the base of his neck to the back of his ear. She heard his sharp intake of breath, felt his muscles tense underneath her. And then when she nipped his earlobe his chest heaved against hers.

"Baby, you better tie me up, or I'll have you under me in less than sixty seconds."

"Patience is a virtue. And don't worry, I'll tie you up." Straightening, she drew a silk scarf across his chest. "When I'm ready."

"You do realize you'll pay for this later."

"I'm counting on it."

"I've created a monster."

She flicked his nipple and he jerked. "And you love it, right?"

"Yes," he said with a chuckle.

"So, I have rules."

"I can't wait to hear it."

"No removing yourself from the restraints just because you can. And no climaxing until I say you can. Got it?"

"Yeah."

"Don't worry." She kissed him on the nose. "This will be fun."

At the look in his eyes her power rush went up a notch, and she straightened her back, letting him take a good look at her sexy lingerie. A drop of sweat beaded at his temple.

Taking his right wrist, she climbed up him, straddling his face. The scrolled iron headboard made it convenient to tie his wrists to either side, and as she did so she could feel his hot breath on her pussy, through the fabric of her panties.

Then, when his arms were secured to the bedposts, she lowered her body, pressing her pussy softly against his mouth, his nose. Letting him feel her, smell her, through the sheer silk. He groaned against her, and she felt his breathing quicken, hot gusts against her swollen flesh.

She rubbed against his face like a purring cat. There was no hurry. *She* could come whenever she wanted to. *She* could take her time. *She* could use his mouth as her personal play toy.

Finally she tore away. The candles cast a soft glow over the room, tempting her with their molten wax. But that would come later. Now she let him watch as she picked up a bar of chocolate off the nightstand and broke off a few pieces. Taking it with her as she slid down his body and placed a piece of chocolate on her tongue.

His stare was locked on her mouth as she tasted the chocolate, showed him how much she loved the experience of it melting on her tongue. After she swallowed she licked her lips, slowly.

The power of controlling his pleasure was electrifying, humming through her veins in an erotic current. It must be like this for Mark every time he did this to her. The thought made her feel special, cherished. *His*.

And then she paused. Because even now, with him tied up before her—her prisoner—he was powerful, full of strength. Beautiful. Was this how he saw her? Was this what he wanted to show her?

Love expanded in her heart as she bent down and took his erection in her hand. She wanted to please him, to take him to the edge of pleasure as he'd done to her so many times. Licking a drop of cum off the tip of his cock, she slid the engorged head into her mouth. He jerked beneath her, but her weight on his hips kept him down. She stroked him, caressing him to the very base of his shaft.

Looking up through her lashes, she placed another piece of chocolate on her tongue. Then she took him in her mouth once more, letting him feel the silky chocolate as it melted, swirled it around his cock before she swallowed.

He moaned. "Yeah, baby. Just like that."

She got off the bed and picked up the remaining scarf. "Shh." She wrapped the scarf around his head and tied it off, blindfolding him.

"Ruby, you're killing me."

She popped the ice onto her tongue and climbed back on the bed. With him between her thighs, she leaned down and used her teeth to draw the ice across his skin, tracing a line over his ribs. He gasped when she reached his nipple and took a metal ring, along with the ice, into her mouth. She tugged and sucked, swallowed the ice as it dissolved in her mouth.

When the metal and his nipple ring were hard and cold she switched sides, letting go only when the ice had disappeared.

Her own nipples were tingling and hard, envious little points beneath her bra. But she ignored the sensation and picked a candle off the dresser.

The small tin candle was warm in her hand, and she lifted it high over his chest. "I'm going to pour candle wax on you now."

He shuddered once but said nothing.

Her eyes were on the flame as she tilted the candle, watching as the ivory wax poured over the edge to land on one of his chilled nipples. He jerked and gasped, his jaw clenched.

"You okay?"

"Yes," he hissed.

She continued pouring, loving the way the muscles in his arms bunched as he jerked against the silk restraints. She moved to his other nipple, watching the way his muscles clenched every time the wax hit his skin. When he thrashed on the bed every nerve in her body gathered between her legs in hot pulses. But she ignored it, instead wanting to draw out his pleasure. Right then, it was so much more rewarding than pleasuring herself.

She lowered the candle, knowing the closer to his body the candle was, the hotter the wax would be when it landed on him.

As if in a trance, she stared at the patterns the wax made on his skin; his ribs and then his stomach were like Jackson Pollock paintings, splattered works of art.

Elation flooded her as she emptied the candle onto him, watching the way his breath caught the instant the molten wax hit his flesh. The way his strong thighs tensed, the way he jerked beneath her. The way he hissed out a groan.

She controlled all those things.

"Tell me how it feels."

"Hot."

"Do you like it, Mark?"

"Yeah, baby. You're doing a damn fine job."

"Thank you." When the small tea light was drained

she placed the empty silver holder on the nightstand and picked up a second candle. Again she popped a piece of ice into her mouth. She scooted down the bed until she was over his knees. Her gaze fell on his cock, which was so hard it looked painful.

"You're mine tonight."

"Yes," he moaned. But the word was strained through his clenched teeth.

"I can do whatever I want."

"I said yes."

"Don't forget. Say Chihuahua if it's too much."

"Just fucking do it, Ruby."

"Say please."

"Pretty fucking please."

"Always the bad boy."

With the ice on her tongue, she sucked his cock into her mouth, sucked him as deep as she could, until he hit the barrier of her throat. She continued to suck him until he was pumping his hips beneath her, until his skin was like fire beneath the icy water in her mouth.

Only when the ice had disappeared, leaving her mouth slightly numb and cold, did she release him.

Glancing at the tea light in her hand, and then at him, she said, "Did you like the candle wax?"

"Yes," he said.

"I want to see what happens when I drip it on your cock. Do you want me to do that?"

He groaned, but didn't answer.

Smiling, she drew his thighs open. She had the candle in her hand, hovering about two feet over his body. She tipped the votive, watching the wax splash onto the skin of his strong thigh. The muscles there clenched, but she gave him no time to recuperate. Instead she kept pouring: his other thigh, his hips, and then, when his breathing was deep and audible, she stopped.

His skin gleamed, his chest rose and fell. He made her entire body tremble with desire.

She asked again, "Well, do you? Do you want me to pour hot wax on your cock?"

"Yes." His voice was husky, rough. "Do it." His jaw clenched. "*Please.*"

"Good boy." She tilted the candle and watched the wax fall onto his erection.

He cried out. "That hurts." But the small, euphoric smile on his face told her it hurt in a good way.

She continued pouring and wax splattered on his cock, his stomach, his hips. She watched every muscle in his body twitch and flex, but his smile grew bigger. "I always knew you were a switch, baby," he said. "Didn't I tell you that?"

"Yes, you did." When the votive was empty, she watched the wax as it dried on his strained erection. "I'm jealous, really. Will you do this to me one day?"

"Payback is a bitch, and I can't wait. But when I do it, you'll be spread wide for me. I'll pour it on your breasts while I make love to you. I'll fill your pussy with my cock while I pour hot wax on your nipples. Would you like that, baby?"

Her pussy was aching at the thought, and her entire body was alive with desire for him.

Grinning, she retrieved another piece of ice, and, running it across his erection, she let the ice harden the wax on his skin. His breathing was heavy as she continued, from the head of his cock to the base and then over his balls, until the sac contracted in her hand.

She set the candle aside and emptied a dollop of the jasmine oil into her palm. Mark's hands wrapped around the scarves and he pulled, but he didn't free himself.

With his cock in her hand, she began to rub the jasmine oil into his skin. She wrapped her fingers around his shaft and stroked until the muscles in his stomach began to twitch, until his breathing was choppy. Until the wax came off in little pieces in her hand.

Now he was smooth again; silky and hard. She continued to pump him, increasing her speed as he ground against her hand. Soon he was meeting her rhythm, faster and faster until she heard his breath stop, felt his body go motionless. Her eyes were locked on his erection. Through his warm skin she felt his essence pulsing through him, and she watched as it spurted out of his body in powerful, warm jets.

When he'd stilled she climbed off, untied the scarves from his wrists and removed his blindfold. Her heart in her throat, she looked down at him, felt her chest swell. He'd done it. He'd trusted her enough to let her do this.

"Are you okay? Can I get you anything?" She used the scarf to clean his stomach, kissing the muscles just under his ribs when he jerked, as if it tickled.

"Just you, Ruby," he said as he reached for her.

But she dodged him, setting aside the oil and scarves. "It means so much, Mark, that you let me do this."

"It's your turn now."

She paused and raised a brow. "Is it, now?"

"Hell yeah."

Giggling, she let him pull her into the bed on top of him, and she kissed him gently, slowly, with love. After a minute she pushed him back and looked down into his deep brown eyes.

"There will be rules," she said.

In a flash, he had her on her back. "I'm in charge now, doll."

"Not *now;* I mean rules in general."

He narrowed his gaze. "Like?"

"No other women, obviously."

He nipped her ear. "No problem there, baby. All I want is you."

"When you're on tour we need to see each other at least once a month."

"Or more." His hand was spanning her hip, and she shivered.

"When I ask you how your day went, I want a real answer. None of this 'I'm too tired to talk' crap."

"Fine."

His fingers were inching closer to her aching center, and she spread her thighs. "No matter what I say during our fantasies, you don't own me," she whispered. But when she felt his fingers spreading her labia so he could slip a finger into her pussy, she knew her words were false. She belonged to him, heart and soul.

"E-mail," she said, trying to concentrate. "You have to e-mail me every day."

"E-mail, text messages, phone calls. Postcards. Whatever you want." He slipped a second finger inside her and her eyes fluttered shut. "Hell," he said. "If I thought you'd agree, I'd tell you to quit your job and just come with me. But I know you'd never go for it."

"No, I wouldn't. But I can make my own schedule. Travel." She could barely think, not when he was kissing her, toying with her nipples, her clit. She let him bring her arms together over her head. He had her so out of her mind, she barely noticed him tying her wrists together with the silk scarves that had been restraining him only minutes ago.

Or maybe she didn't care that he was taking charge. She stretched her body, arched her back so her breasts peaked for him. He tied her to the headboard and she smiled, loving it.

Fingering the silver lock on the necklace around her throat, he gazed down at her. "But you're mine right now, aren't you, Ruby?"

She nodded. "Yes, Mark."

"And I'm yours." He kissed her softly before breaking away to get a candle and some matches. "But, as I said earlier, payback is a bitch." He struck the match, lit the candle, and blew out the match flame. The scent of sulfur drifted up in a puff of smoke.

She caught the gleam in his eye, and a delicious wave of desire washed over her; she wrapped her hands around the silk scarves, pulling tight.

"Are you ready?" he asked.

She smiled, giving him her sassiest look. "Bring it, Mark *Rufus* St. Crow."

With a wicked grin, he did.

THE DISH

Where authors give you the inside scoop!

From the desk of Elizabeth Hoyt

Gentle Reader,

Whilst researching my latest novel, TO BEGUILE A BEAST (on sale now), I came across the following document which was written in a Suspiciously Familiar hand. I append it here for Your Amusement.

THE GENTEEL LADY'S GUIDE TO CLEANING CASTLES

Written for the Express Purpose of Guiding the Lady of Quality who may, through no fault of her own, be hiding under an Assumed Name in a Very Dirty Castle Indeed.

1. If at all possible, the Genteel Lady should choose a very dirty castle *not* inhabited by a Male (one cannot use the word *Gentleman*!) of a foul and disagreeable disposition.
2. Even if the Male in question is rather attractive otherwise.
3. An apron, preferably in a becoming shade of light blue or rose, is important.

4. The Genteel Lady should immediately hire a large and competent staff—even if it is against the express wishes of the Disagreeable Male. Remember: if the Disagreeable Male knew anything about cleaning, his castle wouldn't be in such a deplorable state in the first place.

5. Tea is harder to make than one might imagine.

6. Beware birds' nests hiding in the chimney!

7. The Genteel Lady should never deliver the Disagreeable Male's luncheon to him in his tower study by herself. This may result in the Lady and the Male being closeted together—alone!

8. Should the Genteel Lady dismiss the Above Advice, she should not under any circumstances participate in a Passionate Embrace with the Disagreeable Male.

9. Even if he is no longer Quite So Disagreeable.

10. Finally, the Genteel Lady should never, ever engage in an Affaire d'Coeur with the Master of the Castle. In doing so she puts not only her virtue in peril, but also her heart.

Yours Most Sincerely,

Elizabeth Hoyt

www.elizabethhoyt.com

♥ ♥ ♥ ♥ ♥ ♥ ♥ ♥ ♥ ♥ ♥ ♥ ♥ ♥ ♥ ♥

From the desk of Annie Solomon

Dear Reader,

Everyone always asks me where I get my ideas. Sometimes I get them straight from the newspaper. Or a song lyric might start an idea rolling. Places often give me ideas, especially if they're new to me. But in the case of my latest, ONE DEADLY SIN (on sale now), the idea for the book came from a tour guide to Iowa.

My brother was moving, which was sad because we live next door to each other, and also happy, because it meant he was taking a job that was exciting and challenging and something he always wanted to do. As a parting gift, someone had given him a guide to interesting places in Iowa, and while flipping through it one day—trying to ignore the boxes that were piling up in his living room—I happened across a famous midwestern legend about a monument in an Iowa cemetery. A monument that supposedly turned black overnight because the man buried beneath it was guilty of crimes of the heart.

That got me thinking. What if the person buried beneath the angel was innocent? What if someone wanted to prove it? What if proving it cost that someone his or her life?

That's the nugget that got me started on Edie Swann, the tattooed, Harley-riding heroine of ONE DEADLY SIN.

They say you can't go home again. For Edie, going home is murder. Out to revenge her father's long-ago death, she's caught in her own trap by a maniac who wants to see the sins of the past paid in full. With Edie's blood.

You can check out an excerpt on my Web site, www. anniesolomon.net. You'll also find more on the legend that started the story circling in my head. And while you're there, don't forget to check out my blog for behind-the-scenes stories in the life of a writer.

Happy Reading!

Annie Solomon

♥ ♥ ♥ ♥ ♥ ♥ ♥ ♥ ♥ ♥ ♥ ♥ ♥ ♥ ♥

From the desk of Lilli Feisty

Dear Reader,

Have you ever had a crush on a rock star? Have you ever watched *American Idol* and your heart began to pitter-patter as you saw a performer belt out a song, straight from his gut? Have you ever stared at a musician's fingers as he strummed his guitar and thought, "Wouldn't it be fabulous to be tied up by that rock star as he did wicked things to me?"

Or maybe that's just me.

It all started when I heard Robert Plant. I'd never even seen him, but when I listened to him sing I fell in love with his voice. He sounded so soulful, so sexy. I wondered why he wanted someone to squeeze his lemon, but my mom assured me it was because he liked a citrusy tea. Being thirteen, I believed her. It didn't stop my crush, though. I'd just lie on my bed, listening to Led Zeppelin, in bliss. And when I caught sight of Plant onstage, swinging his hips in those low-slung jeans, I was toast. I never got over my fascination with musicians, and I suspect few of us do.

Enter Mark St. Crow, the hero in my May release, BOUND TO PLEASE. Mark's a hot, tattooed musician with a tendency to, well, tie women up and do wicked things to them. Of course, I couldn't make his life easy so I made Mark fall for Ruby Scott, an event planner who longs for stability and all the things Mark's lifestyle could never allow. Oh, I admit it was fun torturing them both (even though they sometimes liked it) and while I did so I got to live out my not-so-secret rock-star crush, with a heavy dose of spicy romance thrown in.

I hope you enjoy BOUND TO PLEASE! You can find out more information about me and my writing at www.lillianfeisty.com.

Lilli Feisty

Want to know more about romances at
Grand Central Publishing and Forever?
Get the scoop online!

GRAND CENTRAL PUBLISHING'S ROMANCE HOMEPAGE

Visit us at www.hachettebookgroupusa.com/romance
for all the latest news, reviews, and chapter excerpts!

NEW AND UPCOMING TITLES

Each month we feature our new titles
and reader favorites.

CONTESTS AND GIVEAWAYS

We give away galleys, autographed copies,
and all kinds of fun stuff.

AUTHOR INFO

You'll find bios, articles, and links to personal
websites for all your favorite authors—and
so much more!

THE BUZZ

Sign up for our monthly romance newsletter,
and be the first to read all about it!